Naval Maneuvers

Dee S. Knight

ISBN 978-1-936556-38-0

Published 2018
Published by Black Velvet Seductions Publishing

Naval Maneuvers Copyright 2018 Dee S. Knight
Cover design Copyright 2018 Jessica Greeley

Visit us at:
www.blackvelvetseductions.com

Dedication

For my dad, who proudly sailed the seas for 24 years, for my second father, who believed "once a Marine always a Marine," and who demonstrated the finest qualities of the Corps in love of his family, and to my own hero who has always shown the best military traits in living life and loving his women. And to all the men and women who serve daily, and to their families: thank you!

Weighing Anchor: Lifting the anchor and allowing the ship to move from the point where it was secured. Weighing anchor implies going away from an old place and toward someplace new.

Dropping Anchor: Using an anchor to keep a vessel in a particular place for security and stability.

Anchor Home: The position of the anchor when the ship is underway. That is, the ship is moving forward and is under control and not adrift.

Weighing Anchor

Chapter One

"And what is your name, pretty?" Mel Crandall addressed the dinosaur bones in an undertone, bending nearly to face level. The skeleton displayed an open mouth and rows of fierce, sharp teeth.

"Roger," a man standing next to her said in a low voice. Startled, she looked up. *Up* being the operative word. She stood a decent five feet ten inches, and he beat her by a good half foot. She studied him. He ignored her.

The guy had a solid profile, strong chin, chiseled cheekbones, and a straight back with muscular shoulders. Short brown hair. He wore glasses and stared straight ahead, but glasses couldn't disguise the laugh lines that radiated from the corners of his eyes. His posture was near perfect and he was not overweight, as evidenced by the trim fit of his jeans and red polo shirt that clung enough to give evidence of a low body/mass index number.

As a doctor, she immediately noticed body characteristics before actual looks. But with this guy, examination in lieu of admiration was hard. Men were often put off by the fact that she paid attention to whether they looked sallow or flushed, or if their hands were cold or warm before she "saw" them. She noticed if a man's eyes were dilated or glittered with fever before she registered eye color. Dates started with mini examinations before she relaxed enough to enjoy personalities, but that's just the way she was. Men had to take it or leave it. Sadly, most left it. Which was why she talked to dinosaurs at the Smithsonian Museum of Natural History all on her own.

Mel moved on to the next exhibit, a shorter built specimen but still tall and with a nasty spiked tail. "I wonder what you looked like," she murmured. "What color were you, what did you eat, and what's your name?" She bent to read the exhibit information.

"Gray. Grass." That same guy had followed her. Rather than having a strong profile, she was beginning to think he was a weirdo. "Annnd, Roger."

Quickly, Mel moved to the next exhibit. "And you are—"

"Roger."

He stood beside her again! Mel started to look for a museum guard but saw none. Great. Planting her hands on her hips, she turned to him. "Stop following me," she said loudly enough that people in the general area turned to see what was happening.

The guy said, "Hold it."

Hold it? *Hold it*, as in "Wait a minute, little lady?" She opened her mouth to lay into him when he turned and removed his glasses, showing her the richest, most chocolatey brown eyes she'd ever seen. The words stuck in her mouth.

"I'm sorry, what?"

In a lower voice, she said, "You're following me from exhibit to exhibit and talking to me. I want you to stop."

"I didn't realize…" He wiggled the glasses at her. "I'm working here and I'm afraid I didn't notice you."

Well. What was worse, that he was a pervert following her place to place, or that he wasn't a perv and hadn't even noticed her?

His brow furrowed while he studied her. "Yes. Yes." Then he shook his head. "Roger."

Again, with that *Roger*.

"Gotta go. Later." Then he smiled at her. "Just a minute, okay?" He folded the glasses and put them first in a protective case. Squatting, he placed a briefcase on the floor and opened it. He stored the glass case inside a pocket. Then he removed something from his right ear—an earbud? —protected it and also put it in the case.

Mel watched all of this with curiosity. He expected her to wait for him? What arrogance. And yet, wait she did. When he stood, holding the case in his left hand and smiled once more, her heart stuttered. The guy was drop dead gorgeous—at least to her understanding of the word. Normally, she appreciated the male form, mostly from a medical viewpoint. This man she enjoyed with pure pleasure.

And good God. He hadn't been talking to her, he'd been talking to whoever was on the other end of that earbud. Embarrassment flooded her.

"I'm sorry," she said. "I thought you were..." She slid her hand between the two of them and then to the exhibits.

"No," he said. "*I* apologize. I shouldn't be testing this stuff around people. The last time I did it a kid thought I was calling him Roger." His voice had a soft drawl to it. Western Virginia or North Carolina, maybe? *Somewhere in the mountains.* It felt like a cool stream as it ran over a body hot and tired from hiking: refreshing and invigorating, at the same time soothing and relaxing. She wanted him to talk more.

Stop that! She laughed. "I thought you were naming each dinosaur." He smiled, and dimples indented his cheeks. His eyes crinkled and Mel's breath caught. This guy should come with a warning label. *Approach with caution. Could bring on lustful intentions and ultimately, broken hearts. Take only in small doses and in public places.*

He held out his hand. "David Stimson."

She took it gingerly, half expecting lightning to bolt between them. Nope. Nothing. So much for romance novels. He had a nice hand, large and warm with healthy pink nails, and she grasped it firmly. "Melissa Crandall."

"Nice to meet you. Do you mind if I wander along with you?" Grasping the briefcase with his left hand, he deftly, he moved to the left of her.

"No, please. It's a free country." She walked to the next dinosaur re-creation. "And this one is..." She half waited for his pronouncement.

"Not Roger," he said, stopping her heart with that killer smile again. He leaned over to read the information. "*Torosaurus latus.* It says here that these bones were dug up in North Dakota, but that the Torosaurus roamed from Canada to Texas, and that he had the biggest head of any land mammal."

"Well, I guess that's *some*thing to be proud of," Mel responded. David laughed, and she found herself smiling back. When she moved to the next exhibit, he strolled along with her, hands behind his back.

He pointed to the next specimen. "Poor guy. Starved to death."

"Oh, yeah? How do you know?"

"Can't you tell? He's all bones."

Mel covered her face, groaning. "Oh my gosh, that's so bad." She looked up into his smiling eyes and nudged him with her shoulder. "Admit it. You've been wanting to say that ever since you came in. You just needed a straight man."

Giving a one-shoulder shrug he said, "And here you are."

He took her elbow and she had to admit, while there was still no flash of electricity, she did feel a change. His hand was warm and there was a *tingle* going on. Yeah, definitely a tingle.

"Let's go and see if that guy over there is named Roger."

"David, truthfully? I don't think *any* of these guys are named Roger."

"Oh." He slowed to a stop. "Well, I guess that decides it then."

"Decides what?"

"Since I inadvertently caught you up in my test, I think I owe you lunch."

"You don't, really."

His face fell just a little. "I wish you'd let me buy you lunch. Or… let me put it this way, would you please have lunch with me? I heard about a great burger place just a little way up Pennsylvania Avenue. Nothing fancy but good, I heard." David stood back and held his hands up. "Totally platonic, all public."

That voice. Mel was lost in the rich body of it, the smooth softness of the rounded consonants and muted vowels, like being in the embracing mists that creep through mountain glens, until one doesn't know which way is front or back. If she didn't watch it, she'd be falling in lust with the man just because of the way he sounded. She was *not* that kind of crazy woman.

Mel stared up into his hopeful expression. "If you make me go to lunch by myself," he said, "I'll only have my earbud and Roger to talk to."

She took a moment. This was *so* like nothing she ever did. But he was cute and funny, and they'd be in public. Plus, his voice alone moistened her panties. She *wanted* to go, to see if that tingle remained. Certainly, she'd never met anyone quite like him or anyone who made such a huge impression—in more than one way. She didn't live in D.C. and never had to see him again if she didn't want to.

But… Taking his outstretched hand, she admitted that if tonight went well, she just might want to.

***

Melissa's auburn hair had swished her shoulders when she tossed back her head to stare up at him when she thought he was following her on purpose, and her green eyes had glittered with indignation. But the magnetism that held his gaze had much more to do with her curves than with her eyes, beautiful as they were. David's immediate reaction had been to wrap his arms around her and haul her up against his body. They were in the Museum of *Natural* History, and what could be more natural than a man's instinct when it came to a woman?

They'd moved from exhibit to exhibit in a leisurely fashion until he couldn't stand not touching her anymore. He'd taken her elbow to get closer and that bare touch tightened his groin. He wasn't looking for any action while in D.C.—he was there for work, not play. Getting laid had been the furthest thing from his mind when he entered the museum to test their new equipment. Until he'd met the gaze of the woman he'd inadvertently stood beside.

As she'd turned back to give the last dinosaur and parting look, David had given her one. Curvy in all the right places, she showed her shape to good effect in tailored tan slacks and a green, fitted knit top. She wore low-heeled shoes and her head fit under his chin. In heels, he'd barely have to bend down to kiss her. She'd fit him well, body parts to body parts. Or close enough.

David couldn't believe Melissa had agreed to lunch. She hadn't let him hold her hand all the way to the restaurant, but he could wait for that. There was something about this woman, something special. He'd felt it right off the bat, and he sure as hell meant to stay around her long enough to figure out what she was all about.

They ordered burgers at a bar table while sipping a red wine for her and a beer for him. "To Roger," he said holding his glass up to toast.

She gave a wry smile. "You didn't make up that whole routine, did you?"

Grinning, David said, "What? Just to meet you, you mean?" Holding up three fingers like a Boy Scout. "I swear I did not pretend to be running a test just to meet you." They clinked glasses and he tasted the draft beer he'd ordered. "I *would* have made something up to meet you," he said, his voice low and a little growly. "But I'm ashamed to admit I truly didn't notice you were there until you accused me of stalking you."

"That's not very satisfying to a woman's ego," Mel replied. "Suppose I'd been standing next to someone else who wanted me to believe he knew the names of all the dinosaurs in the exhibit?"

"If I'd seen you as you'd been walking off with someone else, I would have thought he was some damn lucky guy. Then I'd have had to trick him into trading places."

"Trick him?"

"How else would a guy willingly leave you?"

Blushing, she focused on her wine. "Now I've embarrassed you," he said. Hesitantly, he reached across the small table to wrap the ends of her fingers in his. To his relief, she didn't pull back. "Sorry. When I see something I like, I tend to get carried away."

Her lips turned up. "You see something you like?"

"I think you know I do." With a great deal of willpower, he removed his hand and picked up his glass again. "Tell me about yourself. Do you live here in town?"

"No, in Virginia. How about you?"

"Also in Virginia. What do you do?"

Mel twirled her wine and David tried not to envy the glass as she raised it to her lips. This attraction made no sense. He didn't know the woman yet instinctively knew they'd launch fireworks in the bedroom. The question was, did she feel anything like the same?

"Let's not talk about jobs," she said. "Let's guess what we each do. Since you were testing some new gadget, you must be a mad scientist working on a device that will control colors."

David rested his chin on his fist. "Colors? Why would anyone want to do that?"

"To change perceptions. I heard you say 'Grass. Gray.' Obviously, you are trying to make us all see things in grayscale. It would make the whole world grumpy." She jerked up in her seat and snapped her fingers. "Oh! You work for a pharmaceutical company that produces anti-depressants. So first you make us all depressed, living without color and then your company sells the pills to correct the problem they created."

"Damn! Now I'll have to kidnap you because you've guessed our nefarious plans." Actually, running off with her didn't sound like all that bad a plan.

"Smart ass," she said with a laugh. "So, what do you think I do?"

"Novelist, obviously. You have an active imagination." He took up his beer.

Melissa preened. "I *did* win my fifth-grade writing award."

He tipped his glass to her. "See? I read people very well. And what do you write?"

"Romance," she said. "Sexy, steamy romance." She smiled at him from under her lashes. His cock rose at record speed, crashing into the zipper of his jeans. He held his breath for a moment, willing himself to relax and knowing he couldn't arrange himself without her noticing.

"I'll have to get you back for that, Melissa," he whispered.

Impishly she smiled. "Call me Mel," she said.

"I'll definitely be calling you. Mel." He flashed her a smile.

Thankfully, their food arrived, giving him a needed distraction. "Man, that *is* good," David said after taking a bite and swallowing. "So, are you visiting our nation's capital for the day or longer?" *Say longer.*

Mel used her napkin to dab at her mouth. "I was in town for a lecture and decided to take a few extra days. I'll be leaving on Sunday."

Sunday. Two days away. "Do you have plans?"

"Not really. Whenever I'm up here I like to hit whatever special exhibit the museum has going. But today that was interrupted by a man who likes to name the dinosaurs."

"Sorry," he said sheepishly.

She laughed and picked up her burger. "No worries. I'm enjoying this. And it's not like I haven't been to the museum before. I like archaeology and paleontology and all that old stuff, so I take advantage whenever I can to learn about it."

"Me, too. It's one of the great things about living in Virginia—history of all kinds is everywhere. Have you visited the Ruther Glen site?"

"No, but I've read about it. Fascinating." She picked up her wine glass and looked at him over the rim. He couldn't help but feel that he was being studied, just like those whale and dolphin remains in Ruther Glen. "So, are you a Virginia native?"

David couldn't hold back a tiny internal smile. She was interested in him as more than a specimen to examine. *Thank you, God!* He liked this woman—her scent, her smile, her intellect. "West-by-God-Virginia."

"Ah! Country roads lead you home much?" She bit into a French fry.

He held out his hands to stop her. "Please! There should be a limit to the number of times any West Virginian has to be reminded of that song."

She glanced down and then back up, looking a little shy and ridiculously sexy. "What are your plans? Are you going to be in town for a while?"

I definitely have plans. "I still have a bit more work to do, but just for the afternoon. I'm free for the rest of the weekend. Can I see you later, maybe take you to dinner?"

Mel rested her wrists against the table edge, hands on the table. Leaning forward she focused her gaze on his and he felt the intensity. "I don't do this, you know. I don't go out to lunch with strange men and certainly not to dinner. But…" She bit her bottom lip and David couldn't help but focus his gaze there. He wanted to do that. He wanted to take that full bottom lip between his lips and bite down gently. And then he wanted to take her mouth and stroke her with his tongue. The whole notion was fucking crazy.

Instead, he reached across the table and took her hand. "Look, Mel. I feel something going on between us. You might not believe this, but I don't do this kind of thing either. I have never asked a woman I don't know—someone I just met—out to lunch."

She choked out a laugh. "Somehow I doubt that!"

David shook his head and tightened his grip on her fingers. "I don't, I promise. But with you…? It's like I've known you forever. Like we aren't strangers. Do you feel anything like that?"

It *felt* like forever before she squeezed his fingers and nodded. "I like you, too. Where would you like to meet for dinner?"

Relief rushed through him. "Where are you staying?"

"In Georgetown."

"Hey, me, too. I just arrived yesterday and wanted to try that place on M Street. It's… um… Hmm. It's a guy's name. It's…"

"Clyde's?"

"Yes! Actually, I already have reservations there for seven. Will that suit?"

She raised her brows. "You have reservations for a place but can't remember the name?"

He smiled. "Don't need to know the name. I know how to get there."

"Touché." She thought a moment. "I think seven will suit."

"Great. That's great." David hoped his grin didn't look too stupid. He was a grown man but for the first time, he felt something settle inside. This woman was special. He could see a relationship in her. Hell, if he were more romantically inclined, he might see his future in her, but it remained to be seen if anything could take root. Maybe tonight she'd give him a reason to find out.

Chapter Two

"You're doing *what?*" Sissy Buchanan's disbelief came through loud and clear. "Tell me you're kidding."

"I'm not," Mel told her. Trying to hold a cell phone conversation while dressing for dinner was no easy feat but she was managing. Until time to add earrings. "Sissy, I'm putting the phone on speaker."

Since she seemed to be throwing caution to the wind by dining with a man she'd just met that afternoon, she'd decided to pamper herself—something she rarely did. She'd had a manicure and facial in a day spa up the street from her hotel and then luxuriated in a long bath with a floral bath salt. After adding the dressiest outfit she'd brought with her—a black pencil skirt and cream-colored silk blouse—she felt special and beautiful and ready for whatever the night could hold. And she hoped that by dessert she would know what she *wanted* the night to hold.

"He's nice," she told Sissy while attaching the back to a gold love-knot stud earring. "And if you met him, you'd know he was okay. I feel it. I'm a good judge of character, you know."

"No, I *don't* know. Let's see. Was it you or me who dated that guy in med school who said he was a graduate student in anthropology but ended up being a junior who wanted to date an 'older woman' in order to get some sexual experience? *You.* And who fell hard for the lifeguard at the beach last time we went because he seemed *so nice?* You again. And who—"

"I get it, thanks." Mel huffed out a breath. "But this guy, I don't know. There's just something about him, something I like."

"You mean," Sissy said in a gentler voice, "that since you spit up with Tony you're lonely."

"Tony was almost a year ago, Sissy. I think if I were going to freak out over someone because I was lonely it would have happened before now."

Her friend heaved a dramatic sigh. "Fine. I've done all a best friend who's not there to tie you down can do. Speaking of doing something, what does this Prince Charming do?"

Ah, there's a good question. "Don't know. We didn't get into jobs."

"Good God, Mel, what *did* you get into?"

"Well, I think he works for some research company. He was testing a pretty specialized gadget when we met. His name is David Stimson and he's from West Virginia, although he lives in Virginia now."

"Where in Virginia?"

"Um… Don't know?" Sissy sent another of those sighs through the phone. "Look, when we finish I'll send you his phone number. And we're going to Clyde's tonight. That's a restaurant in Georgetown. Everything in public and safe."

"I want to hear from you tomorrow morning. Or tonight. Call me tonight before you go to sleep, no matter how late."

"That will disturb Mike."

"Mike isn't going to mind. By the time I finish with him, he'll sleep like a baby right through a nuclear attack. I'm going to–"

"Lalalalala! No sex talk, please. For those of us not getting any, it's depressing."

"Okay. I give. Have fun tonight. *Be careful!*"

"I will. I'll be back at work on Monday morning and tell you all about it." She pressed End, took another check in the mirror, picked up her bag, and left to find a taxi. She planned to arrive early and maybe have a glass of wine at the bar to gain a little courage.

Despite what she'd told Sissy, it did make her nervous knowing she was going out with a man she knew absolutely nothing about. But in the past, she'd gathered all kinds of information on the men she dated— well with the exceptions Sissy had made her recall—and look where it had gotten her. Not that she was dying to have a man, but she was thirty-three and one of the few single or unattached women she knew. The only thing worse than being a third (or fifth) wheel at dinners and parties was being set up, something she'd strongly discouraged for the past year. She wanted to be part of a couple but not if it meant blind date after blind date with men she had nothing in common with.

She didn't know anything about David but at least *she* chose him as her date, her walk on the wild side. No doubt this was a one-time thing, but if she were ever going to form a loving duo with someone, she first had to get used to dating again. David seemed safe and she sensed he'd be fun to spend time with. The best part was, after she went home she'd probably never see him again. It might be mercenary, but she could use him for practice and hopefully have a nice evening, too. She couldn't deny that there was something about him that attracted her.

When she arrived, the hostess directed her to the bar. Before she found a seat, however, she found David. He was just lifting a glass of something amber to his mouth when he spotted her. Carefully, he set down the glass and stood, a look of pure appreciation on his face. He raised his hand in greeting and she started forward. When she reached him, he took both of her hands and leaned in for a kiss on her cheek.

"You look beautiful," he said, mouth to her ear.

"Thanks," she said, returning the kiss to his cheek. "You clean up nicely, too." And indeed he did. Simple, navy blue slacks paired with a white button-down shirt and blue blazer would seem preppy on some men, but on him the look was easy sophistication.

"You're early," she added.

He smiled. "You, too. I'd like to think that's because you couldn't wait to see me again."

"Of *course.*" She looked to his glass and then smiled up at him. "Also, maybe I needed a little Dutch courage."

He laughed. "Join the club. What would you like to drink?"

"White wine, please."

David raised his finger to the bartender and asked for the wine. "So, what did you do this afternoon?"

The rightness of the question struck Mel immediately. It didn't feel forced. The tone was friendly, familiar. No Dutch courage needed after all. She felt totally comfortable.

The bartender brought her drink and she took a sip before answering. "Nothing too much. Some reading and relaxing." No way would she spill the beans that she'd primped for their date. "How about you?"

"I've seen more of D.C. basements than I ever wanted to. Then I switched places with my partner. We were supposed to test the equipment outside the city, too, but I couldn't have made it out to Leesburg and back in time to meet you."

"What in the world are you testing?"

Waggling his brows, he said, "You know I can't divulge any more of the secret plan than you've already guessed."

"Okay, I give. Please thank your partner for making the trek in your place so we could have dinner."

"You're also taking his place at dinner. And I did thank him for that. I'd much rather sit across the table from you than from Todd, believe me. No comparison!"

"Wait! He gave up dinner?"

"He'll grab something on his way back. A burger and beer will make him as happy as eating here."

"Hmm, I think I like this Todd character," Mel said. "And I think I like you, too, David Stimson."

He took her hand and pulled her in for a soft kiss. His lips caressed hers with only a slight pressure and then he pulled back, not demanding anything, just giving pleasure. A very subtle scent—woodsy and fresh—enveloped her. She wanted more.

"I *know* I like you, Melissa Crandall."

His words sent a warmth throughout her body. His look sent a flood of heat to the spot between her thighs. What she wanted from the night was becoming more apparent by the minute. An end to her long dry spell. With this man. Only with this man.

Mel had never been one to throw caution to the wind. But tonight, she just might.

***

When Mel walked into the restaurant in that form-fitted black skirt and slinky white blouse, David had nearly dropped the glass of scotch he'd been nursing. Her hair skimmed her shoulders and she wore minimal makeup and little jewelry. Nothing took away from her stunning good looks. He'd bussed her cheek when what he'd wanted to do was take her lips in a heated kiss and mate his tongue with hers. Then he'd wanted to lift her onto a bar stool, spread her legs and play a little hide-and-seek with his cock and her pussy. But… They were in public and he limited himself to holding her hands and giving her a quick, admiring glance to show her how much he appreciated her. In a polite, gentlemanly way, of course, no matter how his blood had heated and started flowing to the lower regions with his first glance.

Drinks had been fun, dinner really excellent with superb service and food. Conversation had flowed as it never had with any woman on a first date. David couldn't believe his luck. How many women had he met in the last few years and felt no connection? Well, no emotional connection.

He'd had plenty of *physical* connections, but nothing beyond a series of one-night stands and a couple of girlfriends he'd hung out with—fun times with a bit of fucking in between. Nothing serious. Nothing he'd *wanted* to be serious. But now, this woman fell into his lap, and he knew an instant closeness.

"Do you want to walk up the street and see what's what?" he asked as they left Clyde's. With only a little second guessing he reached down for her hand and happily noted that she linked her fingers with his. When had he ever hesitated over something as simple as reaching for a woman's hand? This weird attraction was turning him into a pussy.

"Sure. Georgetown at night is fun." They strolled along, wending through Friday night crowds and eventually mixing with a younger set wearing Georgetown University tee shirts. They found a table in a dinky bar that featured music.

"I remember these days," Mel shouted over the music. She used her pointer finger to sweep over the crowd, indicating the youth of the audience.

"Fondly?" David shouted back, struggling to scoot out of the aisle as a burly young man pushed past to reach a table nearer the stage.

She smiled and leaned forward to reach his ear. Her breath warmed his neck as her lips brushed his earlobe. His cock sprang to life. He gripped his beer bottle so as not to slide his hand around her waist and pull her onto his lap. "Oh yeah. It was great *then*. Now? Now, I just feel old."

David met her gaze. "No way," he mouthed. Then he leaned closer to her ear, hoping he aroused the same feelings in her that she had in him. "I don't know how old you are, but you aren't *old*, you're mellow. You're refined." He leaned back far enough to see her face but not so far as to miss her scent. The soft flowery fragrance had driven him and his cock crazy all night.

"Mellow and refined. Is that supposed to be a compliment?" She smiled, and God help him, her gaze dropped to his lips for a brief moment.

That was all the invitation David needed. He took her mouth in a firm but gentle kiss, giving her the chance to step back mentally if she chose to. To his relief, far from breaking the kiss, Mel slipped her hand to the back of his neck and held him where he was.

David tilted his head for better access and drove his fingers into her hair. Using his lips to explore every inch of her lips, he felt rather than heard her moan. Without his asking, she opened her mouth and gave him her tongue. He sucked in a breath and moved closer, brushing her breasts with the back of his hand as he moved his arm up and over the top of her chair to brace her back and pull her even closer. Exploring her mouth, his tongue stroked and tangled with hers, stoking the raging fire inside him and causing his cock to ache like a son of a bitch. He didn't know how much more of this he could take.

Breaking the kiss on a gasp, Mel leaned forward, her mouth to his ear. "I don't know how much more of this I can take." David smiled. She'd just read his mind. He hoped she couldn't read too much of what he was thinking, or she'd run for the hills.

He nuzzled her delicate jaw up to her ear. "Want to get out of here?"

She nipped his ear lobe. "Roger," she said.

He pulled away and laughed, gazing down at her, stroking his thumb across her cheek. "I'm at the Marriott, not far from here." Mel's eyes lit up. He hated having to squelch her enthusiasm. He held up a finger. "But… I have a roommate." He couldn't help it much if he sounded like a pussy, it was the truth. The government didn't squander money. At least not on him and Todd. "Sorry."

"It's okay. We'll go to my hotel?"

Instead of answering, he grinned and pulled her to her feet. Taking her hand, he steered them through the crowd and to the front door. Once on the sidewalk, he noticed her flushed cheeks and the glimmer in her eyes. She was beautiful and for tonight she was all his. He grinned at the thought and leaned down to take her mouth again, hoping his damn dick would cooperate until they reached his hotel room. Then he stepped to the curb and held up his arm for a passing cab.

In the back seat, Mel reached for him immediately and he embraced her. "You must think I'm pretty fast," she said.

"You're perfect. I think this *taxi* is too damn slow, though." He nipped at her neck until he reached her ear. "I want you, Melissa."

"I hope so," she whispered against his neck. "I think tonight is a pretty sure thing."

Chapter Three

This is stupid. This is so damn stupid. But I want him. I want tonight.

When the cab dropped them off at the main entrance to the hotel, Mel thought David would whisk her through the lobby and upstairs as though they were being chased. And they were, as far as she was concerned, chased by lust that threatened to burst into flames. Instead, arm wrapped around her waist, he ambled to the elevators.

"I have to say, I'm a little disappointed that you're not hurrying me along." The elevator dinged, and the door slid open. They slipped inside and stood at the back wall.

"What floor?" David asked.

"Ten."

David pushed the button. "Now, as for hurrying you along, I don't want you to feel like I'm a horny teenager who can't treat you like a lady because he's so anxious to get in your pants."

Mel huffed a frustrated sigh. "*I* feel like a horny teenager at the moment. It's been a long time and I would appreciate a little reciprocation here."

David laughed and then took her hand and pressed it against the front of his slacks. "Does this not feel like reciprocation?" Good God! The bulge currently undercover in his pants was large and long. She stroked along his length. David sucked in a sudden breath. "Do that once more and you'll see just how horny I am. And how like a stupid teenage kid who can't control himself."

"I like you out of control," she whispered.

"I have to tell you, it doesn't happen often. Shows you how special I think you are."

The ding alerted them to the fact that they were stopping. Mel swiped her hand bank and tried to look like she hadn't just been groping her date. The doors opened to show two couples laughing and talking. "Going down?"

"Up," David ground out.

"So I see," said one of the women with a quick glance at David's crotch. Looking totally unembarrassed, David grinned before repeatedly punching the Close Door button.

"Where were we?" he murmured.

"Waiting until we're inside the room," Mel answered. She folded her hands in front of her and did her best to appear respectable.

"Fortunately, then," he said, taking her hand once again, "we're finally at the right floor." When the door opened this time, he hurried her out. She directed him to the right and the end of the hall. In three seconds flat, she had the keycard in the slot and the door opened. He closed it behind them.

"Do you think those people knew what we are about to do?" Now that they were where she'd wanted to be for the last hour, Mel suddenly felt shy. This was not something she did. Ever. She really had no idea who this man was or what in the world led her to this moment.

"Undoubtedly," he said.

She walked to the window where the curtains remained open and looked at the view over Embassy Row. She'd meant to make this evening count and now she wasn't so sure of what to do. Running to her hotel room—which only a few minutes ago had felt right—now seemed a bit tawdry.

David came up behind her, his hands warm on her shoulders. "Are you having second thoughts?" he asked quietly. "Did seeing those people embarrass you? Is it something I said or did?"

"No. It's just… Like I said, I'm no college student anymore. For a few minutes, sitting in that bar and kissing you, it took me back. But here and now? I don't know. This seems weird."

"Look, Mel, I like you. I mean, I *really* like you. For me, being with you tonight wasn't about getting you here for sex. Although I'll admit, I'd dearly love to have sex with you, too." The proof of that statement poked her in the butt. "But if this makes you uncomfortable we won't stay. Want to go somewhere and grab a cup of coffee? Or… Well, I'll just leave, if that's what you want."

Is that what she wanted? His sweet offer and the fact that he wasn't trying to ignore her doubts and push her into bed added to her original feeling that he was one of the good guys. Mel turned and wrapped her arms around his waist. "No, I want you to stay. But"—she worried her bottom lip between her teeth—"it's been a long time for me."

"We'll take it as slow as you want," he whispered, studying her eyes. Mel raised her head and kissed him.

David started slow and easy but soon tilted his head and slid his tongue into her mouth. Stroking her tongue and teasing the roof of her mouth had her wanting more. His hands skimmed her back and she stepped into him. His erection pressed her stomach. Her nipples prodded his shirt and when he moved, that tiniest bit of friction sent her into overdrive. His woodsy scent enveloped her.

Before she knew it, their kiss was heated and hard. His mouth ate at hers. She pulled his shirt from the waistband of his slacks and ran her hands up his back, against his heated skin. David palmed her breasts. Running his thumbs over her nipples, he slid his mouth down her neck to where it met her shoulder. As though he knew just what to do—and why wouldn't a man who looked like David not have had lots of practice removing a woman's blouse? —he unbuttoned her favorite silk blouse and coaxed it off her shoulders and to the floor. Next came her bra, which he'd unhooked do deftly she hadn't even noticed.

He took half a step back and for a moment just gazed down her body. With shaky fingers, Mel reached behind her and unzipped her skirt. It puddled on the floor atop her blouse.

"My God, you're so beautiful."

Mel laughed self-consciously. "But like I said, no longer the college coed."

David used his finger to raise her chin. "Better, Mel. So much better. Back then it was all passion and nothing else. The desire to see what all the talk was about. Now we know. There's still passion, absolutely, but within the context of life and feelings, and caring about the other person because we *choose* what we want. We choose *who* we want. We don't just react anymore."

Her smile was slow, but her heart raced. Was it possible that she'd accidentally run into the man who could make her feel again? Who could make her trust in a post-Tony world? She traced the laugh lines at his eyes, marveling that this man could be both funny and serious. That he could play and yet be so intense. That he could make her forget her past and want to dive into the unexpected.

"I don't know. My body seems to be reacting to yours pretty well right now."

He laughed and then sobered. Taking her hand, he pressed it against his erection. "I think we're on the same page."

She sucked in a breath. He was long and thick and glorious. "And you choose me to share your passion?"

"I most definitely choose you."

"Well," she said as her smile grew, "in that case, I think you have on far more clothes than you need."

"Not too many clothes to do to you what I want. We had dinner but no dessert. That's because all I could think about all evening was having *you* for dessert. And I can't wait any longer to taste you."

***

It took all of David's willpower to keep from picking Mel up and throwing her onto the bed. She was skittish all of a sudden, though, and he didn't want her to feel steamrolled. She'd said that it had been awhile, and he wanted this experience to be as good as possible for her. But fuck if he didn't want his mouth on her, and right now. Pressing his hands under her ass, he lifted her. She wrapped her legs around his waist, placing her pussy in the exact spot that threatened to make him blow. He couldn't make it to the bed fast enough.

Gently, he laid her near the center and then ran his hands down her torso and across her hips, hooking a sexy pair of black panties and pulling them down and off. He heard a sound and looked up. Mel had turned her head to the side.

"Melissa," he commanded, "look at me." She faced back toward him and finally met his gaze. He hoped all of his desire shone in his eyes. He wanted her to know just what he thought. "You are beautiful." He swept his hand out to indicate her body. "If you haven't heard that lately then you must know some stupid, dumb-ass men."

Spreading her legs, he took a long, hungry look at her pussy, already glistening with her juices. His cock, that thought by now it had been forgotten, nearly danced with glee to be so close to Mel's heat. "I don't want you to be nervous, so I'm telling you what I intend to do, okay?" She nodded but he still saw the tension in her shoulders. "I'm going to eat you"—the catch in her breath make his lips twitch—"and bring you to orgasm like that, with just my mouth." Heat filled her gaze. "Then I plan to use my cock and do the same thing. I want you to feel the passion,

Mel, and I want you to find release, and I want you to know that it's me here doing it because I want you. *I want you.* Are you okay with that?"

"Please, David." Her words were little more than whispers, but they were music to his ears.

They hadn't turned on a light when they entered the room. With the curtains open, glow from the city did a pretty fair job. He didn't need much light for what he was about to do, anyway. Unerringly, David placed his palms on Mel's thighs and gently pressed her legs open. He bent to her pussy and licked along her soft lips, lapping up her juice. Teasing her opening with his tongue, he was rewarded with another rush of juice. Mel was primed and ready to be fucked, there was no question.

Her fingers sifted through his hair, gently but decidedly pressing his head into the sweet vee between her thighs. He set to work with renewed energy, knowing Mel was into it. He momentarily gave up her pussy to seek out her clit with his lips, and added two fingers to her tight, wet channel. Stroking inside and forward brought him to her sweet spot. With a gasp, she arched her back and grabbed his hair, both pushing and pulling him. He had no intention of going anywhere, urging her clit into his mouth and sucking it hard before scraping it very lightly with his teeth.

She went off like a firecracker, crying out and releasing her cream over his hand and chin. He ducked his head and fed, using his thumb to press firmly on her clit while his tongue and lips took care of her juices. She bucked hard but he knew how to ride a woman and he didn't give up until he knew she'd had everything she could handle. Inhaling deeply, he became drunk on her scent—some kind of floral concoction, sex, and woman. There couldn't be a headier fragrance and it made him hurt, literally. He had to get inside her.

Scooting off the bed, he grabbed his wallet from his back pocket and yanked out the condom he kept there. Then he broke the record for stripping and rolling it on. For a second more he looked down at Mel, limp and spread out across the middle of his bed, her eyes half opened and glassy from her orgasm. He'd never seen a more gorgeous sight. Long, long legs, narrow waist, and round breasts, still firm and high. And then there was her face, delicate and oval, now rosy from the glow of what he'd done to her. What he'd brought her to. *Him*, he'd done this. It was stupid, but David felt a sense of satisfaction he hadn't felt with any other woman.

He knelt between her thighs. "Mel," he said softly. "I want to fuck you now. I *need* to. Do you want me? If not, sweetheart, tell me now."

Mel focused her gaze on him and raised up onto her elbows. "Condom?"

David smiled. "On. I wouldn't do anything to hurt you."

"I want you, too."

Dearer words had never been spoken. He touched her again, to be sure she was still wet and ready for him, but he needn't have worried. Juice leaked from her pussy and down to her ass. He used the tip of his cock to spread it along her furrow and then took a slow exploration, fitting just the head of his cock into her pussy. Holding back nearly killed him. Goddamnit, she felt like heaven.

"More," she whispered.

"I don't want to hurt you."

She smiled. "I know how this works, David, and I need it. I *want* it. Please."

David gritted his teeth and tried to strike a middle ground. Taking it easy was agonizing, but she *had* said it had been a while since she'd had sex. He leaned down and kissed her, fusing his mouth to hers and wrestling his tongue with hers. She wrapped her legs around his waist and arched her back, taking him the rest of the way at warp speed compared to his cautious entrance. A groan worked its way from the back of his throat and he eased back, pulling nearly all the way out and then pushing back in.

"Yes!" She turned her head to give him access to her neck.

More quickly, he pulled out. Drove in.

Pulled out. Drove in.

His balls drew up and he felt the orgasm building at the base of his back, the beginning pressure that would make him blow. *Mel first.*

Mel unwrapped her legs from his waist dropped them to his side. David hooked her knee with his arm and stretched her impossibly higher, wider. His balls slapped her bottom with each thrust. A sheen of sweat coated her chest. Her eyes had closed. Her breathing came fast and shallow.

"Melissa, look at me."

With what appeared to be a great effort, she opened her eyes and met his gaze. He was so close, so damn close. "Come for me, sweetheart. Come now."

Unbelievably, she did, hard and greedy, gripping his cock until he could hold back no longer. He shot off, staring right into Mel's eyes and feeling as though he'd just engaged in more than a quick fuck. No, this wasn't a random, unmeaning one-night stand. This was more. How he didn't know, wasn't sure, but strange as it seemed, he'd just cracked open a door to his future.

Chapter Four

In her sleep, Mel dreamed of a tongue stroking her pussy lips and her clit being fondled. She'd been so close to coming, that when she woke to find through her sleep-filled haze that she, in fact, jerked her hips in time to David's tongue and fingers, she hadn't even been that surprised. Just incredibly turned on.

Panting and moaning his name, she clutched his hand that tweaked and rolled her left nipple while the fingers of his other hand toyed with her pussy. His hair wasn't so short that she couldn't grab a fistful and use it to press him into her burgeoning orgasm. Her hips bucked wildly with a mind of their own, and without warning her orgasm broke, sending flashing lights behind her eyelids and fireworks from her pussy to every nerve end in her body. Her heart pounded, and her breath came in gasps.

As Mel fought to bring her breathing under control, David climbed up her body. Her flavor painted her tongue with his deep kiss. Along her stomach, his erection nudged her into awareness that he had taken care of her and not himself.

"You need some relief," she whispered against his lips.

David chuckled. "That would be nice, but don't worry about it. I had two condoms with me." He smiled. "If you remember, we put them to very good use. Plus, I *wanted* to eat you again. You taste fucking good." He turned his head to get at her neck and covered one of her breasts with his big palm.

"Let me take care of you the way you just did for me," she said. Mel had never enjoyed oral sex because she knew about anatomy and what happens with a man's penis. But after all the pleasure David had brought her she was willing to repay him in kind.

"It's okay," he said. "I'll take care of myself later."

Mel reached between them and ran her finger over the tip, slick with pre-cum. David whispered, "Oh, shit, that feels good." He rolled his hips, rocking against her and placing his penis closer. Mel scooted out from under him and pushed him onto his back. Then kneeling on the bed, she pushed her hair behind her ears and bent over him.

"You don't have to do this," David said. At the same time, he stroked her hair back and applied just enough subtle pressure to keep her from moving away.

"I want to." She hoped that was true. She hoped she didn't gag, or jerk away, or say or do anything inappropriate to the moment.

Suddenly, the tip of his cock was at her mouth. Mel slid out her tongue to lick him.

"Oh, fuck yeah. Do it again."

She ran her tongue over him again and then she opened her mouth to take in his head. Running her tongue up and over the rounded, satiny head, and listening to David hiss on an intake of breath, she took heart.

Here she couldn't allow herself to be a doctor. She pushed from her mind that the tool she held in her mouth was what David used to evacuate fluids or release ejaculate. She didn't think of the blood vessels filled to capacity that caused his penis to swell, or the millions of nerve endings that brought him pain or incredible pleasure. His heavy sacks rapidly tightening up against his penis weren't producers of semen. Mel lost herself in the sensations, the steely, satiny feel of him as she held him in her mouth. Nothing in the textbooks hinted at the emotions crowding rational thought from her brain. And those emotions had taken over.

Mel slid her head down his long, long length. When she neared the back of her mouth and started to gag, she stopped and allowed her throat to relax. Feeling his pubic hair tickle her nose sent a thrill of victory through her. She wrapped one hand around his thick base and used the other to caress his scrotum.

"Oh, God, yes. Just like that." David held her hair back. As she ran her mouth back up, using her lips to suck lightly and her tongue to trace the large vein under his cock, she snuck a glance at David. Propped up on one elbow, his gaze locked on hers. Even in the dim lighting, she could tell.

"I wish we had more light. But from what I *can* see, your lips around my cock is about the sexiest thing I've ever imagined."

Silly pride filled her. Tearing her gaze from his, Mel bent to her task. She swirled her tongue across the crown and then engulfed him with her mouth and lips. Down she went, taking care to tongue him every inch of the way. She gave the base of his cock a twist and then started up, sucking hard while whirling her tongue wildly under his cock and along the vein.

She became mindless. Swirl, down, bob, up, all the while, sucking and tonguing. She couldn't get enough. He tasted good. The way his cock filled her mouth, his taste, his scent, the little sounds of David's moans and his whispered encouragement were all she knew. All she wanted. God! Why hadn't any of her friends told her how addictive this could be, how consuming?

How fucking sweet. She hummed in pure satisfaction.

"Mel!" David tugged on her hair, pulling her off.

"No. Let me finish you!"

His voice gruff, he said, "It's okay." He took himself in hand and roughly yanked two strokes before coming on his stomach.

When he finished, and his breathing calmed, Mel climbed out of bed to wet a cloth. She wiped him clean and put the cloth aside. He took her hand and tugged her back into bed. "You surprise me at every turn." He pulled the sheet over them. Lying back down, he wrapped his arm around her. She snuggled into his arms as though that was where she was meant to be.

"I think I just surprised myself. If you only knew how different this whole night has been for me. My friends wouldn't recognize me. I've gone crazy."

"I'm grateful you decided to go crazy with me. But right now, sweetheart, I think I have to—"

"Go to sleep." Mel's eyes closed, and the world went dark.

***

Daylight, not city glow woke Mel. They hadn't bothered closing the curtains last night, using the illumination from the capital city to provide all the light they needed. And they hadn't needed much, since being up close and personal required little artificial brightness. She smiled and stretched, noticing a decided soreness in muscles that hadn't been used in a good while.

After their initial romp, where David used his tongue, mouth, and fingers to bring her off, she'd wondered if the actual sex could possibly feel any better. She needn't have wondered. David proved himself a master of making her body sing. His cock was large and long and had stretched her tired old vagina, and then made it feel things it had never experienced before. In short, he was a magnificent lover.

And they hadn't stopped there. After falling into an almost drugged sleep, he had woken her hours later. Spooning her from behind, he'd lifted her leg over his hips and fingered her to another climax before slipping inside her again, and bringing her off a second time in about the same number of hours. Finally, later, he'd used his mouth again. Mel knew all of the ins and outs of the human body, but as a scientist and doctor, she'd never taken the time to ponder how many orgasms a woman could handle in one night. She'd never had need to, until meeting David.

She knew now that it was more than four. When David brought her to climax with his mouth and then she'd done the same for him, all preconceived notions about what constituted good sex flew out the window. David wasn't just good, he was stupendous.

Fabulous.

Spectacular.

Mind blowing.

All of her knowledge of the human body didn't prepare her for the trembling that had wracked her body or her desire for more from this man. With seeming pleasure, he'd driven her crazy with his mouth, licked her pussy as though he couldn't get enough, rubbed his soft hair over her mound, and planted kisses and tiny nips on her thighs. And he'd used his cock to send her mind into oblivion. No one had ever been able to do that. Her mind never turned off, even during sex. Not until last night.

She knew next to nothing about David except how he made her feel—and not just in bed, but out of bed, too. She wanted so much more. This was not about a night of doing a wild and crazy thing for her. This was about wanting to get to know David Stimson outside the sex.

Turning over, she saw that she was alone in bed. And there was no sound coming from the bathroom. Sitting up, she saw her phone on the nightstand indicated a message. Mel picked it up and checked her texts.

"Well, shit." The text was short and sweet: *Thanks for last night. It was great. Had to work this morning. Will try to call later. David*

What the hell?? She'd been dumped, and even less ceremoniously than Tony had dumped her, which she hadn't thought possible. Obviously, with a brush off this clichéd, she'd not been much more than a one-night stand. Even though a very brief, meaningless interlude was what she'd first anticipated for the night, somewhere between the fucking and the fellatio she'd started to feel something for David. They'd talked and laughed. They'd held each other and touched each other. She'd really wanted to spend the day and the next night with him. And she'd thought he felt the same connection.

Of all the times to find out her mother had been right all those years ago. Once you give the man the milk, he won't want to buy the cow.

***

"If this is a wild goose chase, Chief, I'm gonna kill you." David rubbed his eyes with the palms of his hands. He didn't have to check his watch to know that it was two seconds past too damn early to be up. After he and Mel had spent a good part of the night going at each other like animals, he'd planned to be able to sleep in this morning, maybe slip out and come back to surprise her with coffee—and a box of condoms—and spend the day doing something fun. He hadn't anticipated being shocked out of a sound sleep wrapped around the woman who'd rocked his world by Chief Todd Baxter, USN.

"Fuck, Commander, I wouldn't have interrupted your weekend for anything other than a real problem. The equipment worked just fine last night. I got back from Leesburg and all was well. Then this morning I was woken up by some strange beeping shit. It's the transmitter."

David picked up the pocket-sized piece of equipment. He flipped the on/off switch and high-pitched beeping filled the room. "Fuck." He turned the transmitter off. Running his hand through his hair, he ran through a mental checklist of what could have screwed up a piece of equipment that had performed perfectly until now. Equipment they needed to work perfectly again before they deployed in a little under a month.

"Thoughts, Todd?" David scratched his ear. *His* only thought was that he hoped he could explain this cluster fuck well enough to Mel, so she'd forgive him for skipping out this morning.

Todd shrugged. "I'd say it's not the chip that's bad, but I have no way to test that here."

"Where is the nearest place to test it?"

"Maybe the Navy Yards? But really, the best place is back in Norfolk."

Shit! "I'd rather not go back to Norfolk if the problem can be solved here."

Todd grinned. "Got plans today, Commander?"

"*Had* plans, but…" Damn, he'd give Mel a call and see if she might be free for dinner again, assuming he and Todd could get this fucking piece of equipment working. "It doesn't matter. Getting this thing operational is the first concern. Get on the horn and see what you can find out, will you?" The chief nodded and turned to his phone.

David stepped aside and pulled out his cell phone, sending a quick text. *Taking longer than I thought. Might not be able to make it tonight. Will try to call later.*

Would she understand that this wasn't what he wanted? That he wished he were there in her warm bed with her hot body under his? He wasn't into sexting, or even into sexual innuendo, but surely after yesterday and last night, she had gotten the impression that he wasn't just fooling around with her for a night. In one short day, the woman had gotten under his skin. He didn't know how or why, but he didn't want to fight it, he wanted to explore it. Quickly, he added another text. *Sorry this happened.*

"Sorry, XO, but we have to return to Norfolk." Todd stood before him, concern in his face. "The Navy Yard doesn't have the expertise or the equipment. This *might* be in my area of expertise, but if we need an EE we're shit out of luck up here. Plus, I'm not sure anyone up here has the rights to work on this thing. It's not top secret or anything, but it's not for public consumption, either."

Todd held a mechanical engineering degree but if they needed an electrical engineer they should head back to their own base. "Yeah, I get it. Okay, let's get out of here."

Todd had the good grace to look chagrined. "Sorry about your plans."

"Me, too. But if it's meant to be, she'll understand."

"We are talking about a woman, right, Sir? If she *does* understand, you'd better grab onto her. I haven't had much luck with woman understanding the Navy." Todd began stuffing things into his duffel bag.

"You've been seeing the wrong kind of woman, Chief. This one is different." He hoped. Before starting his own packing, he tried her phone, calling this time. It immediately went to voice mail. Huffing a frustrated breath, David Googled the hotel and called there.

"Ms. Crandall's room, please."

After a few seconds, the clerk came back on the phone. "Ms. Crandall's checked out, Sir. Are you by chance Mr. Stimson?"

"Yes."

"She left you a message should you call. It says, 'Received your message loud and clear. Roger and out.' I hope that makes sense?"

David thought back to the texts he'd sent. Then he tried to think of them as Melissa would have read them. *Fuck!* "Yes, I understood. Thank you." Well, was he royally screwed?

Roger that.

He wanted to be with Mel, but his first responsibility was to the Navy and his position as XO—executive officer of his ship. Tucking his phone into his pocket, he had to admit that Todd was right about women. They were a fickle bunch, with no understanding of what a man had to do.

So much for Mel's being different.

Chapter Five

"I can't believe he blew you off like that." Sissy said. She closed a chart she'd been reading and held it as she slid a hip onto Mel's desk.

"'Thanks for last night. It was great.' That's what the text said. Then he used the old *I have to work* excuse." Mel pulled the file for her next patient from the file cabinet and opened it on the desk. "I'm not all that upset." *Liar!* "After all, it was one amazing night. I'd never expected that it would go further." She might not have "expected," but she sure as hell had hoped.

She shrugged. "He was a good ice breaker." More like an ice melter. He'd heated her up and wrung her out. He'd made her feel beautiful and special and better than she really was. Just the thought of what they'd done to each other increased the tempo of her heart. Why had he left her?

"*Still,*" Sissy emphasized, her hand gesturing toward Mel before propping it on her hip. "Look at you. You're gorgeous, you're an independent woman, you're single, and you're a respected doctor. What's not to love? It was a pretty shitty way for him to leave."

Mel smiled. "First, beauty is in the eye of the beholder. Maybe he didn't think I was beautiful."

Her friend snorted. "Puh-leeze."

"Thanks, but your opinion isn't shared by all the men on earth. Second, he might have *guessed* I'm an independent woman and single, but he doesn't know for sure and he doesn't know I'm a doctor, respected or otherwise."

Sissy walked around the desk and fell into the visitor chair. "What? You spent an evening with the guy and your profession never came up?"

"Nope." Mel grinned. "Other things came up. Several times."

Flapping her hands like a fan in front of her face, Sissy said, "Tell me all. Don't leave out any important details."

Picking up her pen to jot down a few notes before her patient arrived, Mel said, "I don't kiss and tell. Though I will say I won't think of David when I see a little breakfast sausage. But he might come to mind when I walk past the deli counter and see a salami. A long, thick, luscious looking salami."

"Oh, my."

Mel laughed. "What are you mooning over? You go home every night to Mike's salami."

"True." She stared dreamily into space before focusing again on Mel's face. "But it's been so long since you went out—much less went *home*— to any salami that I'd feared you were going to become a vegetarian. I worried you'd end up with a home full of cats instead of a man. Tony really is in the past, huh?"

"Duh. I told you that he is." Tony had left her in bed one morning with the old *it's not you, it's me* scenario, and then had trotted off to another woman. She could never forgive and forget that, but she'd let the humiliation shut her off from the world. No more.

"I know. But working with your ex all the time has got to be hard, and since you haven't dated, well, it leads friends to think that maybe the past isn't in the past. It might lead *exes* to think the same." Sissy looked out the door into the hall. "And speaking of exes…" She rose to leave. "I might have dropped the hint that you were having dinner with someone while you were in D.C."

Horror filled Mel. She wasn't the type to play games and she could only imagine what message Tony took from Sissy's little tale. "You didn't." He would think that she had put Sissy up to the story. His ego would certainly let him believe that she was trying to make him jealous, so she could get him back.

Sissy wiggled her fingers. "Yup. Bye" She slipped out the door just as Tony knocked and came in.

"*She* was in a hurry," Tony said with distaste. He'd never liked Sissy, though she and Mel were best friends. Without being asked, he took a seat in front of her desk.

"What can I do for you, Tony?" She took in his blonde hair, never a strand out of place, his light blue eyes, chiseled chin, and great physique. Even with all that, Mel wondered what had attracted her enough for her to date him for over a year. He didn't compare to David, not in any way. *And you should stop that, right now. Do not start comparing every man to David Stimson.* That way madness lies. Shakespeare damn well knew what he was talking about.

"Nothing," he said. "Just thought I'd stop in to see how you enjoyed your trip to D.C." He picked at a piece of lint that Mel was sure wasn't there. Tony would never allow anything as mundane as lint on his slacks.

"The lecture was good. Dr. Antworth explained a new technique for post-surgical care that I'll write up for our next surgical team meeting."

"Good. That sounds good. And, uh, how was the rest of your weekend? You stayed a few extra days, right?"

Mel put down her pen and leaned forward, elbows on her desk. Was he asking out of standard curiosity? Other than professional discussions and the usual *hi, how was your weekend?* chit-chat, Mel couldn't remember the last time Tony had inquired about her free time.

"Yes, I took an extra day. Went to the museum."

"Ah yes, your penchant for archaeology." His condescension, on top of David's curt, so unimaginative dumping after a night she'd considered beyond magical, stepped on her last nerve. Anger snapped through her.

"Yes, but this time I met someone. Someone who rocked my world, actually." Tony's eyes grew large. "In fact, we spent the last night I was there fucking like rabbits. He gave me more orgasms than anyone ever has, and in more imaginative ways. Did you know there is more to sex than the missionary position, Tony? I could draw you a few diagrams if you like."

He shot out of the chair. "That's disgusting," he said in a low voice. "I thought more highly of you than this, Melissa. Good day." Before she could open her mouth to say more, he was out the door.

"Hey, that went well," she said to herself. Then she bent to the chart to prepare herself for her patient.

***

"Hi, Mom." Mel held the phone between her shoulder and ear while she carried a carton of milk and a box of cereal to the kitchen table where her bowl and spoon awaited.

"Are you eating dinner?"

"Yes, just getting ready to sit down but I wanted to call first and let you know that I'm back from D.C. Heard a great lecture and had some down time." Although, as she remembered, David hadn't had much *down* time. Heat swept through her as a sudden memory of his cock pressing deep inside her almost knocked her for a loop. She plopped the milk down and sank into her chair, willing away thoughts of their night together. She was talking to her *mother*, for God's sake. "Sorry, Mom. What did you say?"

"You're having more than cereal, I hope."

Mel laughed. "Mama, I'm a doctor, I think I know what I can eat and stay healthy." She could just picture her mother's straightened back and forceful face.

"I've been your mother longer than you've been a doctor. I think I know what's best for you. Sweetie," she added, to soften her dictum.

"Yes, ma'am." Would her mother have approved of her date and overnight with David? Would she think that sleeping with a stranger who had sparked her back to life was good or bad for her health?

"Did anything exciting happen while you were away?"

"Kind of." She poured a serving of Cheerios into the bowl and then sprinkled sugar over the small, oat circles. She'd loved the cereal since she was tiny, though her mother normally allowed it only for breakfast, and only on very rare occasions as dinner. "I met a very nice man at the Museum of Natural History. We had lunch and then he took me to dinner, too. It was fun."

"Melissa! That's wonderful. Will you see him again, do you think? Where does he live? What does he do?"

"Slow down, Mom. He was just a serendipitous meeting. We got caught up in talking about so many things that we didn't actually get around to where we lived or what we do. But he was very handsome, and I had a lot of fun. You could tell that he smiles a lot—he had great laugh lines at his eyes." And a fabulous body. "And, most important, he wasn't in the military. He works for some corporation."

"Oh, honey. I don't know why you have such a dislike of the military."

"I don't! I admire it. I admire the people in it. I just know that my significant other can't be a part of it. I couldn't live with it like you did, Mom."

Silence met her claim. Then her mother said, "We can't help who we fall in love with, Melly. If this man was so nice I'm sorry you won't see him again. I know lying, cheating Tony"—Mel smiled at her mother's description—"broke your heart, but you'll find the right man eventually. It sounds like after having dinner with this new guy you discovered that a whole world is still out there for you."

Her mother didn't know the half of it. After dinner Mel had discovered a whole *fabulous* world.

"Now hold on. Before I let you go, your dad wants to say hello." Her mother covered the mouthpiece, but Mel could still hear her "Henry! Pick up. Melly's on the phone."

While she waited for her father, a retired Marine Corps colonel, Mel recalled how wonderful it had felt being held again, being kissed, feeling cherished. Her mom was right. She could find the right man, and now her heart was ready if he dropped out of the sky and into her lap. He'd be professional and independent, good looking—or good looking enough. Mel was no appearance snob—and first and foremost, he would not be in the military. She'd had quite enough of life at Uncle Sam's beck and call.

***

"Off for the weekend, XO?" Todd Baxter leaned on the rail of their ship, watching the men and woman taking passes for the weekend or those just getting off ship to explore Norfolk, Virginia for a few hours as they hurried along the dock.

"I am, Chief. How about you?" David shifted his duffel bag. It was light, with just enough civilian clothes to get him through a couple of days.

"Nah. I offered to take the duty for one of my guys. He thinks he's found the love of his life and wants to spend time with her before we ship out."

David smiled. "Oh, to be that young and stupid again." Although he'd been in that position himself three weeks ago when he'd met Melissa. She'd seemed perfect. Until she hadn't answered his texts or phone calls. Knowing that she wouldn't even give him a chance to explain meant that he'd dodged a bullet.

Todd nodded. "I'm giving him time with her but not without a stern warning about girls who gravitate to sailors and for all the wrong reasons. I made sure he had a supply of rubbers, too, and knew how to use 'em."

Todd's stern, fatherly expression made David laugh. He slapped the chief's shoulder. "You're a good man, Todd. I hope he listened to you. The wrong Navy-town girl will leave a guy broke and unhappy. They should spend as much time in boot camp talking about women as they do fighting."

Todd grunted. "The only safe woman is a man's ship. She'll always welcome him with open arms, even when he's drunk and stupid."

"You don't want to settle down? You're pretty close to retirement years, aren't you?"

"Oh, I've got my twenty years in and a few more, but I don't have any desire to leave the Navy. The first time I left the mountains of North Carolina and found my ass on a ship, I knew this would be my life. They'll have to carry me off some old tub feet first to get rid of me."

David laughed again. He liked the chief, but he couldn't agree with him. Not many years separated them—he was thirty-five and the chief was somewhere under forty. In a couple more years David would be eligible for retirement, but he wanted a wife, a family. He wanted someone to come home to. Melissa Crandall had seemed a likely candidate. Their night together had been pure dynamite. *Some*thing had happened between them, he'd been sure. When he'd slipped his cock inside her tight, hot pussy, it had been more than fucking. There'd been a connection. He'd wanted more. He'd thought she felt that, too.

"So, where are you off to this weekend?" Todd's words brought David back to the present.

"Richmond. There's a series of lectures this weekend about recent Revolutionary War finds." He shrugged. "Thought I might explore some of the battlefields and sights around the city. Keep my feet on the ground a bit longer before we pull out next month."

"Have fun." Todd slapped the railing a couple of times and then turned. "Don't do anything I wouldn't do," he said with a smile.

David smiled back, lifted his duffle onto his shoulder and stepped onto the gangway. He didn't plan to do anything exciting. After all the work he and Todd had been involved in with that special communications unit they'd tested in D.C., as well as managing their normal work on board ship, he was tired. A few lectures about a topic that fascinated him, a few good meals and some great Virginia wine, a quiet weekend exploring in the Commonwealth's capital—that was all he wanted. All he expected. He'd crashed and burned with a dark-haired, green-eyed beauty in D.C. despite his body going off like a brick of C4. He didn't need any further excitement in his life.

Chapter Six

Opening French doors to a deck that overlooked the hotel's private garden courtyard, Mel mentally patted herself on the back for choosing the Birkstone boutique hotel in Richmond's Shockoe Bottom. A trellis of roses led to a bench at one end of the garden. More roses and espaliered camellias lined the wall of the brick side of the hotel at the other end.

Inside, her small suite boasted a sitting room, wet bar and microwave, and a double-sided gas fireplace, viewed from the bedroom, too. The bedroom was tastefully furnished. A king-sized bed centered along a wall offered a great view of the fireplace and convenience to the bathroom where she could shower in a tile and glass stall or relax in a deep soaking tub. She planned to make good use of that baby later on, after the lectures. Honestly, she would be happy skipping the lectures and relaxing here for the next three days.

She picked up the brochures for the lectures she'd traveled a couple of hours to hear. It seemed that in an area between Yorktown and Williamsburg, three house foundations had recently been uncovered along one of the thousands of creeks in the area that drained into either the York or James rivers, and then into the Chesapeake Bay. What made these foundations interesting is that evidence of a Native American village existed a scant mile away. Scientists from the University of Richmond and William and Mary University concluded that the English homesteads and the village were contemporary and apparently existed in harmony. Work was still going on to determine what more could be gleaned from the remains.

"No, I'll go," she said out loud. "But I'm coming back with a good bottle of wine. Then I'll have a long soak in the tub, read a bit, and go to bed with the fragrance of flowers surrounding me." Slinging the straps of her bag over her shoulder, she headed out. "And by morning, hopefully, I will have stopped talking to myself."

Twenty minutes later, she entered the Virginia Museum of Fine Arts and followed the signs to the designated conference room. A large group of people stood around, cups in hand, mingling, something Mel was okay at doing when she had to. Today she'd enjoy just keeping to herself, feeling no pressure to converse or be social.

Mel found the table that held the coffee pot and cookies. She poured a cup and then wandered over to another table that held copies of books about the Williamsburg-Yorktown-Jamestown area, several written by the day's lecturer. She bought two and stored them in her bag. By then she was ready to select her seat. Turning, she found a pair of brown eyes staring at her from across the room. Rich, dark, intense brown eyes that she had been seeing in her sleep for weeks. *It can't be.*

Yet it was. David Stimson stared back at her. She nodded, acknowledging him but not moving to meet him. Instead, she turned to her right and walked up the aisle to take a seat in the center, two rows back from the lectern. Flustered at the way her heart sped up when she saw him, she now determined to ignore him. Of course, she would be polite if he saw fit to speak to her, but she would not approach him. Nor would she speak first. She would ignore him. Absolutely, totally ignore him. The night they had together was very nice. *Very* nice. But he'd dumped her. Dumped her in a way guys dump women they picked up in bars. She did not go to bars. She did not get picked up. She did *not* get dumped and then forgive and forget.

She did not.

Oh, God. He was sitting behind her. She could smell him, detect that unique fragrance that was only his. When he'd held her so tightly they seemed to become one person, his scent had been imprinted on her. She closed her eyes and tried to inhale without looking stupid. The Styrofoam cup in her hand shook with the trembling of her hands. Hoping she could do so without appearing weird, she stood and moved down several seats to her right. There. That was—

Damn him! He'd moved, too. Without giving herself time to think, she stood and walked to the back of the room where she tossed out her half-full cup of coffee. Her left hand grasped the strap of her bag in order to keep from shaking. She wiped her right hand, suddenly sweaty, on her slacks.

"Don't like coffee?" asked a male baritone. Not David. *Thank God!*

Mel spun around to find a very nice-looking man in a navy blue colored three piece suit and gray tie. His clothing shouted professor. The bump in his nose said it had been broken at some point. A slight ruddiness marked his cheeks. From exercise or something else. Hmm. Maybe drinking? He appeared trim, but he leaned on one leg more than the other, showing an injury or weakness of some kind. Finally, she looked back to his eyes. They were clear and open, and light blue instead of chocolate brown.

"I let it get cold, I'm afraid."

He held out his hand. "Dr. Samuel Myers."

She took his hand and felt his subtle squeeze her have it. "Dr. Melisa Crandall. "You're the presenter today."

He gave a wry smile. "Guilty. Are you on staff at William and Mary or Richmond?"

"Neither. I'm a medical doctor but also a fan of archaeology and what's being done in the state."

"Ah!" He struck a very professorial pose—right arm across his chest, left elbow resting on it while his fingers lazily stroked his lips. "An amateur. Interested parties are always welcome, of course." His eyes narrowed as he took a harder, more appreciative look at her. "And at the site, too. I'd be happy to show you around if you're ever in the Williamsburg area."

A hand suddenly found its way to Mel's back. A soft, woodsy scent assailed her nostrils, and she knew just who stood beside her.

"There you are, Melissa. I've been waiting for you to come back to your seat." He stuck out his hand. "And you're Dr. Myers, aren't you? We're really looking forward to your talk." The men shook hands. Mel tried to extricate herself from David's arm, but his fingers dug in and she was trapped.

"The doctor was just saying that he would tell me more about the site during dinner." The lie rolled off her tongue like a No 2 pencil off a desk. Despite the professor's startled glance, she couldn't find it in herself to be sorry. She wanted David to know that she'd gotten past him and his luscious body. "You are not invited," she ground out.

"While I wouldn't be averse to din—" Samuel started.

"Not possible." David interrupted without even a flinch. "Did you forget, Mel, that we already have plans for dinner?"

She snapped her head around and glared at him. "*We* have nothing to do together. Not today, not ever."

"*Yes*, we do."

"*No*, we do—"

"Excuse me, please," the professor said. "The lecture is about to begin." He hurried off, leaving David and Mel alone at the back of the room.

"Look what you've done now. I could have had dinner with an *interesting* man." She wanted to stomp her foot like a child. She wanted to have on her highest heels and stomp her foot right on David's instep. But she wore flats and the effect wouldn't be the same.

He leaned closer. "Now you can have dinner with me," he whispered.

Oh! The man infuriated her. Why was she so incensed to see him? Why so nervous? *Because you were the dumpee and not the dumper. He was proactive and you were reactive. Which of these positions holds the power, idiot? Take charge!*

Mel closed her eyes to gather strength. "Look. You're here and I'm here. That doesn't mean we have to talk to each other or have anything to do with each other."

"What if I want to? What if I see this as a golden opportunity to make you listen to me?"

Mel started back to the seating area. "What if I don't want to listen to you?" She turned and held up her index finger. "And don't sit behind me. It's creepy and stalker-like, and—"

"Distracting?" He smiled as though he knew just what he did to her emotionally and physically. David leaned closer. "Good. That's what I want you to feel."

"Excuse me," she said trying to scoot by a man sitting in the third row.

"May I ask you to move down one seat so we can sit together?" David asked the man. "I'm with her."

Inwardly, she groaned. Why in hell hadn't she stayed in her room and soaked in the tub?

***

"That was interesting," David said as they walked out of the conference room. He'd only heard every third word or so. Her soft floral scent had wafted over him, robbing him of any interest in whatever that prick of a professor was talking about. The dick had tried to pick up Mel with that cheesy effort "I'll share my very important, elite, professorial thoughts with you if you'll have dinner with me." Not quite the "I'll show you my etchings" line, but the principle was the same.

"It was, yes." Mel tried to move away by picking up her steps but she was no match for him. He'd run a few marathons. Keeping up with a five-foot-ten woman was nothing.

"Where are you going so fast?"

"Away from you, please."

"Don't think so." When they'd first met in Washington, he'd been fucking knocked on his ass by her—her beauty, her intellect, her humor.

Her body. He thought he'd done everything right. Then the whole weekend went to hell. He wanted to know why.

"We need to talk." David didn't touch her, but he did kind of crowd her into the main lobby of the museum. A noisy group of school kids filled the area. He had to get her alone. "Let's have some coffee and talk, like civilized people."

"I don't think I can be civilized with you." But she had stopped and not torn out of there and away from him.

David leaned down and tilted his head to look into her eyes. Green as a forest, they were, and just as thick and forbidding.

"Mel, let me explain what happened and then you can explain where and how I fucked up. That we're both here like this, well, it's like a sign, you know?"

She laughed and then slapped her hand over her mouth as though she didn't want to. "A sign? That's the best you can come up with?"

A coil of tension unwound inside David's chest. He smiled. "I'm under pressure here. Give a guy a break." Now he dared to touch her. Reaching out his hand, he stroked her arm, just enough so she knew he was there. "How about that coffee? Or an early dinner? I just want to talk to you."

She stared off into space. She might have been looking at the poster extolling the Faberge eggs the museum had on display, or she could have been looking for an escape route. Then she flicked her wrist and glanced at her watch. "It's only three-thirty. Too early for dinner. But the museum has a café where we can get coffee and dessert."

The words had his cock rising because he remembered what he'd had for dessert after their dinner in D.C. Sweet, sweet Melissa.

If Mel were the dessert, he'd eat her any time of day or night. But he didn't think she had that in mind. Damn it. "Dessert? Before dinner?"

"Life's short."

Chuckling, he fell into step with her. "I think I could go for some chocolate. We have half an hour before the next lecture. Plenty of time." Plenty of time for coffee but not long enough for their talk. And not nearly the time he wanted just to take in her beautiful face, soft hair, sexy body. There might not be enough time in the world for that.

"That's what I had in mind." Mel checked the sign at the broad staircase and started down.

"You don't mind if I tag along?"

She shrugged but she didn't slow to wait for him "It's a free country."

"Good. Then I'm with you."

She sighed. "Why am I not surprised?"

He nudged her shoulder. "Tell the truth. You're happy to see me, aren't you?" Her hard expression softened somewhat. He was sure that slight smile wasn't his imagination.

"That remains to be seen."

"On…?"

"On whether the bullshit you're about to spout about why you dumped me in Washington makes any sense." She blushed when a little girl passing by twittered. "Now look what you made me do. I hardly ever curse in public." They reached the bottom. The entrance to the café was just on their left.

He stopped and faced her, hands on her shoulders. "Mel, it's not bullshit. I told you it was work and it was. Kind of an emergency with that gadget. You know, the one I was going to use to take over the world? We had to get it back to the lab."

"Right."

"It's true. And I told you how much I enjoyed our night. I told you over and over in texts and would have said it if you'd ever answered my calls."

"'Thanks for last night.' That's what you said."

What? She was upset over that throwaway line? *What the fuck??* "So, if I'd said, 'Last night was the best of my life, you're a sex goddess!' you would have responded to my calls? You would have been there when I called the hotel to explain what was happening? *That's* what you mean?"

She shot him a chagrined look. "Well, like that it does sound kind of silly. But you needed to be in my place. A hot stranger had left my bed after a night of sex with the stereotypical dump note. And not even an actual note, a *text*. What am I supposed to think?"

"And when I texted more and left messages?"

"I don't know. I didn't read them or listen. I deleted them." She backed up and David dropped his arms to his side. "Look. I enjoyed our night in D.C. I went willingly and I had a good time. No harm, no foul. Let's just leave it at that, okay? This"—she flipped her finger between them—"is a bad idea. Despite what happened in D.C., I'm not a convenient lay for you just because we're both here."

He planted his hands on his hips and shook his head. "Believe me, nothing about you has been convenient."

She placed her hands on her hips, too. "And what is that supposed to mean?"

"That I don't *see* you as a convenient lay. You're not easy, Mel." Legs braced, feet apart, David stared into her eyes. "But you're worth whatever trouble it takes to be with you. Know why?"

"No. Why?"

"Because you're beautiful and you're fun. You're an intelligent woman who knows her own worth, and I find that to be sexy as hell. It might not have been the same for you, but that night in D.C. *was* one of the best nights of my life."

Mel stood there, her mouth hanging open and then she shut it. Finally, after what felt like an eternity, she held out her hand. "Come on. I'll buy us some coffee and maybe a piece of cake."

Chapter Seven

Once Mel got past the idea that David had unceremoniously dumped her, she started feeling fine. Better than fine—*great.* They shared a piece of chocolate cake and had coffee. Choosing to give up the second lecture and talk instead, they strolled through the museum.

In the garden, David took her hand and said, "It's been a while since I've enjoyed myself so much." Grinning down at her he added, "At least three weeks I'd say."

"Yes, the weather *is* nice." The way they'd fallen back into the easy camaraderie they'd shared a few weeks ago amazed Mel. She couldn't remember anyone she'd felt so comfortable with so quickly. Her anger simply vanished once she'd heard his explanation. After David explained, she'd felt like a real jackass for not reading his texts or listening to his voicemails. Childish, that described her.

David slipped his arm around her waist. She liked the feeling. "Yeah, the weather is fine, but I think you know what I mean."

"I don't get here often, but I love Richmond." Mel glanced at her watch. Her little fantasy of seeing him again was about to end. The rush of disappointment surprised her but no good could come of extending their time. He'd explained why he'd left as he had and she'd apologized for not giving him a chance to do so weeks ago. The man was like sex on a stick. He made her pussy clench and her nipples perk up for attention. If she stayed with him much longer, she'd fall back into bed with him, and she'd already experienced a turn on the wild side.

"It's been fun seeing you again, David, but I have dinner reservations and have to get back to my hotel."

The evening she'd originally looked forward to—dinner, a hot soak, reading and then settling into bed—alone—now held no appeal, but she'd meant it when she said she wasn't available for a night's sex just because they'd been thrown together again. They'd shared a very nice afternoon but now it was time to go back to her life and let him get back to his.

"*Nooo,*" he said. "You aren't going to make me dine alone, are you?"

"I'm afraid so." As soon as the thought occurred to her she tried to swallow it down but the words slipped out anyway. "I'm sure there are any number of girls available to keep a mad scientist like you from eating dinner alone. You wouldn't even have to look very hard to find one." She hated the very idea of his spending the evening with another woman, but she had no strings on him.

His victorious grin was immediate and he backed her up against the side of the building beside large glass doors leading into the lobby. "I think you just said I was sexy." One arm braced above her head and the other still at her waist, his breath fanned her cheeks. "Is that what you were saying, Mel?"

She tried and failed to stop her heart from racing. His eyes were the color of the dark chocolate of the cake they'd just eaten, and so heated and intense, it scorched her wherever his gaze landed. Points south heated, too. Keeping her voice from showing how much she wanted him to kiss her took all of her effort. "I'm sure some women would think so." She tapped his chest with her index finger. "But don't be vain."

He chuckled and leaned impossible closer, his mouth to her ear. All of her defenses crumbled. The scent of him invaded her mind. She wanted to drown in him, wanted to consume him and have him consume her. She shivered with sudden need.

"Didn't we already talk about the difference between us and college kids? There's only one woman in this city, no, in this whole fucking state that I want to find me sexy, and I'm standing with her right now."

He moved his hand from her waist up and over her arm and shoulder to sweep it under her hair. His lips nuzzled the tender skin beneath her ear. "Do you, Melissa? Do you find me sexy?"

It was so much like a pick-up scenario. *Oh baby, I only want you to find me sexy. Do ya?* So cheesy. So lame. So damn intoxicating. If they hadn't been steps away from the museum crowds, she would have ripped off his shirt and slid her leg up over his hip.

Time to end this. "You are delusional."

He leaned back and looked into her eyes. "Too fast? No matter. I meant what I said. I know what I want. And you're it, Mel."

"You mean tonight."

He studied her eyes. His gaze dropped to her lips and back up. She started to squirm under his inspection. "I mean at least for tonight. I have the whole weekend."

"If you don't get called away for 'work' again."

He brushed his thumb across her cheek. "Nothing is going to drag me away this weekend. How about you?"

"I came for the lectures and a weekend of relaxation."

He smiled, showing his dimples, and her heart nearly stopped. "I know the best form of relaxation in the history of man."

Did she want to spend the night with him again, even knowing that his lines were pretty much that—just lines? Or should she follow her mind and common sense that insisted the guy was a player? Her heart won out. No way would she let him take advantage of her, but she wanted to spend more time with him. She couldn't resist. Laughter and conversation with him were addictive.

"How about dinner? I'm sure the restaurant would accommodate one more." He opened his mouth to speak and she cut him off. "But it's just dinner. We go Dutch and say good-bye afterward."

He narrowed his gaze and seemed to think about her offer. "Here's a counter offer. It *might* be 'just dinner,' I pay, and we'll decide what to do after we eat...and after one kiss."

"I'm staying downtown. After dinner, you take a taxi back to wherever *you're* staying, one kiss with *nothing* afterward. It's good night and that's it."

"You drive a hard bargain. And by the way, I'm staying downtown, too."

"Good. That will make your cab fare less expensive." She raised one brow, daring him to contradict the terms she'd set for the evening.

"You're stubborn. Has anyone ever told you that?"

She thought of Sissy, her mother, her father, and several doctors at the hospital, all of whom had railed against her stubbornness at one time or another. "No," she said. "I'm generally considered to be the soul of flexibility."

With his hand on her waist once more, he guided them back to the museum's parking lot where she had left her car. "I'm *sure*."

His tone was not lost on her. She smiled in victory.

***

The restaurant sat directly over the James River, on pilings at the end of a cobbled street. Water flowed beneath them, and sitting at a window, with the one-hundred-eighty-degree view they had, David might have believed they were on the bow of a ship, except sea legs weren't required. Because the fall line was west of the city, the James was still tidal at Richmond, though the ebb and wane of the tide wasn't felt as strongly there as farther downstream. Still, the unstoppable tide fought the natural, seaward flow of the river.

Light from hundreds of bulbs lining the roofline of the restaurant shimmered in the swift moving water. Watching them could mesmerize one, but not as much as Mel's beauty entranced him. He'd fucked up the last time they were together, but he wasn't about to screw up this second chance.

They sat in a mostly abandoned corner of the restaurant, in the time between early and late dining. She was finishing her coffee, her movements graceful. He loved watching her do even simple things, like putting the cup back onto the saucer, patting her mouth with her napkin, resettling in her chair, knees together and hands folded in her lap. Someone had taught her all of the ladylike actions. But he knew that in bed she shed her lady persona and became something passionate. Something bewitching.

They still hadn't touched on anything personal, even after all the time they'd spent together. When he was on a date, the woman usually grilled him about what he did, how long before he could advance to the next rank, and in one case, how much a lieutenant commander made a month. What he'd talked about with Todd Baxter held for officers as well as enlisted men. There were some women who made a habit of seeking out military men. The benefits were pretty great—medical care, allotment checks every month like clockwork, and reasonable housing in many cases.

Unfortunately, long absences were sometimes seen as an advantage of hooking up with a navy man—they were away from home for long periods of time, providing freedom for a spouse to cheat that wasn't as easily available with a civilian. David had long ago avoided talk about his career in an effort to ward off undesired interest.

But Mel interested him. He didn't mind curiosity in reverse. "Did you take ballet as a child?" he asked.

She tilted her head and looked at him. "I did, for about four years. Why do you ask?"

"It shows. You have a real grace about you tonight."

She laughed. "So, I was klutzy before?"

"Oh yeah. You were a mess. It was all I could do to keep you in bed."

"As I remember, you were the one who had trouble staying in bed," she said wryly.

He slapped his hand over his heart. "I apologize again. Not gonna happen this weekend, I promise."

"But then, since you won't be in my bed I won't know, will I?"

David lowered his voice. "Did our night mean so little? It affected me, Mel. I guess I hoped it had had the same effect on you. Are you telling me that it didn't?"

Her eyes darkened and he swore he found desire in their green depths. Then she seemed to regroup. He saw it in the straightening of her shoulders.

"Dinner was delicious," she said, pushing away her cup and saucer. "Thank you."

"My pleasure." He leaned closer, placing his arm on the back of her chair. "What now?"

She quirked a smile his way. "You call a taxi and go to your hotel and I go back to mine where a hot bath is calling my name. Then I shall retire for the evening."

"Don't retire. I have a much better idea. Will you keep an open mind?"

She leaned back. "Maybe."

He'd take it. "Maybe" was always better than no. "I think we should take advantage of the pleasant night to window shop. Some of the stores lining the street looked interesting. We could walk off dinner."

"I don't know." Mel glanced out the window. "It's pretty dark. You might try to take advantage of me."

He jerked back and widened his eyes, expressing shock. "You might take advantage of *me*." Then he smiled. "But I'll chance it."

He saw the moment her expression softened and her mouth turned up in a half smile. "If you're brave enough to risk it, then I guess I am, too."

David stood and helped her with her chair. Standing so close, her gentle perfume worked its magic on him. His heartbeat kicked up a notch and other parts of him came alive, too. He placed his hands on her shoulders and gave a light squeeze. "Of course, I could help us work off our dinner in other ways. Does your tub fit two?" Instead of pulling away, she leaned back into him. Hope had him sliding his hands down her arms and to her hands.

"I'll bet you could. Aerobic exercise is good for you, you know."

"I have heard that. Thirty minutes three or four times a week."

She turned her head. Her hair drifted across his chin and he linked their fingers. He had to get her out of that restaurant and fast before he embarrassed them both. "You can do better than three or four times a *week*, can't you?"

He chuckled. "You already know the answer to that." Reluctantly, he stepped back from her. "We should go before we cause a scene."

The startled look on Mel's face told him that like him, she had forgotten where they were. "Good Lord," she murmured.

David needed to adjust his cock, straining painfully against his slacks, but there was no way to do it there. He took her hand and led her to the front of the restaurant. Before they reached the door, Mel tugged his arm. He turned and she stretched up to his ear. "Just so you know, our night affected me as much as it did you."

That was what he wanted to hear. He dropped a kiss on her lips. Once outside he led her to her car and kissed her thoroughly. "I want to make love to you, Mel. All night long and all day tomorrow. In bed, in the shower, against the wall, anywhere we can fit together. And we fit together so damn well. I want you. Do you hear what I'm saying?"

She looked up, her eyes glazed, and nodded. "Yes. Where is your hotel?"

He smiled. "Right up the street. Where are you staying?"

"Right up the street as well."

"Not the Birkstone," they said in unison.

David smiled. "That's another sign that we're meant to be together. I hope their sundry shop has the one item I need…"

She smiled back. "If not, I know where there's a Walgreen's nearby."

"So, we both just parked in the garage that the hotel uses? That was handy."

"Yup." Mel pulled on his hand, laughing. The sound was music to his ears. "Let's hurry," she said, "I've always had a fantasy about a very special room service guy. Will you give me room service?"

"I'll be your room service guy, pool boy, pizza delivery guy, or boy toy for as long as you'll let him." His dick yelled at him to cut out the chit-chat and get her to the room already. His heart said to take his time and savor being with her. He decided to follow his heart. She sighed, but she slowed to his pace.

"We've never talked about our jobs. I'm a doctor, specializing in pediatrics. If you're allowed to say, what do you do…" She cast a short glance his way. "You're not really a spy, are you?"

"No." The moment of truth came crashing in. Did he trust her? From the very beginning, he'd felt a strong attraction. When they'd had lunch in Washington and he'd asked her to dinner a sense of near desperation had clutched him when she didn't answer right away. And he hadn't stopped thinking of her ever since. But… She hadn't given him a chance to explain what had happened. She'd taken off without trying to reach him—taken off while leaving a kind of snarky message with the hotel front desk.

Still, he was planning on spending the rest of the weekend with her. Hell, he planned to spend a good part of the weekend *in* her. That implied some level of trust, didn't it?

"Not a spy. More like a vice president of a large corporation. Pretty much at the beck and call of the president for whatever needs doing. Thus, my testing of equipment in D.C."

They pushed through the revolving door of the hotel lobby. "Corporate guy. You're a professional. That's what I thought and I'm glad of that."

Huh. *What does that mean?* And just like that, he decided not to reveal anything further. "You've been thinking of me. I knew it! Keep it up, please." They stopped just inside the main door. "Shall I give up my room?"

"I think so, yes." There was no hesitation, no hint of doubt in her eyes. A niggle of worry ran down his back. He wanted her. Hell, he was afraid he was falling in love with her. And before they went much further he needed to be completely honest about his job and who he was, what his life was. Then she rose up to give him a quick kiss and all rational thought fled from his mind.

"I'll be right back," he whispered against her lips.

Just as he wanted, she smiled and said, "I can't wait."

First stop front desk and then the sundry shop. He hoped like hell they carried condoms because a trip to a drug store would be a very painful proposition. *And* he planned to need a lot more than the puny two condoms in his wallet. A great deal more.

Chapter Eight

The heat of the water contrasted nicely with the coolness of the air and even created a steamy mist over the tub. Of course, some of that steam might be a residual of the fire they'd created in the bedroom. They'd hardly entered the room before they were naked and fucking like animals. Now they took a break in the tub in preparation for what she hoped would be another round.

David sat at one end and Mel reclined at the other, her legs on either side of his. They'd been there for a good twenty minutes, give or take, and she just wanted to close her eyes and take a nap. But then, she really resented sleep since it would take up her time with David.

She tapped his thigh with her toe. "Have I told you what great form you have?"

He stroked her ankle. "Not in so many words, but when you shouted 'Oh, God! Oh, dear God!' just a few minutes ago, I got the hint that you liked my form."

His foot rested perilously close to her clit. Mel squeezed his big toe playfully. Wait a minute. She never did playful. There'd been a change in her attitude toward David, one she wasn't used to, one that felt abnormal and yet somehow right. *She* felt right with him. Was it just the phenomenal sex? Mel didn't think that was all of it, though the thought of how he played her body made her tremble.

"Are you getting cold?"

She shook her head. No need letting him know how very *hot* she was getting. "I *meant*, your body. Your muscle tone is excellent. I noticed your posture right away at the museum and you carry yourself with confidence. I would say that you make enough money to afford a great gym and that you use it." Did he stiffen slightly? The sensation came and quickly left, making her think she imagined it.

"How about my feet?" he asked, lifting his leg and sticking his foot out of the water. "Have you noticed my feet?" He stared at her with wide eyes and a smirk.

"I told you I'm a doctor. I notice *everything* about someone physically. And I can tell a *lot* about your feet, smart ass." With a firm grip, she lifted his foot into her lap and massaged his arch. Through the water, she saw his cock start to rise.

David smiled. "Careful there. You know there's a correlation between the foot and the genitals."

She quirked her brows. "I'm a doctor. I know it all." She pressed more firmly. David hissed in a breath.

His smile turned from amused to primal. "So, don't tell me you notice everything and didn't see that pole straining toward you."

Laughing, she dropped his foot and grabbed the sides of the tub. "I think we should get out of here so I can examine that pole more closely. As a doctor, I mean."

"I always follow doctor's orders," he responded. He rose, water sluicing off his body. His biceps bulged in the arm he used to push off the side of the tub. The ridges marking his abdomen tightened with the effort of rising from the warm water, and his thighs rippled as he changed from sitting to standing. With each inch of his body revealed, Mel's mouth became drier. With the impressive ridge of his erection at nearly eye level, the butterflies in her stomach changed from flapping wings to stomping around in army boots. It seemed inconceivable that this beautiful man was hers.

Hers. She liked the sound of that. They'd known each other only a very short time, but thinking of them together felt natural.

He held out his hand. "Don't tell me you're suddenly shy."

She took a breath and reached for his hand. "Not shy, just anticipating."

"Me, too," he said in a low voice. "Sitting here with you so close and yet not close enough? That's been killing me." He grinned. "But now you're all relaxed and boneless. Totally at my mercy." She stepped out of the tub and wrapped herself in a large fluffy towel.

Before the cool air penetrated the cocoon of her wrapping, David led her to the carpeted floor before the fireplace. He switched the unit on and an immediate flow of warm air surrounded them.

"You're shivering," he murmured, rubbing the towel up and down her arms.

"I'll be warmer as soon as I can touch you." He directed her hand to his cock, silky, hard, and warm to the touch. She sighed. "Yes. You make me so hot."

"God, Melissa, I'm burning for you." David brushed her hair aside and licked her neck, then kissed his way from her jaw to her ear. Her heart pounded. Her pussy tingled.

"Smooth talker."

He swept Mel onto his lap. She straddled him while he took her mouth over and over. His tongue stroked hers, exploring, searching until she released the moans she could no longer hold inside. She needed air. Pulling her mouth away and gasping for breath gave David the opportunity to kiss a path down her neck and across her collarbone. When he sucked her breast into his mouth and lightly nibbled her nipple, Mel dropped her head back and spiked her fingers through his hair. His cock slid over her butt cheek. Her pussy skidded over his abdomen. An orgasm built, spiraling up, just moments from bursting through her.

"Huh-uh. I need to be inside you when you come." David grasped her rear cheeks and kneaded them. His cock landed between them, stroking her from behind all the way to her clit. She lost it.

David took her mouth once more in a hungry, rough kiss. He didn't play with her tongue, he dominated it. She didn't know up from down, but she felt that kiss. She knew the mastery of it, the command. His control and power excited her.

When in all of that he'd managed to find a condom and slide it on, she didn't know. Mel had barely come back to awareness when he lifted her hips and fit her over him. She opened her eyes only to watch him close his. He sucked in a ragged breath and then, grasping her hips, raised her up and thrust her down. Again, up and down. His arms strained as he sought to move her faster and faster.

Mel draped her arms over his shoulders, feeling his muscles bunch and relax with each move. On her knees, she took the brunt of their motion onto herself. She leaned into him, scraping her sensitive nipples across his chest hair, and pressing her clit against the root of his cock with each downward slide.

Only the sound of their pants filled the air. A light sheen of sweat lubricated their bodies as they glided over each other. David wrapped his arms around her waist. His hands grasped her butt, increasing their closeness and urging greater speed. The stubble on his chin scraped her cheeks and along her neck. Open-mouthed, she sought to stifle her cry on his neck as her orgasm tore through her, destroying every inhibition left in her.

David clutched her to him, going deep and staying there, right where her body wanted him. His cock pulsed as he gasped for breath. She knew exactly how he felt.

When time became a reality, David slowly sank to his back taking Mel with him. She reclined over him, limp and satiated. He rubbed her back. "Cold?"

She shook her head. "No. Good thing. I don't think I could move to get up and find a blanket."

Mel roused herself enough to prop her head on his chest. If he kept that light back rub up, she would be asleep in no time, and she didn't want to waste a moment of being with him.

"Hmm. Tomorrow night I vote we skip the hot soak and get right to the hot *stuff*." He tipped her nose with his index finger. "That's you, by the way."

Mel smiled. "You're pretty sure of yourself, aren't you?"

He studied her a moment. Brushing her hair behind her ears he cupped her cheek. His eyes burned with desire and his expression held no sign of levity. "I guess I'm hoping I can be. There's something between us, Melissa. If you don't feel it too, tell me now."

Her heart trip-hammered. "I feel it, David. I"—she took a deep breath—"I think it's good. I do."

His lazy smile lit her up inside. He leaned forward to kiss her. "Then if you don't mind, do you think we could give up the floor for that king-sized bed over there?"

***

"Mel? Wake up, sweetheart."

"Hmm?" Mel rolled over, looking all sleepy and yet still thoroughly fucked. He'd woken her twice last night, each time he'd rolled over to find her sweet, sexy warm body next to his in bed. She fit him perfectly, concave to convex, soft to hard, strength for strength.

He kissed her neck and then left little nibbles all along her jaw. She made cute sexy little sounds and turned over to snuggle against him. David had been up for over an hour. He'd enjoyed a cup of coffee. The Birkstone was a cut above, by having a great rich roasted coffee instead of the crappy stuff he usually found. But now it was time to get going if they were going to make the morning lecture at the museum. He bent over Mel with a towel tucked around his hips, fresh from cleaning up.

"Oh, you're up," Mel murmured. Then she reached up and tugged on the towel, letting it drop to the floor. As soon as she touched his cock he hardened, ready for action. She giggled. He smiled at the lighthearted sound, but his smile froze when she licked her lips and then took hold of him like she meant business. She ran her hand up his length and back down.

"You really *are* up," she said. She pulled back the covers. "Come back to bed."

He'd thought they should get up and find some place for breakfast, but fuck that shit. Without a second thought, he grabbed a condom off the nightstand and slid under the covers. Mel immediately snuggled up to his side, throwing one arm over his waist and her leg over his hips. She used her knee to nudge his cock, bobbing and anxious to be let into her pussy to play.

"When you come awake, you really come awake," he said. Turning his mouth to hers, he took her in a long kiss.

"Part of being a doctor," she responded. "But waking up is not normally this good." She sucked his bottom lip between her teeth and gave a little nip.

"For me, either," he whispered. He ran his hands down her side, stopping to tweak her nipple, already hard as a pebble, and then sliding around to her ass. What a fine ass she had, too. Supple yet firm, as though she exercised to keep in shape. Just for him. *Only* for him. He liked the thought of that, although he'd never—ever, *ever*—entertained ideas like that about any other woman. With Mel, it seemed right.

Maybe. He'd wait and see how the rest of the weekend went, but more and more he saw a longer commitment as a viable situation. Those were his thoughts, anyway. He had yet to figure out what she wanted.

"David," she whispered. "Make love to me."

"Gladly," he whispered back. He donned the rubber and flipped her onto her back. His fingers glided through her juices when he reached down to test her, and he rubbed her with his cock before gliding into her hot pussy.

"Ohhhh."

Her moan did something to him. He wanted to make her do it again. And again. Every night and morning. "Do it again, sweetheart. I want to hear when I make you feel good."

"I'd be nothing than a bundle of raw nerves making noise then." She smiled up at him and raked her fingers through his hair as she arched her back. "You don't want that."

"You'd be fucking surprised what I want," David said, his mouth buried against her neck. In less than five minutes they'd both found their climaxes. He rolled his weight off her but kept her tightly held to his side.

"Now you have to shower again," she said teasingly.

"Yeah but this time will be more fun because you'll be there, too."

"Hmmm. Makes it worth getting dirty," she said.

And damn if he didn't agree.

Chapter Nine

They missed the morning lecture but David had asked about the afternoon. Mel hadn't wanted to go, preferring to nap after the night they'd shared. In D.C. she'd wondered how many orgasms a woman could have in one night. Now she had to up the number. David had teased her with a long, deep kiss, and then reluctantly gone, promising to bring dinner back with him.

She slept another hour and then took a long soak in the tub to ease her sore muscles. After pampering herself in the bath, she pulled her hair up in a high ponytail, added a short-sleeved moss green cotton sweater, and a flirty little skirt. Smiling, she left off her panties.

Mel knew David would be at least another hour and she couldn't wait to share her good news. She was in love. At least, she was almost positive.

"I don't understand," Sissy said. "You met up with the guy who dumped you in D.C. *By accident?*"

"Weird, huh? It *had* to be a complete accident. I hadn't communicated with him since our night in Washington, so he had no idea I'd be there."

"But weren't you still pissed at him? I could have sworn you were pissed."

"I was." Mel took a sip of the room coffee in order to control her smile. She hadn't forgiven him for the overused dump lines, but he'd worn her down with fun banter and sincere words, letting her know how much their time together had affected him. What women wouldn't have given up her pique after that? And then there were the orgasms. Amazing orgasms that she could still feel like tiny aftershocks in her pussy whenever she thought about him.

Or remembered the scent of his aftershave.

Or imagined his hands on her.

"He convinced me it was all a misunderstanding." She smiled, remembering all the ways he'd demonstrated how much he wanted her. Good thing Sissy couldn't see her. Mel would be blushing to think these things in front of anyone.

"Uh huh. I can just imagine."

"No," Mel murmured, "I'm not sure you can."

"Oh, Lord!" Sissy lowered her voice. "You're making me horny and I still have an eight-hour shift ahead of me so knock it off right now." She leaned closer. "Are you planning to spend the rest of weekend in bed?"

Mel laughed. "I thought you were getting all horny?"

"Spill it, girlie!"

"As a matter of fact, it's not all sex. David said he needed to talk to me tonight. And it couldn't be in a bad way."

"How can you be sure?"

"Because of what we were doing when he said it."

"Oh. Wow. You've got it bad. Or maybe you've got it good, I can't decide."

"He says he wants to make sure we're on the same page." Mel stared across the room, focusing on the opposite wall and on nothing at the same time. She imagined she wore a dopey grin, but she didn't care. She'd never felt this way before.

Her heart pounded whenever she thought of David. She couldn't wait to be with him, and not just for kisses or sex. Well, maybe *somewhat* for kisses and sex, but also just to talk, to laugh, to hold hands. He was a responsible and very intelligent man. She could envision a life with him and that both thrilled her and scared her to death.

He'd gone to the lecture, but they'd shared at least a dozen texts since then. She couldn't get him out of her mind, and now she knew she couldn't get him out of her heart, either. What would she do if David wanted to tell her that he didn't have that same heart-stopping feeling for her?

This is ridiculous. She felt like a teen going through puppy love, with all the highs and lows. She couldn't wait for him to get back.

"I hope this guy is good enough for you. When do I get to meet him?"

Sissy's question brought Mel back to the present. "I don't know. Last night he said he lives down in Tidewater and he's very busy. He's a vice president in some large corporation down there and doesn't get much time off. Plus, he's going away on business." When David told her that he was preparing to leave for an extended business trip, she nearly cried—and that was something Mel never did.

"Sissy, I've never felt this way. I think I'm in love."

"This is all happening too fast, Mel. Maybe his being gone will be good for you. You'll have time to sit back and think objectively before you get in too deep."

Mel smiled. "I think it's too late for objective thought. And here's the best part. I think he might love me, too." Last night David couldn't get enough of her, as though their physical closeness had changed. The way he touched her, held her, spoke of what it felt like being with her, being inside her—they'd formed a connection, an emotional connection that transcended simple sex.

"He's perfect. He's a professional"—at Sissy's *Hmm*, she straightened her back and took stock. No, she decided, wanting a professional for a boyfriend was not shallow. It's just the way it was—" and I know how that sounds, but I mean, I don't want to marry a mechanic, do I? And he's not—"

"Marry? Aren't you getting ahead of yourself?"

Was she? "I honestly think he feels the same as I do." At Sissy's silence, she added, "Look, there's nothing about him that's a negative. He's intelligent, funny, and sexy. And he's also a professional and not in the military. Like I said, perfect."

Sissy sighed. "This is scary. Does he know you're a doctor? Does he think you're rolling in dough?"

"No! He's got a good job of his own. He's wonderful and sweet and—"

"Great in bed." Sissy huffed out a breath. "I don't know what else to say. You sound like a crazed woman. Don't run off and marry him, for God's sake! Guard your heart. You'll be back on Monday?"

"Monday, I promise. And without a wedding band. I can't get married without my BFF, can I?"

"And don't you forget it. At least take a picture of this perfect dream guy and send it to me, okay?"

"Will do. Talk to you later."

***

David swung open the door of their room after only one knock. He took her in with one quick glance and proclaimed her fucking beautiful. He'd been aching for this all afternoon.

Holding up a white bag he said, "As promised, I brought Italian. And

I'm hungry. But not for baked ziti." He dropped the bag on the room's café table and opened his arms. Mel rushed to him. Molding her body to his and feeling her soften in his arms, taking her lips in a greedy kiss that she met with equal hunger—this is what he'd imagined and longed for. What he knew now he would always long for.

"You're mine," he ground out in a raspy voice. "*Mine.*"

Flipping positions so that she backed the wall, he dropped to his knees and reached under her skirt—thank God she'd worn something other than slacks. "You naughty girl. You've gone all commando on me." He nestled his nose to the apex of her thighs and inhaled, taking the scent of her arousal deep into his lungs. He nudged her legs apart and pushed her skirt to her waist and with one, long lick, he took in her taste. She was fucking delicious.

Mel's moans faded to the background as he proceeded to mine her pussy with his tongue. He loved the way she kept herself clean shaven, knowing how much he enjoyed eating her out, something he intended to do several times before they separated on Sunday afternoon. He hated leaving. Feasting on Melissa had turned into one of his favorite things in the world. How could he do without?

By the time he'd switched from his tongue to two fingers lightly stroking her pussy while his tongue sought out and attended to her clit, Mel had stabbed her fingers into his hair and pressed his mouth closer. Her hips rocked against him. She was close. Her moans had changed to sweet little sounds between pants.

Once again, David used his tongue on her pussy and pressed her clit hard with his thumb. Mel screamed his name and her cream drenched his mouth and chin. He lapped at her, taking all she had to give before pressing his forehead into her stomach and catching his breath.

Finally, as shaky as she, he stood up and took her mouth. Their tongues battled for supremacy. Mel pushed into his mouth and he pushed back. "God, I missed you," he said when they broke for breath.

She smiled and smoothed her hand over his hair. "It was only a few hours. But I missed you, too," she said, and then kissed him once more. "I have to admit, after being apart you sure know how to welcome a girl."

"That? That was nothing. I have hours of pleasure saved up to share with you." He laid his forehead against hers. "Did you really miss me? Even with all the texts?"

Her arms were around his neck and she lazily stroked his neck. He loved when she touched him. Anywhere. "They only made me miss you more. I don't know how people stand long distance relationships. If I'd had to go longer than these few hours, I would have died." She took his mouth again, but this time, in addition to the passion, a tiny frisson of worry ran down his spine.

He pushed it away. It's the kind of things lovers say—I couldn't wait to be with you, or I couldn't stand another minute away from you—but in the end, people put away that hyperbole and dealt with the realities of life. That is, people in love do. And he hoped Mel was in love with him because he sure as hell was in love with her.

"If you can wait a few more minutes to eat, we have the microwave to reheat dinner. I think I need some more Mel time," he said with a grin. "Let's get you off your feet." Sweeping her into his arms, he took her into the bedroom.

"And what do you intend to do now that you have me off my feet?" she asked in an innocent voice.

"Have my wicked way with you," he answered with a growl. "But first, naked. I need you naked."

She smiled, exchanging innocence for sexy in a nanosecond. "I'll show you mine if you show me yours."

He'd thought his cock couldn't be any more needy but he'd been wrong. "You're on," he ground out.

Instead of hopping to get out of her clothes, though, she lay back and regarded him. "David, are you...are you clean? That is—"

His hand froze on his belt buckle. "Yes! Yes, I'm good, I swear." Was she implying what he thought she was? "And I can assure you, I'm not the kind of guy who slept around much, but during those times I've never, ever been without a condom." Maybe he should ask about her, but she was a doctor, right? Surely, she wouldn't take any risks.

"Then do you think...I mean I really care for you. A lot. And if you think you care for me, too, maybe we could forego the condoms? I'm on the pill."

Stunned, David wondered the correct thing to do here. He'd never been in this situation before and he wanted to get it right. Instead of continuing to strip, he lay on the bed beside her. He stroked her lips with his finger and took in her scent, which was unique to her.

"Melissa, this is early on. I know we've hardly known each other a month, and we haven't been together for the majority of that time, but

I know myself pretty damn well and I'm not afraid to say the words." She gasped, and her eyes grew wide. "I love you, Mel. Nothing like you has ever happened to me. As impossible as it seems after so little time, I love you."

She was silent, staring at him with wonder. It *was* wonder, wasn't it, and not horror or disgust?

"David, I love you, too."

Fucking yeah. He gave a mental fist pump. Taking her into his arms, he kissed her tenderly, hoping to convey through his lips the sentiments he'd just expressed in words. He loved her damn it, and she loved him back. The world was one hell of a happy place.

When she leaned back from him he said, "So, shall we see what this feels like, skin to skin? It's something I've never felt before."

"Me either."

He wrapped a strand of hair around his finger, loving the way it looked, binding them together for the moment the way his next actions would bind them for forever. This act of sex would be an emotional tie as well as a physical one. She was his woman. *His.* And he was about to claim her. She would claim him, too, and strangely, a calm settled over David with that knowledge.

"Think it will be different?"

"I know it will be because it will be new to each of us, a sign of our love and trust. And when I come," he whispered, "a part of me will stay inside you for days, you and me as one." He kissed her. "We can't get any closer."

In less than a minute the two were naked. David looked into her eyes and saw desire and a depth of feeling he'd never known. Love filled his heart and he knew this is how he would feel forever.

This is the way it's always going to be for us. That was David's last cogent thought before sliding into the wet heat of her body.

Chapter Ten

Mel had never felt anything like it. She wrapped her legs around David's waist and used them to pull him closer, further inside her. Her breath came in erratic pants, her fingers clawed at his back, urging him on.

But David wouldn't be rushed. He seemed to have his own timetable for bringing her off. He pushed in and then pulled out until his cock lingered at the entrance to her pussy. Slowly—ever so slowly—he glided back in. She trembled with desire and the love she knew she held for him. Mel had never been so happy.

"So fucking good, baby. God, you feel so *fucking good.*"

"Yes," she murmured and nipped his neck where his shoulder met it. Stroking that same place with her tongue as he started his slow but purposeful entry brought forth a guttural moan. She dug her hips into the mattress and then thrust forward to meet him.

"David, I love you!" She couldn't hold back. This felt too damn good, too right. This was her man. *Hers.* And she wanted this for the rest of her life, this friction of his loving, his cock making her feel alive, his smile to wake to every morning, his hands sending shock waves of pleasure through her body.

"Melissa. Oh, *God*, Melissa!" David increased his speed, his thrusts becoming hard and fast. He took her mouth in a rage of passion. His tongue invaded and conquered, his lips ate at her mouth. Breaking off, he took her shoulder in an open-mouth kiss, nipping and sucking.

Mel was so close, so very close. Every deep thrust rubbed her clit until she thought she would scream. Instead, she gasped in a breath, sure she would let go, not wanting to so that this would go on and on. His thrusts rocketed her to a state of mindlessness and she gave up all thought, surrendering to pure feelings.

When he bent to take one of her nipples into his mouth and lavishly laved it with his tongue, she felt the stroke all the way to her pussy. But when he lightly bit down, she came apart. The orgasm rolled through her like seismic waves. From far off she heard a keening cry that had to have come from her. Through the fog of her powerful climax, she felt David's drive into her. A strong pulsing deep inside told her he'd released, and warmth spread through her.

He rolled off her but took her with him, wrapping her in his arms and kissing the top of her head. With a languid stroke, she let her hand caress his torso, from his heart, still beating a rapid tattoo under her palm, to his washboard of a stomach.

"That was incredible," she said. "I'll never know anything like that again."

"Hey." He tipped her chin up with his index finger. "Except with *me*. It will always be like this with us. We were meant for each other. You're the other half of me."

She smiled. "Why, Mr. Stimson, I had no idea you were such a romantic."

"I wasn't until I met a certain dinosaur lover a few weeks ago. Since then, romance and her, are all I've been able to think about."

She smiled back gently and ran her index finger across his lips. "It's so soon, though. How can we know it's right?"

"I just do. Can't you tell?" He placed her hand over his heart then lightly touched her left breast with the back of his hand. "They're the same. Same tempo, same power. My heart beats in time with yours."

She laughed. "Maybe that's lust, not love. Ah, at the word 'lust' I notice a slight increase in tempo and power." He chuckled.

"Well, I won't deny that there's a healthy dose of lust mixed in there. How could there not be, you being you?" He sighed, taking a moment to stare at her. "You doctors are scientists, and I am, too. An engineer by training. But even I can recognize love when it strikes me. Maybe you still need a little more convincing." He pulled her to him and kissed her possessively. Melissa melted into him, allowing the fantasy to grow. She knew she loved him, but enough for it to last? Enough for a future? *Stranger things have happened.*

When he broke the kiss, she leaned into him for more, causing him to chuckle. "Maybe you're right," she murmured. "Your convincing is certainly very…convincing." He chuckled again as she scooted down and buried her head against his chest, listening to the strong beat of his heart, knowing that when it sped up it was because she touched him.

With the same certainty she had felt earlier, she knew that he was her man. She didn't want any other, wouldn't accept any other.

David stroked her hair. "My dad always used to tell the story of how he and Mom met. He was visiting his cousin. They went to church and stayed for the dinner afterward. He said he saw a girl across the room and when her eyes met his he just knew. Two weeks later they were married. And they're still married, after forty-two years, so it happens, Mel. Sometimes people get lucky. I think we did."

"That's a great story. They got married so soon because they just *knew?* Why not wait longer?"

"My dad was only there on leave. He had to get back to his ship, so there was no time to waste."

She sat up and faced him. "Your father was in the Navy? How could your mother stand being separated from him if she loved him so much? I could never marry a man in the service."

The intense look in his eyes froze her. "What's wrong?" she asked.

"Maybe I should have told you this sooner, but it never occurred to me that it would be such an issue. Mel, you know that we can work through any problems, right? We love each other."

Mel moved back a few inches on the bed, wishing she had on some clothes with which to shield herself from what David was going to say. Instead, she drew up her knees and wrapped her arms around them, pulling back as much into herself as she could. "Just tell me."

David sat up. "Let's eat first."

"No. What is it you don't want to tell me?"

He swiped his hand through his hair and took a deep breath. His brow furrowed as though he tried to figure out a puzzle he didn't understand. Something was very wrong. Her happiness of a few minutes ago had fled, leaving fear in its place.

"I'm a lieutenant commander in the Navy. Actually, I'm the executive officer on a destroyer."

Oh, God, oh, God, oh, God. This couldn't be happening. He'd *lied* to her. "You said you were the vice president of a company." Her voice was devoid of emotion. She felt drained and empty.

"I said I was *like* the vice president of a company. That's what an XO is. A ship is like a small city. I'm second in charge." He reached for her, but she jerked away. "Mel, it's an important position. I don't see why this is such a problem. Explain it to me."

"My dad was in the Marines. I hated the military life." She sucked in a breath and met his gaze full on. "Not the military itself, you understand. It's fine for some people, but not for me. I swore when I was growing up that I wouldn't marry into the service. They're never home. Life is never stable. My dad wasn't there for anything. Not my recitals, awards, first steps, first date. My mom was so sick twice in her life that she had to be hospitalized. He wasn't there to help her or me."

David just watched her, letting her talk. "And now there's you. I almost believed that you were right, that we *were* two halves of a whole. But I can't be your other half, David. Don't you see? You're a lieutenant commander. So, you have a lot of years invested?"

"Eighteen." He watched her soberly.

"Obviously it's a job you love, or you wouldn't have stayed in all this time."

She examined him again, carefully, seeing things now in a different perspective. His straight posture and strong shoulders bore the stress of a command position—gladly accepted but wearing, nonetheless. The face etched with strength that she'd thought showed a dedicated research engineer now showed the steadfast look of duty. Laughter alone hadn't caused the small lines at his eyes. They'd formed from standing on the bridge of a ship looking across miles of water. For one who prided herself on being such a damn good observer of people, how had she *missed* all of this?

You saw what you wanted to see.

She fought the urge to cry. "If I'd known at the beginning I wouldn't have let it get this far," she said softly. "I can't love you." Her voice broke. "I won't let myself."

David stood and paced alongside the bed.

"Why didn't you just *say* you were in the Navy? You should have told me." Her stomach roiled, and not from hunger. What would she do? How could she go on?

"There are plenty of women who would have dated me for just that reason. It sounds bad, I know, but I had to be sure." He stopped and gave her a wry look. "My salary isn't too bad, and with retirement just a few years away, some women would be interested in that alone. I've met a few who would do most anything to snag someone in my position." He resumed pacing. "That might sound vain, but I don't mean it like that.

"I know that marrying a military man requires a special kind of woman, especially since I'll be gone a lot." He turned to her, legs braced, hands on hips, just as he would stand on deck. His nakedness seemed not to matter at all. "And marriage is what I'm talking about here, Melissa. I was planning to talk to you about it tonight. I told you that I would be gone on business, and the Navy is my business. We're leaving in ten days. We'll be gone for six months."

No! Mel covered her mouth in an effort to hide her sob, but David saw her tears anyway. He came back to sit beside her. "Honey, please don't cry." He tried to hold her, but she turned away.

He let out a huff of frustration. "Mel, I don't want to leave you behind. Not metaphorically, anyway. I know you have a job in Charlottesville, an important job, but I want us to commit to each other. I want to write to you as my future wife and when I come back, I want us to get married. Hell, if I had my way we'd get married before I leave. I know myself, Mel, and I know I love you."

"No." Melissa pushed herself off the bed and quickly began dressing.

"Where are you going?" His brows furrowed into a frown, stubbornness showing in the set of his chin.

"Home." She yanked on her clothes.

David stood up and tried to grab her arm. "Mel, we have to talk about this. We love each other. *Talk* to me."

She faced him, unable to stop her tears or catch her breath. "I'm sorry. I could have dealt with most anything else, but I cannot love you. I hate if I hurt you, but that's just the way it is. We should have known this was too good to be true." She literally threw her things into her suitcase. David started to dress. He'd kept talking but she didn't hear a thing. She had to get out of there before she completely broke down.

"Keep the room," she blurted out. David made another plea. She grabbed her suitcase and was out the door, leaving her heart behind.

* * *

Just like the first time she'd left him, Mel hadn't answered his calls or his texts. With nothing to lose, he'd decided to go to Charlottesville as soon as possible. Unfortunately, a variety of matters arising from preparing to ship out had prevented him from making the trip for eight long days. He'd been miserable for each and every one of them, but he was counting on this effort to convince her that they were meant to be together.

A meeting at the Pentagon had provided him the chance to sneak a visit to see Mel. He found Jefferson Hospital easily enough. If he'd shown up at her house, she could have slammed the door in his face. But facing her at work would make it harder for her to yell, or whatever she might do. He was preparing his heart for the worst while still hoping for the best.

David walked into Jefferson Hospital in his blue winter uniform. Mel had wanted honesty, and here he was, as honest as he could be in Uncle Sam's way.

Entering the building he tucked his hat under his arm. "I'm looking for Dr. Melissa Crandall, please. I think she's a pediatric specialist?"

The receptionist fiddled with her computer for a moment. "Dr. Crandall is on duty today. Pediatrics is on the third floor."

Nerves struck as David entered the elevator and pressed the button for three. What if she *did* ignore him? What if his coming here embarrassed her and hurt his cause instead of helping it? What if—

The bell chimed, announcing he had arrived on the floor. For better or worse. He squared his shoulders and stepped up to the nurses' desk. "Dr. Crandall, please?" The nurse couldn't have been more than in her early twenties. She stared at him with obvious flirtation but said nothing.

An older nurse stepped forward. "Dr. Crandall is with a patient right now but you can wait in her office. It's just around the corner. I'll let her know she has a visitor."

"Thank you." He easily found Mel's office. Placing his hat on the corner of her desk, he looked around, too nervous to sit.

He walked the tiny office, reading her diplomas. She'd attended Georgetown University for undergrad, where she'd graduated summa cum laude, and then the University of Virginia for med school. Her residency had been in Washington. No wonder she seemed to know the city so well. Then she'd settled into this relatively small hospital in Charlottesville to practice in her chosen specialty. Why? What had made her decide to settle here? And why pediatrics? There was a whole world they didn't know about each other.

Except for one thing. They loved each other. He believed that with all his heart and soul. He just needed Mel to believe it too, and trust that they were right for each other.

The door opened, and Mel charged in, a woman in a hurry. Then she looked up and saw him. She stopped. No, she actually took a step back.

"Hello, Melissa."

She took a deep breath and came forward, dropping a file on her desk. "You always call me Melissa when you have something intense to say."

"I called you Melissa when I came inside you last weekend," he said softly.

He stood at one end of her desk. She walked to the opposite side, as though the desk could shield her from him. Not exactly the reception he'd hoped for. She moved then and took her seat behind the desk. He sat in one of the visitor chairs. Even with her reserved attitude, she was alluring and beautiful. It was all he could do not to rush to her side and take her in his arms. If he were sure she wouldn't rebuff him, he'd do it, damn it, and make her see that they belonged together.

"Why are you here, David? I think I made myself clear when I left last week. You didn't come chasing after me, so I assumed we'd come to an understanding." She folded her hands on her desk.

Was she *angry?* Damn it, she was the one who stormed out of the hotel room where they'd just made love. Well, fuck it all, he was a bit angry, too.

"*You* left *me* if I could remind you of that. And not for the first time. And once again, you ignored all of my calls and texts." He took a deep breath. *Shit!* He didn't want to argue with her. "I can't trust that there will be another accidental meeting, so I came up. This is the first chance I've had. I hope that in the last few days you've had a chance to think about us, about what we mean to each other."

Her eyes glistened with tears. "Do you think I've been able to think of anything else?"

David rose and did what he'd wanted to since she'd walked in: he went to her. Pulling her into his arms he finally felt right for the first time in a week. She would relent, and they'd get back on track. He'd make her his wife, after all.

Chapter Eleven

Mel breathed him in and let David's unique smell invade her senses. The wool jacket scratched her cheek, but she didn't care. She hadn't felt whole since running out of the hotel room in Richmond like a coward a week ago. Now, here in his arms, she could breathe easier, at last.

"You look as though you haven't slept," he said against the top of her head, where he rested his cheek.

"I haven't. It's been a horrible week. And you?"

David cupped her face in his hands. "Oh, God, honey. I've never been so miserable in my life. A friend of mine and I wrestled our way into poison ivy when I was eight years old, and I spent a happier week then than I have since leaving Richmond." He placed a tender kiss on her lips and Mel reveled in his gentleness. She wanted much more, but for now, she'd settle for this, just being held by him.

"I shouldn't have run out on you last week."

"That's behind us now." But he looked into her eyes. "But Mel, life has ups and downs. Even if one of us walks out, we have to answer our phones. We have to be able to let the other explain. We have to talk."

Shame filled her. She'd been childish and selfish. Again. "I know, and I'm sorry. I was wrong." She gave a short laugh. "I'm thirty-one. Far old enough to know better. I act my age about most everything except what matters most. And David, we must talk about that."

With his hand in hers, they took up the visitor chairs. "Talk to me," she said.

He took a deep breath and let it out. "Ever since you left Richmond I've been trying to think of what I could say or do to convince you to stay with me. The worry that you would leave forever has plagued me all week. I've had only half my mind on my work. The other half has been all about you. All I could think about was how to get you back. I've missed you so much."

She squeezed his hand. "I've missed you, too." David smiled, but it didn't reach his eyes. Like her, he appeared tired.

"I didn't mean to hurt you, David. But how I live my life is important. Military is the one deal breaker I've always held true. I love you, but if I'd known you were in the Navy, I never would have had lunch with you to begin with."

"I can see your point, I *can*." Keeping hold of her hand as though he wanted his feelings to be passed to her through their linked fingers, he turned slightly to face her more fully. "I know the military lifestyle isn't for everyone. It's hard, more so on the families than on the service member. But…" He flicked a glance away from her and then back. "I want you to marry me." He reached into his pocket and pulled out a small, velvet box.

No, no, no! "David, I—"

He held up his hand. "Just hear me out."

Mel's throat burned with unshed tears. She didn't want to cry, she wanted to be strong in the face of the arguments he was about to make. Hell, she had to fight what her own damn heart wanted her to do. It took memories of her own childhood to give her the strength to hold tough. She nodded for him to go on.

"I found out in D.C. that I'll have my own command after this cruise. And I made another rank. I'll be Commander Stimson, with my own ship. It's what I've worked for, and I'm damn good at what I do. I think I'd make a good commander."

"David, that's such amazing news! I'm so proud of you, and happy for you, too." She placed her right hand atop their joined hands. "I know what having your own ship means. You'll be the best commander in the fleet."

He looked down at his shoes. Gathering courage? Then he faced her gaze with a spark of determination in his eyes. "But I'll turn in my papers if you want me to. The military is an important job, but it's not the only important job. I love you. If it means having to give up the Navy, then I'll do it." He studied her. "If that's what you really want."

Oh, God! He couldn't do that. She couldn't let him do that. "David, you're close to retirement. And you love your work. Don't you see? If I asked you to give up your dreams, you'd be miserable eventually. And I would be miserable if you stayed in. We're at an impasse." Using her index finger, she tapped the velvet box. "Put this away." Now she didn't even bother to stem the flow of tears.

"Do you think the Navy means more to me than you?" he demanded.

"Let me ask you. If we hadn't met, would you even consider giving up your career?"

"No, but—"

"I don't doubt that you would make the sacrifice for me. But I don't want either of us to *sacrifice* in order to be together. We should come together with joy, not with dread."

His lips flattened into a thin line. She saw the frustration in the tightening of his jaw. "Even if it were for this one cruise, I want someone to be here for me, someone for me to come home to. I want that to be you, Melissa."

Mel couldn't stop herself. She leaned forward and kissed him. In seconds he took the kiss deeper. Pulling her onto his lap, he thrust his tongue into her mouth, taking command of her tongue with a greed that shocked her. Even after all she'd said and done, he still wanted her.

He broke the kiss and trailed his mouth down her neck and then back up to her ear. Brushing her hair back, he whispered, "I want you so much. But not just for now. I want my babies growing in your belly, I want us to raise a family and then grow old together. I want every sunrise and sunset to begin and end seeing your face."

And that's when the problem slammed back into her again. Carefully, she stood up and moved to the side of her desk, out of his reach. Away from him and her own weakness.

"If we married and had a family, how much would you be here to help raise them? Who would be responsible for dealing with their insecurities and fears when we had to pack up and move every few years? How would I stand being parted from you when you went off for months at a time?"

He stabbed his hands through his hair. "But I'd be *home* for months at a time, too. You're looking at the glass half empty. Our love would make it full."

"Sometimes love isn't enough, David." Her heart broke with the words. She saw by the devastation on his face that his had, too. But what could she do? She understood herself well enough to avoid making this one huge mistake. Wiping the tears from her face she cleared her throat. "Can you stay long enough to have dinner?"

David stared straight ahead. "No, I have to be back at the base by midnight."

He'd just proven her point. The military, the regulations, the demand on the majority of his time, would always come first.

"I—I wish you the very best, David. And despite what you might think, I'm happy we met."

He stood, ramrod straight and picked up his hat. Tucking it under his left elbow, he finally looked at her again. "Take care of yourself, Melissa."

And before she could say *you, too,* he'd left.

***

"XO, here are the reports on the boiler room maintenance." Chief Todd Baxter handed over the requested forms.

"Thanks, Chief." David took the paperwork and placed it in the appropriate inbox on his desk.

"A moment, Sir?"

David looked up. Todd had served with him on two different ships and on multiple cruises. He was a man worth listening to when he spoke. "Sure, Todd. Take a seat. What's on your mind?"

"Forgive my nosiness, but you haven't seemed yourself since we left port."

David knew he'd been grumpy, though he'd tried hard not to take out his own problems on his men. And he'd really hardly seen the chief, since Todd spent most of his days in the boiler room of the ship, far from David's office and duties.

"And you base this observation on what?"

Todd rubbed his chin and narrowed his gaze. "You don't smile as much. No jokes. No light touch like you normally have. I hear you've even lost at poker, and you *never* used to lose at poker."

"So, you're saying that because I've lost a few hands of cards that something is wrong?"

"Yes, Sir, that's exactly what I'm saying. I might work in the bowels of this tub, but I hear things. And I know something's up." Todd held up his hands in a gesture of understanding. "If you'll allow my saying."

David tossed his pencil on the desk. With a deep breath, he leaned back in his chair. "And do you think I'm going to unburden myself to you, Chief? I know you have several degrees but is psychology one of them?"

"I have a degree in *life*, XO. I don't get the flu often, but I know it when I see it. In the same way, I might never have been in love, but I recognize the symptoms. Non-com or officer, woman trouble hits us all the same. You don't seem particularly happy about the condition."

"Todd"—David leaned forward and folded his hands on his desk—

"has anyone ever told you that you should mind your own fucking business?"

Todd, damn him, didn't seem the least bit offended at David's words or tone. They'd known each other too fucking long, obviously.

"Yes, Sir. Often. But that doesn't change the situation." Todd stood and stepped toward the door. "I just wanted you to know that I'm not the only one who's noticed a change in you. We're all worried, XO. We like you, damn it."

Chagrined, David nodded. "I appreciate it, Todd. I'll try to handle my woman troubles better." He half smiled. "And tell anyone who might be playing poker with me that I won't be easy pickings from now on."

"Yes, Sir. Glad to hear it, XO."

When Todd had gone, David sat back in his chair and let his mind wander. Mel was never far from his thoughts, but he'd had to separate her from his daily routine. However, at night in his bunk, there was no keeping her from his mind. Her face with that killer smile would appear in his dreams. In his unguarded moments, he could almost feel himself inside her, her hot, wet pussy caressing his cock with each stroke, her pants and soft whimpers just before she came, and her curvy, sweet body wrapped around his in the aftermath of their lovemaking. He'd known her only a short time, but she had become a huge part of his life.

Until she wasn't.

David had to admit, even as much as he wanted her, Mel had been right. He didn't want to give up the Navy. If he did it just to make her happy, eventually he would have been miserable. When he'd joined the Navy, he hadn't set his mind on commanding a ship, but as the years went by and his skills increased along with his rank, he knew he'd be good. It wasn't bragging to say that he was a natural leader. He wanted his own command, damn it, and why shouldn't he?

But why shouldn't he also want a wife and family? Why couldn't Melissa see the good in what he had to offer instead of only the bad?

"Get your head out of your ass, Stimson. The woman has made up her mind," he muttered. He picked up the pencil and got back to his reports.

Chapter Twelve

Mel tried to place the thumping sound that interrupted her dreams of David. He had been just about to kiss her when something tore her out of her fantasy and back into real life. It had been a little over a month since he left her standing in her office, wanting with her whole being to run after him and say yes, *yes*, she would marry him. But her more rational side held her back. Was that best, for her or for David? Intellectually, yes.

Emotionally things looked very different. Hell, had she slept for one full night since he'd been gone? She'd started crying at the stupidest things now, like Kleenex commercials, Hallmark movies—which she should swear off of in her current state—and even war movies on TCM. Anything and everything reminded her of David, and that broke her heart. How long before she healed?

Thump, thump, thump! Well, damn, it was the front door.

"Okay, okay," she muttered. She pulled a robe over her pajamas and made her way from the bedroom to the living room. She cracked open the door. The sunlight made her squint but there was no mistaking who stood on her doorstep at seven on a Saturday morning.

"Mom. Dad. What are you doing here? And so early, too." She raked her hand through her hair trying to smooth what she knew to be bedhead. "Not that I'm not always happy to see you, but really? So early?"

"Did we wake you?" he mother asked, though not in an apologetic tone. She brushed past Mel and made her way to the kitchen.

Mel's father followed her in but bent to kiss Mel's cheek. "Hi, honey." Holding up a white box he said, "We brought doughnuts from that place in Gordonsville that you like."

She couldn't help a smile and inhaled the delicious, sugary scent. She linked her arm through her dad's and walked with him to the kitchen. "Hi, Daddy. What's going on?" she asked in a low voice.

"Your mother will explain," he replied.

That's the way things had always been in their household. Her dad, a colonel when he retired from the Corps, might have been a badass Marine at work, but at home, he deferred family business to Mel's mom. He did it with love, though he was no pushover in serious matters. Those, her parents always decided together. But Mel assumed that her dad's attitude had been that since her mother was home even while he was away, that she had the better take on the pulse of the family.

In the kitchen, Mel's mother had the coffee started and was beginning to rinse the few dishes Mel had left in the sink and stack in the dishwasher.

"Mom," Mel said on a sigh, "there's no need to do that. I'll take care of them later."

"Why wait? I'm just standing here waiting for the coffee to brew." Mel sank into a chair, outnumbered and outwitted since she was still fighting sleep. She'd had an emergency that kept her at the hospital into the early morning hours.

"You do know it's Saturday, right? And before I've even had a chance to wash my face?"

In her typical motherly fashion, she ignored Mel. "Do you know that you have no fresh fruit in the refrigerator? And you're almost out of coffee." Her mother sat down while her dad opened cabinets until he found plates. He brought back three and opened the box that he'd placed on the table.

"We should wait for the coffee," his wife chided, as he removed a raspberry jelly, filled doughnut and placed it on his plate.

"I've been smelling these things for the past half hour. Coffee be damned." He picked up the luscious smelling piece of fried, filled dough and bit into it.

"I'm with you, Dad." Mel chose her own favorite, a sugar-dusted confection filled with Chantilly cream.

"Well, all right," her mother selected a chocolate covered, chocolate doughnut, but got up to find a fork.

"So," Mel said between bites. "What do you want to talk about? Nothing's wrong, is it?"

"Yes," her mother said seriously. "It's you, Melly. You're what's wrong. You look awful. And you haven't sounded like yourself on the phone in weeks."

"It's nothing, Mom. Just not sleeping well and I've been really busy.

You know, the regular things that make people look like hell."

"Now, honey," her dad said. "She didn't mean you look like *hell*. Not exactly." Mel snorted a laugh at that. "But we are worried. Is everything okay at work?"

Mel pushed the doughnut around on her plate, suddenly not hungry. Since that first time on the phone, she hadn't mentioned David to her mother. At first, she'd already decided not to see him again. After Richmond, she couldn't talk about him without crying. It would have been too painful to explain what had happened. Roller coasters had fewer ups and downs than her short relationship with David.

"It's a man, isn't it?" Her mother's tone was quiet. Mel stared at her plate and nodded.

Her father's chair scraped the floor he stood up so fast. "I think I'll go for a short walk." Without another word, he hurried out the front door.

"You're over thirty and your father still thinks you're his little girl. He's worried sick about you, Melly, and so am I. Now what's going on?"

"I'm not a little girl. And it's nice that dad worries about me now. That's better than when I actually *was* a little girl." She went to get coffee. Her mother stormed after her.

"What is that supposed to mean? Your father loves you more than life itself, and always has."

Her mother was angry with her and in her mind Mel knew she deserved it. In her heart, though? Well, her heart had had too much to deal with lately and it ruled her head right now. She'd grown up hating the way the Marine Corps had controlled her life. She loved her father dearly, but right or wrong, he was the example she had to follow when it came to husbands in the military, and it wasn't an example she appreciated.

"Well, he always loved the Corps better, Mom, and you know it. Look at all he missed while I was growing up. He was never home, never where we needed him to be. Always off playing war or something." She slammed her cup on the counter and spilled coffee all over. "Damn!" Melissa braced her hands on the counter and stared into the sink. It was unfair to take her anger and pain out on her mother. "I'm sorry."

"You're right, Melissa, your father did love being in the Marines. But it never compared to his feelings for us. How could you *think* that?" Melissa turned. Her mother smiled wistfully, remembering. "He joined up right out of college and we married shortly afterward. I had no idea what being a Marine wife entailed, but I learned quickly enough, and then I loved it as much as he did."

"What?" Disbelief marked Mel's tone. "You loved having him gone all the time? Missing all the important events in our lives?"

Her mother studied Melissa now, just as she had when Mel had been young, searching for exactly what the trouble was. After filling her cup, her mother moved to the table. Sitting comfortably, she crossed her legs and tapped her fingers on the table top before speaking.

"Of course, I didn't love having him gone, but it was inevitable. Part of the job. An important job that a lot of people can't do or aren't willing to do. The responsibility is high, and the pay is low, but it's necessary. When I was pregnant with you we talked about whether he should stay in and decided that he should. Then when I had my miscarriages–"

Shock rocketed through Mel. She'd never asked what had put her mother in the hospital. She should have, but her mother never brought it up and soon, after her mother was back at home, her childish mind filled with other things. "Is that why you were in the hospital those two times? Why didn't you ever tell me?"

"You were too young to understand what was happening then, and later it wouldn't have mattered. When your father got home after the second one, he brought the paperwork to separate from the service. I talked him out of it."

"But *why?*"

"Because, Melissa, it was his *job*. And more, it was our life. He loved what he did and was very good at. You don't make the rank of colonel as fast as your father did by being a nothing, you know."

Mel felt as though she were being scolded. And worse, that perhaps she deserved it.

"What would have been different if he'd been home with us? We had a fantastic support group with the other wives, and your grandma came down and stayed with us. Don't you remember?"

Melissa looked at her mother with a blank expression. "I guess I don't."

"Honey, it wasn't always easy, but I loved being in the service with your dad. We saw so many places and had so much fun. Even at my lowest points, your dad could always make me laugh."

Mel smiled, too, remembering "Roger" the dinosaur. David always lifted her spirits, too. And he was patient with her. Until she'd cut off all hope of their being together.

"It was sometimes a very hard life, but we service families were all in the same boat and it made us stick together. We're still friends with many of them."

"But, Mom. All of those things Dad missed, the time away from home. Moving and leaving friends. What about all of that?"

"Honey," her mother said, "you need to grow up."

Mel suddenly felt stupid. As though everything she had assumed for all of her life was upside down. She'd viewed her life through the prism of childhood and never grew out of the misconceptions. How could she have been so completely clueless?

"Melly, you left friends, but you always made new ones when we settled, and you adjusted well to new schools. The worst thing about it was when Dad was away from home, that's true, but he wasn't gone as much as you seem to remember. And do you think that he didn't *mind* being away from us? I could show you some of his letters that would break your heart because he missed being with us so much." She took a sip of her coffee. "Not only military men are away from home a lot, you know. Your Uncle Lou works for a big company. He missed as much or more with your cousins as Dad did with you." She frowned. "What is this about? Why didn't you ever voice these concerns before?"

Yeah, Melissa, why didn't you? "Because it didn't matter before. Because I wasn't in love before." Her mother's eyebrows rose. "He's in the Navy." She reached for her mother's hand. "What can I do, Mom? I told him I wouldn't marry him. I've been so stupid."

"Melissa Ann. Do you mean to tell me that you turned down marriage to a man you love because he is in the Navy?" Her mother shook her head. "I knew you didn't like the military for some reason, but I had no idea... Don't you remember any of the good times? Don't you remember the love?"

No. That's what she'd left out of her memories, the love she'd been surrounded with in her life, from her parents and even the whole service community in which they'd lived.

"Is it safe to come in now?" Her father's booming voice sounded from the living room.

"Yes, Daddy, it's safe." Mel got up to pour him a cup of coffee, putting it in front of him as he sat. He gave her mother a questioning look and she answered by smiling and patting his hand.

"Our daughter is in love."

A stricken look passed quickly over his features, then he smiled warmly at Melissa. "Sweetheart, that's wonderful. Who is it? When do we get to meet him?"

"That's something of a problem, Dad. He's in the Navy and he's overseas."

"Oh. Well, a swabbie is okay. A Marine would be better…"

Mel's mother chuckled.

"He's the most wonderful man, Dad. I love him so much and I sent him away. I told him I wouldn't marry him." Tears welled in her eyes.

"But, honey, if you love him why didn't you accept?"

"Because I didn't want to be a military wife. I hated growing up in the Corps, and I always thought Mom hated being married to the Corps."

Her father was quiet, swirling his coffee in the mug. "You're right to be wary, Melly. It's not an easy life."

"Henry…"

"No, honey, better to be honest." He looked at Mel. "You'll be married to the Navy as well as to him. Being in the service is especially hard on wives and families. Your man is on board ship I assume?" Mel nodded. "So, he'll be gone a lot. That means you have to be self-sufficient. You have a good career, but will you be happy being alone for months at a time? Moving? Taking care of the children if they come, dealing with crises by yourself?" He took his wife's hand. "It's not a life entered into lightly, Melly. Be very sure."

She tried to be objective. Could she be as good a wife as her mother had been? Could she put up with the Navy in order to have a life with David? He had tried to say that if they loved each other it would be enough. She'd disagreed, but maybe she'd been wrong. "I love him. I'm not sure I can be a good Navy wife, but oh my gosh, I *love* him. I've been so miserable." Her shoulders slumped. "It might be a moot point. I'm not sure he even wants me now."

"We'll help, if you want." Her mother looked at her dad. "I loved your father more than anything in the world. Still do." He smiled and squeezed her hand. "If you and your man love each other like that, then you take the few bad times along with all of the good and march onward together."

"Your mother and I just want you to be happy, Melly. If you love this man, make up your mind what you're going to do about it."

***

The ship had been docked in Naples for a couple of hours. David was in the boardroom going over paperwork with the head of engineering when the Officer of the Day asked him to come on deck. "There's something you should see, Sir."

David was puzzled, but grabbed his hat and excused himself, following the sailor to the railing. Todd was there, too. The man was uncanny. He'd probably "heard" something through that grapevine he had on board and come up on deck to check it out.

"Chief, what's going on?"

"XO, I was about to ask you the same thing." Todd pointed to the dock.

Propped up on the pier stood a huge cardboard sign. Painted in big blue letters he saw, "Lt. Cmdr. Stimson, will you marry me? *Joyfully?*" Melissa stood to the side, holding her hand to her eyes, searching the deck of the ship. When it seemed that she was staring at him, he smiled and raised his hand in greeting. A wide grin split her face and she waved back.

"She sure is a looker, Sir. Does she have a sister at home?"

"She doesn't, Todd. And you're right. She is a looker, and smart, too."

"I have a feeling your woman trouble is about to be solved."

David slapped Todd on the back. "You're damn sure right. That woman down there is Dr. Mrs. XO as soon as I can get her to the altar." He held up his hand and pointed to his watch, then flashed five fingers, six times. She nodded in understanding.

Twenty-six minutes later—David had counted every one of them— he walked off ship in his whites and with a four-day pass in his pocket. He didn't even slow, just strode up and took her in his arms, lifting and twirling her as their lips met.

"I can't believe this," he said, raising his head just enough to speak before kissing her again. "Get married? Are you sure?" She smiled, and he put her down and cupped her face. "Don't toy with me, woman."

"I'm sure. If you'll still have me, that is."

"Are you crazy? I love you," he grinned down at her. "Let's go find a hotel with room service, and not see Naples." She laughed.

"Wait a minute," he said, "how did you find me?"

"My father called some buddies at the Pentagon and tracked the ship down." She tried to hide her smile and failed. "As a Marine colonel, he's not totally convinced I should marry a swabbie…"

He laughed. "I'll overwhelm him with my awesomeness."

She placed her hands on his cheek and he covered it with his own hands. "Just like you did me."

God, he wanted to kiss her, a real kiss and not what they'd be able to do here on the dock. He couldn't wait to see her naked and prove again how much she meant to him. But first…

He leaned over to dig through his duffel bag. Where was the damn thing? He'd carried it with him rather than leaving it at home. Until now it had served only to torture him. There it was!

He stood up, opening the small box and offering her the ring she hadn't even bothered to look at before. Slipping it on her finger, he kissed her again.

Applause and whistles filled the air. David turned back, grinning, and gave a thumbs-up sign to the men watching from his ship's railing. And not only from his ship but from others docked nearby. "Later I'll talk to the chaplain and find out how to get married in Italy. I don't want to wait any longer."

"My father says he wants to give me away, so I promised we'd give him and Mom enough time to get here."

"They'd better catch a fast plane." He picked up his bag and hurried her down the dock to where they could get a cab. "What changed your mind?" he asked as they walked along.

"Strangely enough, Dad told me it was time to weigh anchor and move on with life. He strongly suggested I do it with the man I love."

David grinned as he squeezed Melissa. "I know it's against Navy rules, but I like that Marine already."

"And he'll like you, too." She pulled him to a stop, so she could lean up to kiss his cheek. "Oh, I need so much more than that."

David smiled into her eyes as he took her hand. "There's time enough, now." He looked up the street. "There's a cab. Let's go, love. I don't think I can wait any longer."

Dropping Anchor

Chapter One

"Where the *hell* is the campground?" Carissa Walker stopped to consult the compass. She still headed north, but by her reckoning, the campground should be in sight. She'd spent the morning and early afternoon in a cycle of hiking, climbing and running the trails of the Blue Ridge to the west and south of Asheville, North Carolina. Having had little to eat or drink but a trail mix of her own concoction and a single bottle of water, she was ready for a good meal and an evening of relaxation. But where the hell was camp?

"Lost?"

The male voice behind her startled the shit out of her. She spun around, barely keeping her feet. His gaze held concern, not amusement, thank God, because in her frame of mind she would have been inclined to knock him on his ass if he'd taken pleasure in her situation. She swiped her wrist across her sweaty forehead.

"I guess I am." Then she took a good look at him and forgot all about asking if he knew which direction she should take to reach Paradise Valley Campground. Her mouth dried, and her heart did a sudden little flip.

The man was handsome beyond belief. Dark gray eyes stared back beneath thick, charcoal colored lashes and dark brown brows. His auburn hair was shaggy, hanging over his ears and over his forehead, and his chin was covered with a short beard that showed a few strands of silver. He was over six feet tall because she was five feet ten and she had to look up to see his eyes. And he looked powerful. His slender build and muscular physique could easily be detected beneath his jeans and denim shirt. Good clothes for hiking but Carie's mind formed an image of how he would look without clothes. The wrong thing to envision because she was here for a vacation, not to hook up. She wasn't a hook up kind of woman, anyway. Not anymore.

Breathe! "I must have gone too far west in my hike this morning. I'm staying at Paradise Valley, which by my calculations should be right"– she turned to point behind her–"there. But as you can see, it's not." She tilted her head and blinked, trying to keep her mind on directions and not on how imminently kissable his mouth looked with those full lips. "I don't suppose you can point me in the right direction?"

He unfolded a map he pulled from his back pocket. Moving to his side so she could see, she brushed his arm. An electric shock ran up to her shoulder but didn't stop there. Instead, it zinged and zanged like a pinball on its way to that sweet spot between her legs. The jolt paused long enough to zap her nipples, which became hard and erect and super sensitive against her sweat-dampened blouse. Carie could barely take a breath. Moisture on the lace panties that she wore under her hiking shorts sent forth a waft of arousal. That last might be her imagination, though, because the man gave no hint that he noticed.

Had she made a noise? The man turned his head to look at her, a question in his eyes. Carie had heard of people being drawn to each other immediately, but she'd never experienced it. If desire was a real, live, physical event, she had just felt it. And having felt it, the thought of stripping off right then and there to fuck in the forest ran through her mind. A wood nymph and her satyr having a grand time rolling around in the… She took a closer look at where they stood. Poison ivy climbed a tree to her right and prickly pine needles and cones carpeted the ground. *Real life trumps fantasy once again.*

She cleared her throat. Finally concentrating on the map he held, she asked, "Where are we again?" Jeez. The thing had to have every trail in the area on it. Even with this map, she'd be just as lost.

He studied the paper for a few seconds and then folded it, so he could use one hand to hold it. With the other he pointed. "We're here. I'd say if you head back west about a mile and then turn north you'll run right into the campground." Sure enough, right under his finger was a mark for Paradise Valley Campground. "About four miles should do it."

"Four *miles?*"

"Done in?" He smiled and in the dappled sunlight his eyes twinkled, and his straight teeth seemed blindingly white. He was good looking enough to be a model. *An underwear model.* Yeah, her mind's eye pictured him in only underwear. She licked her lips.

Unfortunately, in her current state—more hair pulled loose from her ponytail than still in it, Redskins ball cap half on, half off, scratches on her arms and legs, and probably smears of grime from where she'd wiped sweat off her face—she must look more like a reject from *Deliverance*.

"I've been out since about ten and I'm not used to these mountains. I usually do my running on flat ground."

"Did you have plenty of water with you and something to eat?"

"Water, yes. But only a cup of trail mix."

He raised his brows until the right brow disappeared under the shock of hair on his forehead. "Where do you normally run?"

"Around D.C."

"Ah. Where there's a coffee shop every few blocks."

Just because she was lost was no friggin'cause for him to patronize her. "I normally run ten to fifteen miles a day with nary a coffee break. This is just my first time here, and I'm not quite used to the ups and downs."

"They do call them 'mountains.'"

And they do call them assholes. Shocks of sexual electricity and hyper-attraction did not excuse a man from being a dick. "You're right. *So* right. Thanks for the help. I'll be on my way now." After consulting her compass once more she started west, the thought of four miles draining what was left of her energy. But she could do it. Four miles was nothing. *Nothing.* She did more than that every day of the week.

A branch knocked the cap off her head just as a vine caught her leg and she fell, sliding on her butt into a shallow ravine. Her hair clung to her neck and face. She pulled strands out of her mouth, off her forehead and back behind her ears. When had she last been this hot, sweaty, and just plain exhausted? *Maintains one, Carie zero.*

Leaves rustled behind her and over her head. "You can make the four miles," he called down to her. "I don't have *any* doubts about it. Or you can walk half a mile to the road and I'll drive you."

Half a mile? There's a fucking road half a mile away? Why didn't he point that out on his little Boy Scout map?

Sighing, she dragged herself to her feet and started up the five yards of hillside that looked more like a mountain. When she was close to the top, he extended his hand. She took it and another spark sizzled up her arm, across her shoulder, ran circles around her nipples and zipped right to her pussy. Good God! He was like a sexual magnetic pole. If she pointed her compass at him, the needle would snap right to S-E-X.

He held her hand for several seconds after she had solid footing, and then he looked anywhere but at her. "The car, um, it's up this way." He handed her the cap she'd lost. Twisting her hair into a tight knot, she jammed it all up under the cap.

He stepped back, staring. Then, shaking his head slightly as though he could erase what she knew he'd felt when their hands met. Suddenly, he turned and started off at a brisk pace. Rushing to keep up, Carie tried and failed to dispel the vision of the two of them naked, having wild monkey sex all over the North Carolina mountains. Now *that* was a memory that would make the vacation worthwhile. A mental Kodak moment that would keep her warm on snowy winter nights for years.

***

The woman's trouble. Big trouble. His incredibly quick hard-on reminded him he already had problems with his sister and mother and Jenny, who thought she owned him. The last thing he needed was another female, especially one whose body screamed "Fuck me!" to *his* body, with only the merest touch of hands. He should let the woman wander the Blue Ridge without the benefit of help. She could become a legend, a tale told over campfires late at night, like the Brown Mountain lights. The wandering sex goddess who seeks out men and then fucks them to death in the underbrush.

"But what a way to go," he muttered.

"What did you say?"

"Nothing." Another three minutes of power hiking brought them out of the woods and onto the edge of a parking lot.

"I was *this* close to civilization?" the woman said.

"You're hiking in a national forest. Uncle Sam likes to make his parks accessible to people." He pointed off to the right. "I'm over there."

When they got closer to the light green Prius, he pressed the unlock button on the key fob and then opened the passenger door for her. "Here we are."

"I'm happy to see that you drive an environmentally sound vehicle."

He closed her door and walked around to climb behind the wheel. Silent, he buckled up before answering. "It's a rental and the only thing they had left on the lot. I drive a big, old Chevy pickup. Sorry."

"Oh, well, it's okay. I'm not a fanatic or anything."

The car was quiet when he turned the key. He backed out of the space and went left out of the parking lot. "My name is Todd. Todd Baxter. Not *Ted* Baxter." She laughed, and he glanced at her. "You couldn't be old enough to have watched original *Mary Tyler Moore* episodes."

"It ran on one of those classic TV channels when I was in college. I think I've seen every episode."

"Even the one where Mary falls in love?"

"I felt bad for her, but thinking of her in love was strange. I don't believe in love."

He glanced at her. "For Mary, or for yourself?"

"Both. I have no interest in entangling myself with a man. Love is a chemical reaction. Chemical reactions can be controlled."

He'd always thought similarly. Until he reached out to pull her out of the ravine. That shock was like a Manhattan Project chain reaction and he wasn't at all sure it could be controlled.

"You're a rare and unusual woman." He made a sharp right and the road curved into the forest again, throwing the road and car into deep shadows. A mile or so farther and they burst into the sunlight again.

"What's your name and what brought you from D.C. to the wild mountains of Carolina?"

"Carissa Walker and vacation with a friend."

"A male friend?"

"Does it matter?"

Todd thought for a moment. He'd never felt the jolt of pure sexual power with a woman like he had twice with this stranger. So, yeah. It *did* matter. "Yes." He glanced at her. "And you know why." If her boyfriend was so stupid as to let her out of his sight for hours at a time in a strange place, he deserved to have a fight on his hands.

A light blush touched her cheeks, but for such fair skin, with red hair and light green eyes, it wouldn't take much to tinge her cheeks pink.

"You know you felt the heat when we touched," he said.

"I don't know any such thing." Her adorable little snub nose turned up. He suddenly wanted to kiss it.

"You've set me right, it seems. No electricity, no spark. Got it." He slowed to turn into the campground. "Where's your camp?"

"You can let me out here."

"All right." He stopped in front of the office.

"Thanks for the lift," she said. "I have to admit that four miles might have wiped me out." She held out her hand. When he took it, he felt like he'd been kicked in the gut. That was desire, pure and simple. Like Disney magic, if Disney made XXX films.

"You can't possibly ignore that," he said.

"Ignore what?" She looked so smug, he knew she lied.

A woman outside the car leaned down and tapped on the window. "Carie, where have you been?" When she saw Todd, her eyes widened, and she smiled. Carie opened the door and exited the car, dragging her hand from his. The other woman leaned in and then sat down, one leg in and one leg out of the door. "I'm Martha, Carie's friend. And you are…?"

"Todd. So, *you* and Carie came camping together?" He leaned down to see Carie's face through the open door and raised his brows. She shrugged and stuck her nose up again, which made him laugh. The woman had more impudence than he'd come across in a long time. He liked it.

"I've always loved the mountains around Asheville, so I convinced her she'd love them, too." Martha gave him what she might have thought was a discrete once-over. She had the subtlety of a sledgehammer. "Are you camping here?"

"No, I grew up in Asheville. I'm here visiting family. I just offered Carie a ride."

"Oh." Martha smiled and showed an impressive set of dimples that Todd believed must serve her well with most men. They did nothing for him, not when compared to the sheer animal attraction he felt for Carie, who stood outside the car watching her friend flirt. "Guess I should have gone hiking with her today."

"She might not have been lost then, and we wouldn't have met."

Martha turned her head. "You were lost? Wait until the office hears about that."

Todd glanced at Carie. Only a flicker of her eyes showed that she cared about the office hearing anything about her. "I could have that wrong. Maybe I was the one lost and she rescued me." Carie shot him a look that made his nuts roast with heat. "Maybe we can solve that puzzle this evening."

"Oh, are we meeting this evening?" Martha asked.

"No," Carie said. Staring into his eyes, she had to have understood the invitation he'd just issued. "I believe Todd just invited me to dinner?"

He smiled. "That's right." Pleasure filled him. If their touch—and the light in her eyes now—meant anything, this would be a night for the record books.

Martha's brows shot up. "But, Carie, you never hook–"

"It's just dinner, Martha."

Martha snuck a look at Todd. He shrugged. "Okay," she muttered, climbing out of the passenger seat. Carie slid back in.

He took a peek at his watch. "It's almost four. Can you be ready by six?" He couldn't believe she would go out with him, a perfect stranger, but he had to ask.

"I think so. Fair warning, I didn't bring any dressy clothes."

"This is Asheville. Casual is in. Shall I meet you here?"

"Six o'clock. I'll be here."

Well, holy shit! She was really going to go out with him. "There's only one thing left to decide."

"What's that?"

He cupped the back of her head and pulled her closer. "Who's going to kiss who first." She raised one brow, meeting his gaze. "Okay, no decision. I'll take the lead." When their lips met, the world disappeared. He touched her soul and merged it with his.

What the hell? When had he started thinking like a princess? He gave up thinking and concentrated on the sensation of her body close to his and the heat that burned from the inside out.

"Oh my God," she whispered against his lips and then raised her head. "How will we survive a whole meal if we can't make it *to* the date without attacking each other?"

"You call *this* attacking each other?" He removed the stupid baseball cap that trapped that glorious red hair. A lot of hair had fallen free of the ponytail she'd caught it up in, cascading around her face to the tops of her breasts. Sweeping it over her shoulders, he imagined it sweeping across his thighs instead as she sucked him off.

He kissed her again, this time pressing his tongue between her teeth and into her mouth. She tasted of raisins and nuts. And passion, as sweet as honey. Only remembering they were in public kept him from sliding his hands under her blouse and capturing her breasts.

Todd broke the kiss, needing air. "I'd better go."

"You'd better." Happily, she seemed to be as short on breath as him.

"But I'll be back." He stroked her hair.

"Six o'clock." Carie leaned into his touch.

"Wait a minute." He took her hand, not wanting to let her go. Too much could happen in the two hours between then and later. "Come with me now."

She laughed. "I can't do that." She looked down at herself. "Look at me. I'm hot and sweaty and—"

"Perfect." Her cheeks tinged soft pink and he couldn't help skimming his thumb across one her blush. "Just pick up a change of clothes. You can shower at my hotel." The flare in her eyes showed she knew exactly what he meant.

"I'll be ten minutes." This time when she got out, she ran off immediately, glancing back only once. Martha followed her friend after giving him a much more careful, shrewd look.

Whatever this attraction was, there was only one way to get past it and that was to quench it. They'd fuck, reduce the wildfire to a candle flame and be done with it. He was a lifelong bachelor, uninterested in any relationship crap. Yup. An afternoon and evening should do it. A couple of days, tops.

At least, that was the plan.

Chapter Two

"Are you out of your mind?" Martha demanded.

"Maybe." Carie gathered up a clean set of clothes from the duffel bag on her side of the stand-up, military tent and put them in a smaller bag whose contents she dumped on the cot. "I'm sorry to leave you alone this evening."

"Hell, don't worry about me. I'm going to the sing-a-long. Met a cute guy at the pool this afternoon. You realize this stranger you're running out with could be a serial killer."

Carie thought about that. Normally cautious, she had considered the same thing. But something told her that he was safe. *Well, not safe. He sets me on fire.* "What are the odds of that? I don't think he's a serial killer."

"Why? Because he's good looking? Remember Ted Bundy."

Hearing the name Ted make Carie laugh. "He's not Ted."

"What?" Martha propped her hands on her hips and moved to the tent flap. "Unless you give me a damn good reason, I am not letting you leave this tent."

"Didn't you say coming down to North Carolina would give us a chance to let our hair down away from the office?" Her friend nodded. "This guy sends sparks along my veins, Martha. My pussy is wet. I would have screwed him right out there in front of the office because when he kissed me I forgot where I was. I have to be with him, Martha. If he wanted to kill me, he had his chance out in the woods before anyone knew where I was." She took a deep breath and let it out. "I want to let down my hair. All over his body."

Martha stared at her, mouth in a tight line. "I want to know his name, address and blood type."

"Of course."

Martha continued her piercing stare. "I could ask Cute Guy if he wants to double with you two for dinner."

"No need. Unless I misunderstood him, I doubt we surface for dinner.

All I want to do is screw him and get him out of my system. I'll be back tonight. Promise. Tomorrow at the latest."

"Don't forget that you've had martial arts training. And don't do anything that will get your name in the papers. It would not do for a JAG officer to be arrested." JAG—or Judge Advocate General's Corps—was the legal arm of the military. Lax as ethics might seem in some parts of the government, JAG did not look kindly on its members being tossed in jail for any reason. Even if charges were superfluous, such embarrassment would be very bad for her career.

Carie laughed. "At least I know where to find a good lawyer." She folded her clothes into a neat package, picked up her canvas pocket book and headed for the tent flap. Martha stared at her a few seconds longer and then moved aside.

Hurrying for the campground office, she half hoped, and half feared that Todd Baxter would be gone. But there he was, standing at the front of his car, leaning on the hood, arms crossed, and one knee bent, foot on the bumper. Looking as good as sin itself, he smiled when he saw her.

"You came back," he said.

"Did you have doubts?"

"Hell, yes. I was already planning the search grid I'd follow to find your campsite." He walked to the passenger door and opened it for her.

"Just a minute," Martha said, coming up behind him. "I want your name and address plus a cell number where you can be reached."

Todd pulled a sheet of paper from his pocket. "All ready for you."

Martha took the paper. "You knew I'd ask?"

"I would have been disappointed if one of you hadn't. That's my hotel receipt, so you know where I'm staying. You see I've also noted the license number of the rental car."

She pulled her cell phone from her pocket and called the number on the paper. A ring tone sounded. Todd smiled and withdrew his phone from the front pocket of his jeans. Holding it up to show Martha he said, "Good enough?"

"Blood type? DNA sample?"

"You think like a lawyer," he said laughing. Carie looked at Martha and raised her brows. "You *are* lawyers? I'll be damned."

"You will be if anything bad happens to my friend." Martha gave him the warning look. The one that had quelled many an opposing counsel.

"I hope you don't *mind* that I'm a lawyer," Carie said.

"Oh, hell, no. I've been screwed by lawyers before." He grinned wickedly. "Just never in bed."

"It's about time, don't you think?" she said in a low voice as she slid into the passenger seat.

"You read my mind." He raised his hand to Martha, who looked like judge and jury standing in front of the car, hands on hips. She shook her head and turned away as he slid into the seat.

"Is she like this with everyone you date?" he asked Carie. Right hand on the back of her seat while he turned to back out of the space, his thumb stroked her hair. Even with that light touch shocks of pure pleasure shot through her.

"We aren't really on a date, and no, not normally. Truthfully, I don't go out that much and it's usually someone we both know."

"Well I'm honored to have made the cut." He slid a smile her way.

"You should be."

His laugh was sudden and full. Executing a sharp left, he turned onto the highway. "I like you Carissa Walker. Your friend called you Carie. What would you like me to call you?"

Goddess. Queen of Desire. Sexy Counselor. She started to giggle and then caught herself with a half cough. "Carie is good."

"Okay, Carie it is." Flipping on the turn signal he made a right and merged into traffic. "I'm staying at the Mountain View Lodge. They have a great restaurant, but there are other good places close by. What do you like to eat?"

"I'm not fussy. Why are you staying at a motel? I thought you were visiting your family."

"I'm here for a family reunion, which means that for the next several days somewhere between fifteen and sixty relatives could be hanging around my parents' place. I need to be able to get away. Know what I mean?

"Good God. *Six* relatives at my house would be enough for me to want a place to hide. Won't they be expecting you tonight?"

"I'll make a phone call. I've been here a week already, so they can do without me a night. Or three."

"*One* night." She held up a finger to emphasize her point. Even with one night she'd have to call Martha and explain. "That should be enough."

His glance let her know that he understood what she meant by "enough." "You think so?"

"Yes. A night should get whatever this is out of our systems. That's what we're doing, right?"

"Maybe a night will get you out of *my* system, but counselor, I think you might underestimate how long it'll take to get me out of *yours*." She snapped her head around in time to see his smiling profile.

"Arrogant much?"

He reached over and squeezed her hand. "Just so we're clear, I wonder if a night will do it for either of us."

Desire, potent as hundred-proof alcohol raged through her system. If there *was* any getting over this feeling, one night sure as hell would not do it. What had she been thinking? "Well. I could be wrong."

"Don't I know it."

"There you go again, full of yourself."

He half shrugged. "If you find I'm not right, you can leave whenever you've had enough."

"Oh, I will."

He shot her another glance. "Now you're just being cruel."

She regarded him objectively. Once she got past his killer looks, she noticed slightly graying temples and lines at his eyes, as though he spent a good bit of time outdoors. All of it added to his handsome visage, his charisma and sexual attraction. But she also noticed a little age.

"How old are you?"

He chuckled. "Are you afraid I can't keep up?"

"Maybe. I am in my prime, you know."

"I'm thirty-eight. And I'd guess you're"—he glanced at her again—"about thirty-two."

She jerked back. "Good guess."

His smile turned to a grin. "I've had a few good looks at you, and with all due respect, I've observed my share of women."

Carie sniffed. "That's a very ungentlemanly thing to say to a woman you're about to fuck."

"Don't say that word! It's all I can do right now to keep from pulling over and jumping in the backseat with you."

Todd turned into the Mountain View Lodge parking lot, at last. He wasn't the only one anxious to get it on. Her hands had been clenched atop her bag and her stomach had churned through every twist and turn of the road.

He stopped at valet parking. "It's faster," he muttered.

She exited the car without waiting for him and headed for the hotel's automatic doors. He caught up with her and took her elbow, swiftly guiding her to the elevators.

Once inside, Todd punched the fifth-floor button and then jabbed the button marked Close Door. "Damn slow thing," he said, drawing her into his arms.

His erection poked her stomach. She stood on the toes of her right foot and slid her left leg up his leg and over his hip. Bending his knees, he pressed the bulge in his jeans to her pussy. Even through their clothes they blazed with desire and she rubbed him like a cat in heat.

Pulling her tee shirt out from her waistband, he had just swept his hands up and under, reaching for her breasts when the elevator stopped, and the doors slid open. They jumped apart and she quickly used her free hand to yank her tee shirt down over her waist. Running her hand through her hair she followed him out and down the hall. Her heart nearly burst from its staccato beat, and she was out of breath by the time they reached his door, though not from the long walk.

Anticipation robbed her of oxygen, and desire made her heart hammer. *The real thing had better match the fantasy.* She had a good feeling that it would.

***

Holy fucking shit. If this key card gave him a red light one more time he'd punch something. Todd jammed the piece of plastic in the slot again and held it there for a painful second. There! The light turned green and the door opened when he pushed. Carie rushed in behind him and tossed her duffel bag toward the bed. Backing him up to the closed door, she unfastened her shorts. She ripped them to her ankles and then used her toes to push them off. Using her hand to rub him through his jeans she wrung a sharp hiss of breath from him. His hands roamed up her arms, feeling her tremble, hearing her moan.

"Please tell me you have condoms," she said.

"I have condoms."

"Thank God," she mumbled, pressing him firmly.

"But not here at the door," he added. He picked her up. She wrapped her legs around his waist and gave him her tongue. No kiss had ever been sweeter, or more full of need.

Todd let her down on the bed and dug in his suitcase for a rubber, his gaze never leaving hers. Her red hair fanned out around her head like fire. Green eyes under heavy lids stared up at him, glazed with lust. She propped her feet on the side of the bed and spread her legs. Touching herself, she met and held his gaze. Her fingers slipped through her pussy lips, wet with her juices. He hoped to hell he had the rubber on right. He'd never seen such a sexy sight, bramble-scratched legs, walking shoes and all. He bent and pushed away her fingers, so he could taste her.

Fitting his mouth from the top of her clit to her pussy, he teased her with his tongue. Through a fog of lust, he heard her gasp, and then he inhaled, taking in her scent—pine and leaves, sweat mixed with sex, a heady, earthy aphrodisiac. Only then did he dig his tongue into her pussy. He used his hands to run up and down her legs, filly legs, long and muscled and toned for a good, long run. Her skin flowed beneath his fingers like satin. He ran his hands under her hips. Flexing his fingers and squeezing her ass, he lifted her to his mouth.

Her cream was a mixture of sweet and sour, a tangy flavor that tantalized his taste buds. He ate hungrily, only barely aware of her fingers digging through his hair and massaging his scalp.

"Oh!" Carie jerked her hips up and cream flowed over his tongue and lips, flooding his senses.

Even with her pussy heaving with convulsions, Todd moved his focus to her clit. He laved it with his tongue and sucked it into his mouth.

"Oh my God. Oh God." She moaned it over and over.

Okay, so he'd made her come. She'd been primed and ready, after all, just as he was. What he really wanted was to have her mindless and moaning while he was inside her, and God knew he was aching to be there.

He stood up and reached under her arms to pull her to sitting position. Yanking her tee off, he reveled at the sight of her tits, full and round and high. "You keep in great shape," he said, taking in the toned shape of her arms and narrow waist.

"Running," she muttered.

"Take off your bra," he said, at the same time ripping his shirt open and off his shoulders. His laced hiking shoes forced him to take the time to bend and undo them before he could get rid of his pants, but it was all done in a matter of seconds. When he looked up, Carie had pushed off her shoes and lay before him naked as the day she was born.

"You weren't this beautiful even in my imagination."

Carie gestured to his cock, straining the rubber that sheathed it. "I could say the same. Very impressive." She smiled. "And the rest of you ain't bad, either."

He smiled back. "Thanks."

"So, here we are. The moment of truth."

"Time to see if that electricity really means anything."

She bent her knees and spread her legs wide. "I really prefer being on top, but I'll give you the privilege if it's what you want."

"There's time for us both to have our preferences." Todd climbed between her legs and sank into her pussy without preamble. He'd had all the foreplay he could stand.

Using his left hand to prop his weight off her, he used his right to caress her left breast, pressing her flesh and thumbing her nipple. Using every ounce of strength—and thank God, he'd also kept himself in top shape—he leaned down to take her mouth.

There was no gentle poking going on with his dick. He pounded her into the mattress, anxious to make her come again. He wanted—he needed to feel her grip his cock the way he'd felt her convulse around his tongue. If he had to recite the steps in breaking down an engine and putting it back together again he would, to keep from coming before her.

Carie didn't lay there like a wet cloth, either. She brought up her knees and wrapped her legs high on his hips, giving him full access to her cunt, hot and wet and tight enough to fit him like a glove. Her hands roved his shoulders, giving a hint of nails now and then.

When her breathing was heavy and labored, he broke their kiss. She thrashed her head back and forth, her lips open and rosy from their kiss, and her eyes shut. She was close. Her hips jerked off the bed, meeting him drive for drive, a wild woman in search of release.

Todd reached between them, finding her clit. Using his thumb to stroke it, he dropped his head to her breast, kissing the inside of the globe with his open mouth and sucking hard. Pressure built at the base of his spine and his balls drew up. Euphoria flashed through him as he joined her in a sudden climax. Ramming into her, a surge of power ran from the tip of his cock throughout his body, a million little short circuits rendering him totally and absolutely helpless.

They stayed like that, connected cock to cunt for what felt like an hour, but what must have been only a few seconds. He'd never had such an experience, never known so much passion or such a strong climax.

He'd never touched a woman and felt electricity as he did with Carie, and now he knew that the magic continued when they fucked. Hell, fucking made it stronger. He worried that even a few nights of bed acrobatics wouldn't be enough for him.

Then he worried even more that she might feel differently. Most women were coy when it came to sex. They might want it, might enjoy it, but his experience was that they rarely were honest enough to show those feelings openly. Some he'd run across expressed what they wanted or when he touched them in a pleasurable way, but Carie was one for the books. Remarkably, she expressed her desire in words and actions, and that was a real turn on. With a rare moment of self-doubt, he worried how he would feel if she hadn't felt the spark of fire he had, or if the pleasure petered out for her before it did for him.

Worse, for his well-being and confirmed-bachelor status, what if it didn't?

Chapter Three

Todd slid his cock out of her and fell to her right. Carie chanced a glance. He lay on his back, one arm over his eyes and the other over his head. His cock, now limp in its latex sheath drooping with a startling amount of cum, lay along his thigh. *My God, the man is built!* His cock was six inches or more at rest and his abs were a twelve pack, not a puny six. He put twenty-five-year-old men she knew to shame.

And holy hell could the man fuck! She'd never, *ever* felt such an explosion of pleasure zing through her at climax. Until now. What was it about this guy? How did he do that?

She shifted her focus to the ceiling and worried. He hadn't said anything since he'd given her the most intense orgasm she'd ever had. What if he didn't feel it? What if he had her once and that was enough? She wanted more, more of him, more of that amazing, shocking sex that debilitated her during her climax and then re-energized her. Now that she knew such a thing existed, she didn't want to stop at one fuck session. Or even one night, maybe. She wanted more. Much, much more.

He lowered the arm over his eyes and let his fingers drag across the skin of her thigh. She shivered with his touch. Stretching her arm, she covered his hand and linked their fingers. Then she drew their hands over the apex of her thighs to the entrance of her pussy that still leaked her juices. His sigh sounded deep.

"You're incredible," he said. "Abso-fucking-lutely incredible."

"I want you again already. How weird is that?"

"Not so weird. If I was able this soon, I'd be inside you right now."

"I don't care who's on top, I just want you."

He started to roll to his side, and then seemed to remember the condom. He quirked his brow at her. "I'd better take care of this."

"I'd welcome a shower. I don't suppose you'd be interested?"

"I'd love to get dirty with you while we're getting clean." He rose from the bed and held out his hand.

She liked his confidence in standing before her naked. She loved especially that he wanted her again so soon. So, she hadn't been alone in thinking that their fuck fest had been beyond fantastic.

Taking his hand, she walked with him to the bathroom. Once there, she started the water. It heated quickly, and she stepped in.

The warm water caressed her skin. Carie ran her hands up her body, across her hips, her breasts, neck and face. Cool air hit her when the shower curtain was drawn back and then his hands—Todd's hands, that could be both strong and gentle, demanding yet giving—followed the same path. Over her hips to her breasts, circling her nipples, encircling her neck. He tightened his grip. For a fleeting moment, Martha's words came back, and the thought of Todd as serial killer formed in her mind. He could choke her right now. If only he was deep inside her at the moment, she would die happy.

You idiot! No fucking is worth giving up your self-control. Yet she wondered.

Before her fevered mind followed that path any farther, he ran his fingers into her hair to hold her for a kiss. A deep, greedy kiss that drove away all other thoughts.

"I forgot to bring a rubber," he whispered before he rimmed her earlobe with his tongue. His erection prodded her stomach. She was greedy for him, in whatever way she could have him.

Carie sank to a crouch, using a firm grasp of his hips to steady herself. Opening her mouth, she engulfed his entire length. His pubic hair tickled her nose, his scent overwhelmed her senses.

Todd groaned when she pulled back, using her tongue and lips on him all the way up to the head, a large and purple knob of baby soft skin. He tasted so good. She took a moment to explore the slit at the top and licked the moisture she found. His hands raked through her hair. The tension evidenced in his touch told her how much she affected him.

She glided her mouth over the head and back down his length again, using her tongue and lips to feel every inch of vein and satin covered steel. He was long and thick, stretching her to her limit, but hunger drove her. Water poured down her back, but not even the shower could erase his flavor, his scent, the texture of his cock as she examined it with her mouth.

He smelled so damn good. She'd read somewhere that the sense of smell was stronger than that of taste, and now she believed it. The world disappeared—there was no water sluicing off her back, no hotel, no city, forest, mountain. The world held only her and this man, his cock in her mouth, his hands on her head. She pulled out, slid in. He pushed his hips forward. She sucked hard, and teased his scrotum with one of her hands.

"Jesus Christ!" He tugged on her hair and pulled his hips back, forcing his cock out of her mouth. She leaned forward, mouth open seeking him again, but he bent and lifted her to her feet. Unstable, she grabbed hold of his shoulders.

"Can you stand by yourself for a minute?"

She nodded, still dazed.

Todd stepped out of the shower, mumbling that he was a "damned shithead" for forgetting the rubber. In moments he was back. He ripped open the foil packet with his teeth and slid the condom on in seconds. Then he turned to her with hunger in his eyes that matched what she felt.

She lifted her leg over his hip. He reached between them to touch her pussy. She could have told him she was wet and anxious for him if he hadn't had his tongue down her throat. He must have been satisfied with his finger exploration because he drove his cock home. Once he pulled out, and then drove in again. Twice. Three times and she splintered into a million pieces. He came with her, banging her back to the tub wall and holding her there with his hips and cock, so deep inside her it felt as though he came in her womb.

He broke the kiss when they came and buried his face in her hair. Her breathing was hard and fast, and she held onto him, her anchor.

When they finally came down, he smiled ruefully, "Do you think maybe we should actually shower?"

She grinned and held up a tiny bar of hotel soap. "Start with me?"

He rolled the condom off and reached out to drop it into the trash. "Gladly."

***

Todd rubbed the soap over Carie's back and down to her ass. *Such a great ass. Round cheeks and firm sweet flesh.* Her right cheek had a tattoo of a dragon.

"A dragon? What's the significance?"

"I joined a group in college. Some of us were dragons and others were dragon hunters."

He caught her meaning immediately. The girls were dragons, and guys were hunters. "And what happened when the hunter found a dragon?" He explored the crack between her butt cheeks, rimming her ass with his slippery finger. She pushed back against him.

"It depended. Sometimes the dragon escaped the hunter. Sometimes she found ways to overcome him. Whoever was the winner, the other did whatever was commanded."

"I'll bet you won a lot more than you lost," he whispered into her ear. She smiled. "I'm competitive."

He slid his soapy finger into her asshole up to the knuckle. She sucked in a breath but relaxed enough to let him probe farther. "And when you won, what did you demand?"

Her breath was hitched, and she took several seconds to answer. "Let's say I never went long without getting laid."

"Oh, I can believe that even without the dragon."

"But I had my share of catered meals and laundry done, too."

Todd slid his finger out and in. Not far, but enough so he knew she liked it. What a phenomenal woman she was. And to think, she lived in D.C., just a few hours from Norfolk. He didn't want to give her up. He had to make her feel the same before he lost her to her friend, her job, and the end of her vacation.

He pulled out his finger and continued the wash job, giving considerable attention to her tits and pussy area. He wanted to fill her pussy. He wanted her skin to skin, without a rubber. He wanted his cum inside her, part of her, absorbed into her body.

A vision of her big with his child flashed to mind. He pushed it aside, but he couldn't ignore the thrill the image summoned. He'd never wanted a wife and family. In fact, he dropped women like a hot match when they became serious. The Navy wasn't always a good fit for family, and after so many years of being suspicious of women and their wiles, he was comfortable being a lone wolf. But the mental picture of Carie carrying his baby inside her, and the knowledge it wouldn't happen, filled him with melancholy. No matter how much he enjoyed his life now, he'd miss that; miss an anchor that grounded him.

"My turn to wash you," she said, taking the soap from him. "And guess where I'm going to start."

Without further preamble, she grasped his half-erect cock and lathered it with soap, rubbing it and his nuts so thoroughly he couldn't help himself—he came in her hands.

"Sorry," he said. "You keep me cocked and ready all the time. I don't even know what to do about this."

She raised her head to kiss him, giving him her tongue and taking his. Instead of slipping her arms around his neck she encircled his hips, running her well-soaped hands over his butt.

He clutched her to him. "You're driving me crazy," he said into her hair. "Since we first met, all I think about is fucking you in every way possible. And then I want to fuck you again. I've never had my mind so screwed up by a woman before."

"The answer is so simple," she said.

"Yeah?" He drew back to see the green eyes of the woman who'd just said she had the answers to all his problems.

"Yeah. Fuck me in every way possible. And then…fuck me again. I haven't gotten you off my mind since we met, either."

She leaned forward and nipped his shoulder. "The dragon surrenders to you."

"I didn't know I was a hunter until I found you in those woods. Now I never want to let you go." Had he really said that out loud? *What an asshole.*

"The electricity means something. It's never happened to me before. I don't want to lose it."

At any other time, that admission would have made him run for the hills. Surprisingly, all he felt now was relief. "Let's get out of this water. I feel like a prune."

She laughed. "I think I could use some food. I have a feeling you're going to demand energy. And I need to call Martha and tell her…?"

"That we're coming back for the rest of your clothes and you'll see her when it's time to go home." Todd knew that time would come. He'd deal with it when saying goodbye happened.

Carie smiled, as though he'd given the answer she wanted to hear. "You know what else we need when we go out for food?"

"Definitely more condoms."

Grinning, she agreed. "*Many* more condoms."

Chapter Four

Though she was at work, Carie anxiously clicked her text feature on her cell phone. TBaxter sat in her Inbox and her heart skipped a beat. It shouldn't matter that Todd had sent a text. After all, they had texted a few times since her vacation in North Carolina three weeks ago. Mostly they exchanged *How are yous*, but nothing more serious or suggestive, though every time she saw his name in her text box, she remembered how he'd made her body sing—and by sing, she meant full out arias, not *Twinkle, Twinkle Little Star*. However, neither had asked when they could get together again. Carie waited for Todd to make the first move but he hadn't taken it. Damn it.

She opened the text and her heart rate jumped.

Carie, if you are interested, what would you think about my coming up to D.C. in a couple of weeks? Let me know, please. Hope all is well.
Todd

A thrill ran through her. Maybe he *did* miss her as much as she missed him. Sure, their time in Carolina had been almost entirely about sex. When they'd had time to breathe at all, they'd ordered room service for sustenance and slept when necessary. In the four days before she left Asheville and he had to reappear at his family reunion, they'd wasted very little time eating or sleeping. Or talking, for that matter. Even so, Carie had come away with an itch for Todd she couldn't seem to scratch.

She'd thought fucking for a day or two—or four—would get that weird reaction to him out of her system. No such luck. She craved him still. When she closed her eyes, she could feel him over her, in her, surrounding her. His scent was like no other man's—clean, fresh, spicy. She could pick him out of a crowd blindfolded simply by following his pheromones. The electric zing when they touched had never left them.

As an attorney, she had developed a real knack for reading a person and knowing who they were. The impression she'd formed of Todd was all good. She wanted to know him better. Something deep inside, some instinct told her that he could be important, a man she could rely on as well as be a partner with. That was another reason she wanted to see him again—she'd never had strong feelings for any man. Todd was different, but it was too damn soon. Feelings that strong didn't develop overnight, yet it seemed they had. For her, anyway. Todd had been much more than a one-night stand for her, but she'd had no notion of whether he felt the same since he hadn't indicated he wanted to see her again. Until now.

Carie jotted off a quick reply—*That would be great. Let me know the dates you're considering so I can schedule time off. Carie*—then she was jarred from her daydream of Todd by a knock at her office door.

"Carie, I need a huge favor." Martha rushed into her office and shut the door. She only did that when something serious was going on.

"What's up?"

"That guy, Dan, that I met camping, remember?"

Carie did remember. She'd met him the last day of their trip. Tall, blond and muscular, he and Martha had evidently been the talk of the camp. "What about him?"

"He's coming up for a week. Next week."

Carie cocked a brow. "Good Lord. What does he do that he can take off another week?"

"He's not taking off, he's working. Something in the city. I don't know what. Anyway, he wants to hook up while he's here. And *I* want to hook up while he's here."

"What's the problem?"

"I have that case down in Norfolk. I'm supposed to prosecute the guy who ran the forklift into the harbor."

Carie perked up. Todd lived in the Tidewater area. She mentally sorted through everything she had scheduled. "I can do it for you if you take the bar fight in Spottsylvania."

"Done!" Martha blew out a breath and fanned herself. "Thanks so much! I really think Dan and I have something worth exploring."

"What does he do, anyway?"

Martha flapped her hand dismissively. "I don't know. Something with computers." She leaned back and crossed her legs. "To tell the truth, we didn't talk all that much."

I know the feeling. Still… Was that disapproval running through her mind? Ashamed, she acknowledged to herself that she and Todd had been the same. Did she know what Todd did? *No.* Did she know anything about him except that he came from Asheville and turned sex into an Olympic sport? *No.*

Of course, one couldn't screw every single second, and while eating they'd shared some conversation, all shallow she admitted. Carie knew Todd liked the Carolina Panthers while she went for the Redskins, and that neither of them cared for baseball at all. She knew that he liked anything beef while she favored chicken more, even though a good hamburger now and then satisfied something inside her. They both got a kick out of wandering through a good hardware store, and they enjoyed reading mysteries.

When they'd been together, more than that just hadn't mattered. Now it did. When he came up, she resolved to talk more. She wanted to know *him,* not just how it felt to wrap her legs around him and feel his cock probing her depths.

Sure. Well, maybe they could talk more after a few bouts of hiding the salami. She smiled at the thought.

"Say, isn't that guy you met in Asheville living down there somewhere?" Martha asked, once more pulling Carie from her thoughts.

"Yes, he is."

"So, this works out well. We can both hook up."

Carie gave it some thought. How better to find out about a man than to surprise him? By showing up unannounced she could see if he's a slob, if he drinks to excess, and whether a woman answers the door when she knocks. She'd look him up once she got to Norfolk. She wouldn't have pulled anything like this—dropping in out of the blue—on a guy she wasn't sure wanted to see her, but Todd had just told her that he did.

Carie leaned forward on the desk. "Martha, what do you think about surprising people?"

"I think the surpris*er* is the one who's usually surprised. And not always for the best."

Crestfallen, Carie agreed. Okay, so she wouldn't show up at his house. Maybe she should get a hotel room instead of staying on base as she normally did when she had to work in Norfolk. Then she could text him and invite him for a drink. In the room. Wearing nothing but a slinky negligee.

That worked for her. "Let me have your case records," she said. She dug through the manila folders in her hanging files and gave Martha the notes she had regarding a bar fight that had ended up destroying property in Spotsylvania, a town about thirty miles south of the Marine base at Quantico.

"My thanks to you and Dan for being horny little bunnies." She now had a possibility of being a horny little bunny, too.

"No," Martha said, looking into space with a starry-eyed expression, "thank *you*! I'll bring the case file right down."

Carie's only concern was whether Todd would be around. He'd suggested meeting in D.C. but not for two more weeks. Did that mean he wouldn't be available? She hoped not, but worst-case scenario, she'd have a free weekend at the beach.

From what little she knew of the case, court time should only take a day, and the trial didn't start until Monday. If she could get away early enough to arrive in Norfolk on Friday afternoon—traffic on I-64 to Norfolk always sucked—they would have the whole weekend.

This madness for a man had never struck her before. If it developed beyond wild, primal lust, they'd be lucky. If it didn't, well, she wanted to enjoy the magic again if she could.

***

Todd rested his hand on the kid's shoulder. "Son, you do what I tell you and you'll be better off. Mr. Jeffers is the best lawyer in Norfolk, and a friend of mine. He'll do all he can for you. You just stand tall and tell the truth."

"Yes, Senior Chief." The youngster twisted his hands. "But I can't help being worried. I swear I don't know how that lift truck ended up in the harbor. It was working fine one minute, and all hell broke loose the next."

"Are you sure you didn't step on the wrong pedal?" Jeff Jeffers asked.

The kid looked from Todd to the attorney. "I don't think so."

Jeffers formed his mouth into a thin line. "Had you been out drinking the night before, on Friday night?"

The boy looked down and then glanced sheepishly at Todd. "We had passes. The guys and I hit a few bars."

"Were you hung over when you climbed onto that lift truck?" Jeffers asked, a little harshly Todd thought.

"Hell, Sir. I had a headache and a queasy stomach, but I wouldn't let that keep me from doing my job."

Jeffers looked up at Todd. "We need to talk." He put his papers back in a black leather briefcase and exited the interrogation room.

Todd looked down at the nineteen-year-old boy sitting morosely at the table, head down and hands folded. Of course, his hands were in cuffs, so there was only so much he could do with them.

"Sit tight, you hear? I'll be back in a minute."

"Okay, Senior Chief." His voice wobbled when he spoke.

Todd took a deep breath. He'd been young and stupid once. He felt for the boy. Closing the door behind him, he joined Jeffers in the hallway. "How's it look?"

Jeffers laughed. "You're shitting me, right? Is this a prank?" He looked around high and low. "Is there a camera somewhere?"

"That bad, huh?"

"Jesus Christ, Todd. The kid was hung over. He's not even sure if he hit the gas or the brake as he approached the water. This is a slam dunk—no pun intended—for whatever prosecutor the Navy sends down." He sighed and shrugged in a way that asked *what-can-I-do?*

"He isn't at fault."

"How do you know that? While we were playing poker Friday night did you have a sudden vision that the boy was going to do something stupid but wouldn't be to blame? Forgive me if I don't put you on the stand." Jeffers shifted his case to the other hand and checked his watch. "I'm supposed to meet the prosecutor in a few minutes. Lucky bastard to get a conviction so easily."

Todd frowned. "Why's he coming today? The captain's mast isn't until Monday."

"Free weekend at the beach is my guess. Look Todd, I really think the boy should just admit guilt and take his punishment. I'll see what kind of deal I can get him."

Todd thought it over. "I don't want it to come to that. It'll maybe lose him a rate and pay, or worse, brig time. Sam is a good kid and if this goes on his service record it will stick with him forever."

"He sank a lift truck worth thousands of dollars and sent the freight on it to the bottom of the harbor. He's lucky no one was hurt. Hell, he's lucky he wasn't *killed.*"

"We've had trouble with that make of truck before. I've worked on the bastards, and they're the worst manufactured lift trucks in the world."

"Why does the Navy buy them?"

"Why does the DOD take the lowest bid for equipment?" Todd couldn't help sounding bitter. The government always proclaimed they bought only the best for their men and women in uniform and then took the lowest bids on equipment, often ensuring he and his men ended up with crap.

Jeffers sighed. "Well, all I can say is, find me evidence. Something other than your intuition. Why are you so protective of him anyway?"

Todd grinned. "Because he reminds me of two kids from the mountains of Carolina. We did things way more dangerous than going to work with a hangover the day after a night of drinking. Luck was on our side, that's the only difference."

Jeffers' face changed from solemn to smiling in seconds. "Jesus, remember that time we stole your dad's old Ford, even though he told us it was unsafe? And the wheel came off when we were headed over the mountain into Tennessee?"

"We were lucky we didn't end up over the bank, down a few hundred feet and into the Pigeon River." Todd laughed. "God damn but we were idiots."

"Good driving on your part, getting the thing to a stop."

"Dad nearly killed me when we managed to get home. But only because he was worried about what could have happened. I *deserved* to be in trouble. I don't think this kid does. We did a stupid thing that could have had tragic results and we got a second chance. This boy deserves one, too."

"*You* should have been the lawyer." Jeffers shook his head. "Okay, we'll plead him innocent and see where it goes." He pointed his finger at Todd. "But find me something to use, damn it! And where is that prosecutor anyway?"

He took a note from his jacket pocket. "Walker," he read. "Where is the bastard? I have to be downtown in an hour."

A vision of the only "Walker" he knew came to mind, her fiery hair spread across his pillow and her emerald eyes filled with need. His cock started to rise just as a voice said, "The bastard is right here."

A second later, her scent struck him. He'd become intimately familiar with the smell of her, the feel of her, the taste of her. With a jerk of his head, Todd found himself staring at the object of his erotic thoughts.

Carie looked like a vision from one of his many dreams—except she was wearing the uniform of a naval officer. She held out her hand to Jeffers. "I'm Lieutenant Commander Walker, representing the Navy in the case against Seaman Second Class Samuel Turner."

"Well, *hello.*" Jeffers held out his hand, smiling like a jackass. "I'm Jeff Jeffers, defense."

She turned to see who else stood there. Her mouth fell open when she saw Todd.

He nodded. "Senior Chief Baxter, Ma'am." Just saying the words and seeing her cheeks blush sent his libido into overdrive. He suddenly pictured her on top, doing wild and crazy fucking things to his body, and all the while he was begging her to keep on, while calling her "Ma'am."

Quickly, she gained her feet. "Nice to meet you Senior Chief. Are you involved in this case?" A look of startled awareness flashed in her eyes. Did she think he had some part in the accident?

"The Senior Chief's a mechanical engineer. He's working with me to clear the seaman's name."

"I see." Her eyes narrowed, and her lips formed a thin line. She spun around to face Jeffers. "I presume you will be ready to go to court on Monday."

"That's the plan. If something comes up, like *evidence*"—he slipped a frowning glance at Todd—"or a sudden desire for a plea, where are you staying?"

She hesitated. "I was planning to surprise a friend, but I'm afraid those plans have changed. I'll be here on base." She thumbed through paperwork in her briefcase and wrote out something that she handed to Jeffers. "Here's the main number. Ask for the female BOQ, and they'll connect you. Or leave a message and I'll call back."

Smoothly, Jeffers pulled one of his cards from his jacket pocket. "My cell number is on there. Call anytime." The bastard grinned—actually *grinned*—at Carie. If he tried anything with her, Todd would have to kick his ass. *Which might not be too hard.* It seems that lawyers sat a lot. Jeff had a layer of flab starting to show around his waist. Todd could take him, easy.

"If you're free for dinner," Jeff said, "I'd be happy to host, show you a bit of Norfolk besides the base."

She smiled. "That's very thoughtful, but I don't think that would be a good idea. We'll be adversaries on Monday."

"If you're looking for a good place to eat, Ma'am," Todd said, "I'd highly recommend Nero's on Atlantic Avenue at the Beach. It's a bit of a drive, but if you leave the base by three, traffic isn't too bad."

She raised her brows. "Three, Senior Chief? Isn't that a little early for dinner?"

He smiled, remembering that she was a bit uppity the first time they met, too. "Early for dinner, but a nice time to walk the beach. The restaurant is at the far end of Atlantic, and they don't mind your parking there mid-afternoon if they know you're coming back to eat. It's quiet but good food and not many tourists. Five or five-thirty is usually best to get a table on Friday night. Gives you time to do something in the evening, too."

"And what would you suggest I do with my evening, Senior Chief?"

"Why, Ma'am, whatever you were going to do if you'd been able to visit your friend."

"Touché, Senior Chief," she said quietly. "I might take you up on your recommendation." She turned once more to Jeffers. "Anything else right now?" she asked briskly.

"Nothing I can think of," he said reasonably.

"Then gentlemen, I'll say goodbye until Monday." Her leaving didn't dispel the fragrance of her perfume, or the profound impact of seeing her so unexpectedly.

"You son of a bitch." Jeffers was nearly whispering. "You've fucked the prosecution."

Todd stepped back, stunned. He thought they'd covered their relationship pretty well. "What the hell are you talking about?"

"Don't fuck a fucker, Baxter. I've known you too long. The way you two looked at each other, and that last little 'if I can recommend a place to eat' shit, was enough to make me want to play music and throw rose petals. Sure, you don't want a cigarette? Because there was sex going on in this hallway a minute ago."

"You're full of shit, Jeffers."

"Just don't fuck up the case because your dick stands at attention for the pretty lieutenant commander." He thought for a few seconds. "Say, doesn't the military frown on officers screwing around with non-commissioned folks like you?"

Fraternization between commissioned officers and noncoms was a serious breach in the service. His seeing Carie could have repercussions for both of them. "Just worry about your own fucking life, Jeffers. And that kid in there."

Jeff burst into laughter. "Son, you've got it bad." He slapped Todd's shoulder. "Let me know if you find anything this weekend. We need a small miracle." And he disappeared down the same hallway Carie had just used.

Trying to put both of them out of mind, Todd pushed open the door to say a last word to Turner. If he kept his wits about him and Carie out of his thoughts, he might find a way to keep the kid from brig time or even a dishonorable discharge.

If he could keep Carie out of his mind. Considering his recent past experience, he doubted that was even possible.

Chapter Five

Carie found Nero's where Todd said she would, as far to the south as she could go on Atlantic Avenue and still be on Atlantic. Beyond the restaurant, the street went into the county and, eventually, down to North Carolina, though far from the Asheville hotel room where she'd lost herself in days of lust.

The place was small but looked inviting. She parked and went inside to let management know she would be back and to make sure her military-issued sedan was out of the way. They seemed happy to let her park. She made her way around the side of the building and nearly ran into Todd, who lounged against the weathered wood siding. He looked better than good in a pale blue polo shirt and jeans. Top-Sider boat shoes with no socks gave him that naturally casual look that no model could successfully carry out.

"I was hoping you'd come," he said.

"You were pretty obvious," she said dryly.

"I knew you were smart enough to *catch* the hint. I just didn't know if you'd follow it."

How could she not? The moment she noticed him she'd remembered the feel of his being deep inside her. But that didn't change a damn thing. They shouldn't be here, not together.

She held her head high and tried to look down her nose at him—nearly impossible since he was taller than she, but she had perfected the attitude long before meeting Todd Baxter. *Senior Chief Todd Baxter.* "I wanted to walk the beach while I was here, that's all." Todd grinned and Carie melted inside.

"Lucky for me, I wanted to walk the beach, too," he said. "Quite a coincidence, huh?"

She snorted in disbelief and slipped off her sandals. Brushing by him, she was glad he didn't try to kiss her or hold her. But then she frowned. Why *didn't* he try to kiss her? She'd wanted to jump his bones right there in that Norfolk hallway. They had to maintain propriety then, but here, no one would see them. What held him back? She knew an unfamiliar sense of self-doubt. Had she mistaken his feelings before?

Nonsense. Carie knew what they'd had was more than mere lust. It had been lust of stupendous proportions, far beyond a few days of burning out. Then what held him back? *Knowing the military regulations preventing officers and enlisted personnel from having a relationship, you idiot.*

Damn. She finally found someone she clicked with, and he had to be an enlisted man in the Navy.

The sand felt good between her toes, cool and squishy. Gulls screeched overhead and on the sand, where they snatched up sand crabs and poked around for scraps sunbathers might have left. Surf pounded to the shore and then surged forward, the sharp white of its foam sharp against the dark, wet sand before the water was absorbed. The sun beat down, making her wish she'd worn her bathing suit under her jeans and tank top so she could take a quick dip, and remembered to bring a floppy hat to shield her face.

Suddenly, something was plopped on her head. She dragged it off to look at it. SFC Baxter was stamped on the inside of a white sailor hat, brim folded down.

"I kept it for sentimental purposes when I made chief," Todd said. When she raised her brows, he continued. "I brought it in case you came without a cover. I remember you were sensitive to the sun when we went to pick up your clothes." He smiled. "And I know you're quick to freckle. Not that I don't like your freckles a great deal. Ma'am."

She cringed at his use of "Ma'am," though it was the proper term for him to use when a superior officer was a woman. But she smiled inside that he'd remembered such a small thing like the sensitivity to the sun suffered by all redheads. Chagrined, she put the hat on and pulled it forward, shielding her eyes from the sun.

"After all that time in North Carolina, how in hell did we never mention what we did for a living?" She couldn't believe her stupidity. Martha had nothing on her for not asking the right questions.

"In Carolina, we had lots of other things on our minds. I knew you're a lawyer. When I thought of you, I never wondered how you spent your time at work. I just thought of how you spent your time with me."

"That's pretty shallow."

Todd laughed. "Not to a man."

Stupid answer. But it had been his very maleness that captivated her. Well, and orgasms. *Who's shallow now?*

"Look," he said, his hand out in a request for understanding. "It isn't as though I didn't want to get to know you better. I did. I do. But when we're together I can't keep my hands off you. I can't stop thinking how I want to touch you, kiss you, sink my cock into–"

"When were you going to tell me you were in the Navy?" she asked.

He sighed loud enough that she heard it over the sound of the waves. "I don't know. I guess when we slowed down enough to talk. There wasn't much time."

There hadn't been. In Asheville, if they hadn't been eating or sleeping, they were fucking. And there hadn't been much eating or sleeping going on.

"I think they should put a plaque on the outside of that room for the fewest number of times the occupants left in four days. I couldn't get enough of you." Carrying his shoes in his left hand, he stuck his right hand in his pocket and strolled along beside her, barefoot. "I still can't."

"You didn't exactly write and tell me that."

He shrugged. "I didn't want to assume too much, not knowing if you wanted me again as much as I wanted you. Call me shy." He grinned, and she burst into laughter. "Besides," he continued, "you're the one who left saying, 'It's been fun.'"

She dipped her head, acknowledging the fact. "And you agreed."

"Carie, I was scared."

He sounded sincere, but *really?* He stopped and stared out across the breakers. She stared along with him, wondering what he saw out there. "I'm pretty set in my ways," he said, and she had to strain to hear him, he spoke so low. "I'll be honest, I haven't been a monk, but sex with you was different. You made me think of things I'd never considered before." He studied her face. "Do you understand?"

"I think so," she said softly. "I wanted you more than anything. I've never had time or energy for a relationship. I've given all I have to my career. But I think I want more now."

Todd reached to cup her cheek but then dropped his hand. "Like I said, I'm not a monk but there's been no one since you."

She wanted him. More, she needed him. "Nor for me. It wouldn't have been the same. Nothing before you was ever that intense. Nothing else has ever touched me." Pain struck her heart. "I want to kiss you so damn much."

Before he could say anything, she turned and began walking again, sticking her hand in her pocket so she wouldn't be tempted to reach for his hand. She'd had to hold herself back from stepping into his arms in the hallway on base. Here, on a near-empty beach, she had to exert even more willpower. "That was then, and this is now. Vacation and real life seldom mix."

"Funny," he said. "Given the chance, I'd mix vacation and real life in a New York minute"

"Me, too," she admitted. "But we can't now. You've ruined everything."

She felt him stiffen beside her. *Idiot! You make a living saying the right thing to sway people's opinion and you screw up like that?*

"This is my fault *how?*" he asked quietly. She hadn't seen him angry, but she had an idea this quiet voice was the prelude.

"You're in the Navy but you're not an officer." It might sound petty, but regs were regs. "Why *aren't* you an officer?" Okay, and that sounded whiny. But damn it, she *felt* whiny. "That attorney friend of yours said you were a mechanical engineer. Weren't you offered OCS?"

"As a matter of fact, yes. After I received my BS and again after I earned my Masters. I didn't accept because I didn't *want* to be an officer."

"Why not?" She spun to face him, the arm holding her sandals outstretched in confusion. She'd never met anyone who would turn down the chance to make more money and have more prestige.

"I like working, using my hands, being with my men—on the job and off."

She started walking again. "Well, too bad you like screwing me. Or you seemed to. God knows, I loved fucking you. And now it's all over."

"I'm surprised at you, counselor. The regulation obviously was written for two people who work together. It's to keep one from having undue power over the other. We don't work together."

"It's military regulations. You don't mess with them. I don't mess with them. *I* work to up*hold* them, not bend them to suit my desires."

"I love your desires." He pulled her hand from her pocket. Linking their fingers, he stepped closer and they continued their stroll across the sand as though the world hadn't just turned on its axis. "Right here, right now, it feels like we never left Asheville. The view is different but we're the same."

Carie opened her mouth for air, suddenly needing more than she had a moment ago. But she couldn't gather the strength needed to take back her hand. "The view isn't the only thing different."

He frowned. "Was I the friend you had planned to surprise this weekend?"

"Yes." She sighed.

He laughed out loud. "You succeeded wildly." They continued in silence for a few more yards, letting the surf, pounding its way to high tide, provide the background to their thoughts.

"All we can do now is talk. So, tell me about yourself," she said. "How did a mountain boy like you end up in the Navy?"

He shrugged. "Too much mountain and not enough water, I guess. How about you?"

"I wanted to be a lawyer and didn't have the money it would take. The service paid for my law school and I paid them back by working in the JAG's office. Then I found I like the military, so I decided to stay. I have six years until retirement, so it's a commitment now."

Todd looked wistfully towards the sea. "I loved the Navy from the moment I got off the bus in San Diego for recruit training. I still do. Everything about it."

She glanced sideways at him. "If you'd become an officer, you might be captain by now with that kind of devotion."

Grinning, he said, "Or that might have been what soured me on the whole thing." He sobered. "My brother was a chief in the Navy. He was ten years older than me, and I thought he could do anything. He's probably the real reason I decided to join up."

"And where is he stationed? Or is he out?"

"He's dead. A car crash fifteen years ago. I thought if I could become what he was, it would be a chance...I don't know, to honor him in some way." He turned his head to look at her. "I've never aspired to be the highest-ranking sailor, just the best sailor."

"Well, that's damned unfair. How am I supposed to argue with something that sounds so noble?"

He smiled. "You aren't, counselor. You're supposed to kiss me, tell me I'm your hero, and come home with me."

"Todd, I want to. I really do. But..." She bit her bottom lip. Who would know? What could come of it except an exceptional weekend with a man compatible with her in every way? "I can't," she whispered.

He couldn't have heard her, but he nodded, knowing somehow what she'd said.

"Well, there's nothing in the regs that say two people eating at the same restaurant can't share a table, or that one of them can't foot the bill. So, can I buy you a great beach dinner?"

Carie forced a smile. "Absolutely." Her stomach roiled with her decision not to accept Todd's offer of the weekend. She didn't think she could eat a bite, but her day had already been so fucked up she didn't want to spoil anything else. They could talk some more over a meal and glass of wine, and then she would head back to the BOQ in Norfolk.

And spend the weekend alone. *Damn it.*

***

The meal had been great. They'd talked a lot, laughed a lot, and consumed two bottles of wine. Todd had discovered that Carie came from eastern Washington state, had a love of all things natural and a vicious streak in her for justice. He revealed that he was a Senior Chief Boilerman and would be shipping out for a six-month cruise to the Mediterranean in another few weeks. That had quieted her. Over coffee, he attempted to liven things up before they said goodbye.

"Have you ever been to the Med?"

"I went to Europe after graduation from undergraduate school. My parents sent me on the Grand Tour reduced to three weeks of hostels and student train passes," she said with a laugh. "I've never been sent by the Navy. I had a tour in Guam and everything else has been stateside."

"So, you haven't served onboard ship?"

"No. Martha has. I don't want to tell you how that went."

He laughed. "I have a hard time thinking of women on ships, even now. No offense to your feminine sensibilities."

"Maybe I should put in a request to serve on *your* ship and go the Med with you." She said it with a smile, but he saw fire in her eyes.

He reached across the table and took her hand. "I can only tell you that in close quarters like we'd find on a destroyer, there'd be a hell of a lot of fraternization going on between us, regs or no regs. Don't you know how hard it is for me to sit across the table from you and know I can't have you in my bed tonight?"

"Todd, please. We can't." She squeezed his hand before slipping hers away.

He sat back in his seat. "I understand. I respect your decision. Just know this. I love my life. I love my work and my men who serve with me. And I've never regretted for a single moment not going to OCS—until tonight."

Smiling, she picked up her cup and held it with both hands at her lips. "Without getting too much into the case—"

"Because that would be inappropriate," Todd said, smiling back.

"Right. But I'm curious as to why you were there."

"He's one of my men. It's my job to help him if I can."

"And you think you can?" Her eyes took on an impersonal, business look. She sipped and then set the cup back in the saucer.

"I do."

She quirked her brows in a disbelieving manner. "I think this is an easy win for me. I don't think you and Mr. Jeffers can beat me."

Suddenly it all became too much—her coming to Norfolk, and then her decision not to be with him. Now she offhandedly made a comment that made the life of Seaman Turner sound like a game.

"I believe we will... *Ma'am*." She looked as though he'd slapped her. He softened his voice and continued. "I think he's innocent, and I am going to do everything in my power to prove it."

Stiffly she said, "Feel free. I think it's time I head back." She stood. "Thank you for a delicious meal." Slinging her purse over her shoulder, she walked away.

Shit! He'd acted like an ass. Throwing money on the table, he rushed out after her. "Wait!" He ran across the parking lot, now filled with cars. She turned and looked at him, hand on the open door of her rental. "Carie, I'm sorry. That was a stupid thing to say. I can only plead frustration."

She stared past the restaurant and to the ocean, saying nothing. "Carissa." He whispered her name and used his finger to tilt her head to face him instead. "Forgive me?"

"I want you every bit as much as you want me," she whispered back.

"I know. But you made the best decision. Doing the right thing means doing it even if no one would find out whether you did or not."

She laughed. "I'm worried that I understand that."

He smiled down at her, loving the way she laughed out loud, openly. He loved the way her eyes crinkled when she smiled. He loved that her face was fresh and natural, instead of covered with makeup. Her smell, her shape, her fierce sense of right and wrong—he loved everything about her.

Damn. He loved her. Impossible after only meeting her twice, despite their first meeting having lasted for days. But he'd never felt anything like he did with her, in bed or out. She understood the Navy, the demands, the duty. He didn't want to be apart from her, and that was straight from the heart. How had that happened so fast?

"See that truck over there? The green one? Well, keep that in sight behind you because I'm following you back to base."

Carie shook her head. "You don't have to do that. It's still daylight."

"I want to. I need to make sure you get there safely."

"I love your chivalrous attitude."

"How about breakfast tomorrow? I know a great place near the base and I have to be there tomorrow anyway. About eight?"

"I'll be ready. But tomorrow I buy."

"Fair enough." He stared at her a moment longer, wishing they could kiss.

Kiss, hell. You want to take her home. But following her to her temporary quarters would have to do. Tomorrow would be another day. He surprised himself by admitting he'd rather spend it with Carie at arm's length than in any other way without her.

Chapter Six

Carie took a gulp of strong, black coffee and reflected that the only way having breakfast with Todd could have been any better was if they had woken up together and *then* eaten. She chafed at the way she had tossed and turned in the bunk in the BOQ the night before, unable to sleep, knowing how close he was—just a few miles away in some part of the city called Ghent—and she was there on base, in a mostly empty building reserved for single female officers.

She knew she looked like hell that morning. The touch of worry in Todd's gaze when he studied her face across the table told her all she needed to know about the dark circles under her eyes. When had she ever let a man affect her like this?

"I didn't sleep worth shit either," he said finally.

"So how come you look fresh as a cucumber while I look like death warmed over?" Even her tan slacks, her favorite silk coral-colored blouse with the cute tulip sleeves, and her comfiest dressy shoes didn't give her that fresh, peppy feeling.

"Years of standing watch at all hours of the day and night." He smiled. "And I wouldn't say you look like death warmed over. Exactly."

She laughed. "Didn't your mother ever tell you that there's a time for honesty and a time to keep quiet?"

"Yeah, I got that whole Thumper's mom 'If you can't say something nice' speech a million times. But I thought you were a woman of the law, counselor, and that only the whole truth would do."

"You got it wrong, sailor. I like a pretty compliment the same as any woman, even if it is a white lie to spare my feelings."

Todd's gaze turned blistering. "You are the most beautiful woman I have ever laid eyes on, Carie Walker. And that's no lie."

Her eyes widened, and she stopped breathing. *He's going to kiss me.* Todd was going to stand and lean over the table to kiss her. His intense gaze, the way he braced his hands on the tabletop, the tension in his shoulders told her what he aimed to do. The little hole-in-the-wall restaurant was packed, and she didn't care. She waited, hoping, wanting.

"Hello, Todd. Who's this?"

What? Carie blinked, pulled from the magic. Todd's whole bearing turned hard and cold. The fire left his eyes. In fact, the only light in their depths now was of anger. She'd never seen him like this.

"Jenny. I didn't expect to see you here."

The woman licked her lips nervously and glanced from Carie to Todd. "I'm here with Mary."

"My sister, Mary," Todd explained. "Since she was ten she's liked to think she can run my life better than I can." He cast a look around the crowded establishment, and then raised his hand in greeting. Carie turned to see a dark-haired woman sitting alone in the back. The woman tipped her head in greeting but didn't smile.

"I didn't realize you had family here." There was so much they didn't know about each other. How could her feelings run so strongly for this man when she knew next to nothing about him? Last night, alone in the dark, with a need for Todd pulling her like the tide pulled the moon, the awareness that she might love him crossed her mind. It concerned her that the concept felt comfortable and right in the light of day, too.

"I wish I didn't sometimes," he muttered. "Jenny, this is my very good friend, Commander Walker."

"Commander!" The woman gave a more appraising look at Carie. "Mary didn't tell me you were expecting company, Todd. I thought you might come over for dinner last night."

"There was no reason for you to think that. And I don't usually report my comings and goings *or* my company to my sister." At her crestfallen look, he seemed to relent. "The commander is here for a problem at work."

Her relieved sigh made Carie wonder just how close the woman and Todd were.

"I know your ship is leaving soon, Todd. I'll expect you for dinner several times before then." She focused on Carie. "I just hate when the Navy drags him away."

"Oh, I'm sure."

Todd made a disgusted sound. "Excuse us now, Jenny. Carie and I have some work to do."

"Carie…?"

The sudden switch from commander to her first name must have indicated a friendlier status to Jenny. Confused, she glanced back at Todd's sister. "Are you *friends?*" she asked, addressing Carie.

"I'm afraid so." Much more than friends if her pussy had anything to say about it. Or her heart.

"But you don't live here, in Norfolk."

"No."

"All right then. That's fine." Jenny's smile as she turned and left was a bit smug. What was she to Todd?

Todd examined her eyes. "I'm sorry about that."

"Interesting fan club you have, Senior Chief," Carie murmured as soon as Jenny took herself back to her table.

He sighed. "I've been gentle, direct, firm, even cruel, I'm sorry to say, and she doesn't accept that I am absolutely uninterested in her as anything other than a friend of my sister's. Mary talked me into taking her to a couple of events after I came home from the last cruise just because...well God only knows why. Everyone but my sister could see we don't suit. Anyway, much to my regret, Jenny has latched onto me."

"Well you *are* a god among men," Carie teased.

"It's good to know you recognize that," he teased back. Then he sobered. "She's a nice woman, but only as a friend." Todd looked into Carie's eyes. "She needs to find some other poor SOB to be with. She doesn't need me. Hell, if she really knew me she wouldn't *want* me. Sorry she interrupted us."

"It's okay. If you were visiting me in D.C. we'd be besieged by hundreds of men ready to drag me away to their caves."

His look turned primal. A growl emanated from deep in his throat. "They'd have to get past me first."

"I was kidding," Carie said, surprised.

"Good." He took a breath. "There's no one I'm interested in but you, Carie. I want you to know that."

Her heart swelled with longing. "I feel the same about you. I wish—"

"Don't wish. I know why we can't be together." His mouth formed a thin line. She wanted to kiss away the tension in his face, his shoulders, and hell, his whole body.

"I don't want to let you go yet," he said. "If you aren't doing anything right now, do you want to come with me?"

She didn't even ask where. "Yes."

His smile told her how pleased he was with her answer. He picked up the check.

"Oh no you don't," she said. "I told you that breakfast was my treat."

He handed her the check without argument. "A woman who wants to pay is one I can get behind." He leaned closer as they stood. "And over, and under, and any which way."

Her blood ran hot. A whiff told her that her pussy moistened. He seemed to notice, too. His eyes dilated.

"Be a good boy."

"Yes, Ma'am." Unlike the sarcasm with which he'd said the word the night before, today he made it feel like a soft caress. The word sent shivers through her. How she'd last the day without touching him, she didn't know. But she knew she wouldn't pass up the opportunity to spent time with him.

***

"Is this something?" She held up a narrow strip of tubing with half a clamp stuck to it. Her brows were raised in question.

"I don't think so, but put it in the bag and we'll look closer back in the garage."

Todd didn't understand how they'd made it through the last two hours without dropping to the ground and having a good fuck, but they had. Only the task at hand—scouring the path Seaman Turner had taken with the lift truck, looking for any remaining evidence that might show why his accident had happened—kept him from a powerful, painful erection.

Carie had been a good sport, walking the area with him, searching the ground though he wasn't sure she knew what she was looking for. She wasn't dressed for time on the dock where wind off the water blew anything and everything their way. But she hadn't complained, just helped him look for that unknown clue that might help Seaman Turner.

"So, tell me more about your time in college," she said, continuing along the invisible line Todd had designated for her search. They walked in parallel about six yards apart from the garage to the edge of the concrete where the lift truck went off into the brink.

"Georgia Tech was a great school, and I loved Atlanta. But you have to know how different it was for me, a serviceman, older than most of the other undergrads."

"I'll bet girls flocked to you."

He let the silence hang for a moment, uncertain of how to answer. "Girls *are* attracted to a hot guy." Her snort made him smile. "But to find a girl willing to go beyond looks and appreciate what I wanted wasn't so easy."

"And that was…?"

"Someone who understood how much I wanted to learn, that I wanted a degree. And more than that, that my life and mistress was the Navy. Any woman would have had to take third place. Not many were willing to do that."

"But you got in a lot of fucking before they discovered that." She sounded unhappy. Could she possibly be jealous? God, he hoped so because that would mean she cared.

"Yes, Ms. Dragon, I did."

"Dragon…?" She stopped and looked at him. And then she laughed, throaty and full. He grinned back and willed himself not to walk over and kiss her until she wrapped herself around him.

When she stopped he stared intensely. "Empty fucking, Carie. Only when I met you did I have sex that really meant something. That spark of electricity between us goes deep."

"I know," she said in a low voice. "I think…" She stopped and bit her lower lip. "I think I'm in love with you, Todd."

He sucked in a deep breath. His heart raced. "I know I'm in love with you, Carie. I don't understand how it happened, but the moment I helped you out of that ravine in Carolina I knew you were the one."

She looked as though she would cry. He started forward without realizing he was. "Don't cry, sweetheart." He wrapped his arms around her. She felt soft and warm and sweet in his arms, right where she belonged.

"What are we going to do?" Pleasure ran through him as she stretched her arms up his back and pulled him closer.

"I don't know. But there will be an answer somewhere. Just give us some time."

She stayed silent. He could only hope she considered his suggestion, that they hold on until a solution presented itself.

"You're here for work, sweetheart. Let's concentrate on that right now."

She nodded against the front of his shirt. "You're right. A young man's future is at stake." She pulled out of his embrace and wiped her nose on the back of her hand. "That's one thing that made me realize I love you, that you care so much for Turner's welfare."

"And what about you?" he asked. "You're here to prosecute the case, and yet you're spending your day helping me look for something that will prove his innocence."

"I'm an idiot," she said with a wry smile.

"You're damn wonderful."

"No, I'm— Is this something?" She walked a few feet away and Todd followed. Holding up a long piece of metal rod, she shot him a questioning look.

"I'll be damned. I think you've found something important, Carie. Put it back where you found it, so I can take a couple of pictures to show the position and locations." Using his phone, he took several views. "Let's go back to the garage."

On the walk, Todd tried to re-create what might have happened to the lift truck the day Turner sent it crashing into the harbor. They had recovered the equipment and it waited now in a roped off area of the base's maintenance garage.

Carie's eye grew large when she saw it. "He's damn lucky he wasn't killed," she said with awe in her voice.

"It's a long way from the operator's cage to the ground, so you're right. He *was* hurt but he was lucky." Todd took a long look at Carie. "Sanders!" A young sailor who had been standing watch over the evidence came running up. "Bring me a pair of coveralls. The smallest size you can find."

"Yes, Senior Chief." The young man ran off. He didn't salute or address Carie since she wore civilian clothes. No one could tell she was his superior. As it was, it didn't matter. She was with him. And by God, Todd was going to find a way to make sure she was always with him.

"I don't want you to ruin your clothes,"

"Wait a minute. Am I supposed to climb under there with you?"

"I want you to be sure of what we found." And under the hulk of ruined equipment, they'd be out of sight.

The sailor came back holding a set of denim dungarees. "This is the best I can find, Senior Chief."

"They'll do. Thanks. We'll be examining the lift truck now, so there's no need to stand watch. I'll let you know when we leave."

"Okay, Senior Chief." Sanders left.

Todd crouched before Carie. She slipped off her pumps and braced herself on his shoulders as she stepped into the jeans.

Her aroma tempted him, with his face so close to her pussy. He inhaled deeply and fought to keep his desire under control.

Standing, he pulled the denim up over her body, managing to brush his knuckles over every luscious curve.

"This is different," she said. "You putting clothes *on* me."

"It has its own allure," he replied. "All this time I've been missing a real turn-on." Finally, he fingered the shirt collar while she snapped up the front.

Under the bench along the wall, Todd found two dollies. Helping Carie down onto one, he stretched out on the other, with the metal piece they'd found on the dock. "Push with your feet," he directed, "and let's see if we have a match."

He slid up under the part of the machine that housed the hydraulics.

"We found right away that the hydraulics were trashed," he explained to Carie when she slid in beside him. "The theory was that it happened after the truck hit bottom. But—" he held the rod up to the destroyed linkage. "Look here," he said. "It fits."

She reached up and twisted the rod a little left and then right. It fit perfectly.

"And what does this mean?"

"The linkage for the hydraulic lines broke off before the truck went off the edge of the dock."

"Is it common for linkages to break like this?"

"No. But I've worked on these things enough to know to look for something wrong. This brand of truck is known for giving trouble. We have constant maintenance problems with them."

"What would have happened, assuming this broke as you think?"

"Turner would have hit the brakes and nothing would have happened. The brake pedal would have felt the same, but the hydraulics wouldn't have responded."

"So, he could be innocent."

Todd twisted to look at Carie. "I'd bet on it, Carie. Look, I wouldn't protect a sailor who did something wrong through malice. What happened to Turner would have happened to me." He shrugged. "Except I might have thought to turn the machine into something to stop it. One of the concrete stanchions or something. He was too inexperienced and probably a little panicked."

She was quiet. "I still have to appear in court on Monday."

"I know that." He reached over and brushed a strand of hair behind her ear. "I wouldn't expect you to do anything against your beliefs. I just wanted to provide a perspective of things as I see them."

She turned her head to kiss his palm, and the dam on his libido threatened to burst.

"I can't see you for the rest of the weekend," she said. "I won't be able to hold back if I do. Beyond that, everything that's happened since my coming here could be seen as compromising the case. It'll be bad for me and if I can't continue, someone else will reopen the issue."

His heart sank. "I understand. I appreciate your helping me today."

Maneuvering the dollies so they were side by side, he kissed her, deeply, intensely. She responded with passion unmatched by anything he'd experienced. Maybe because they had admitted their love? He didn't know. But their tangled tongues and heated breath stirred something new and wonderful in him. He loved Carie. She loved him. Somehow, they would work things out so they could be together.

Chapter Seven

"The government calls Senior Chief Todd Baxter," Carie announced clearly in court Monday morning.

Todd, looking absolutely killer in his whites, walked up to the stand and took the oath. She knew he must have been surprised to find that morning that he was appearing as a government witness instead of for the defense, but she wanted his testimony on her side of the ledger instead of having her weakly agreeing with the defense's theory. Perception was everything, and this way she seemed stronger.

"Do you know Seaman Second Class Turner, Senior Chief?"

"Yes, Ma'am. He's in my squad."

"And is he a reliable sailor?"

"He's young, but a good man. I've had no complaints."

"So, it surprised you to find that he ran a lift truck off the dock and into the harbor?"

"Yes, Ma'am, it did."

"Do you have any theories about how that incident might have happened?"

He presented his theory about the broken hydraulic linkage and explained his experience with that brand of lift truck.

"And, Senior Chief, in your opinion, this broken linkage is the cause of the accident, not negligence on Seaman Turner's part?"

"That's correct."

"If counsel may approach?" she asked the captain in charge of the court. He gestured her and Jeffers forward.

"Sir, I saw myself how the rod Senior Chief Baxter refers to fit perfectly to the lift truck. In fact, I found it myself on the dock, about halfway between the garage area and where the truck went into the harbor."

"Did you know about this?" the judge asked Jeffers.

"I knew what had been found, but not that opposing counsel was the person who discovered it."

"Sir, I believe this to be an accident and not an act of negligence on the part of the seaman. The government is prepared to drop charges."

"And you've cleared this through your office?"

"Yes, Sir."

The judge looked shrewdly at Carie. "Is there anything else you want to say regarding your being on the dock searching for evidence with the Senior Chief?"

"No, Sir. I was just trying to cover all bases." She wanted to shrug but one didn't do that to a captain unless you were a captain yourself. "Justice doesn't always come as a conviction, Sir."

He had the mojo to shrug and he did. "Case dismissed."

A single glance showed that Todd stared at her. She nodded briefly and then turned away. Seeing him and not holding him was far too painful. She packed her briefcase, left the courtroom and climbed into her car for the return trip to Washington D.C. Best to get away than to stay here and torture herself, or Todd.

***

Two weeks later—two weeks with no phone calls or emails from him—she saw a message in her personal email account.

Richmond is a large city where it wouldn't be unusual for perfect strangers to meet. Especially, I understand, near the Birkstone Hotel in Shockoe Bottom. My former XO stayed at the Birkstone a couple of years ago and said it was very nice. And discrete. My ship departs on the 3rd. I have leave from the 28th through the 2nd. Will you be my perfect stranger?

She replied immediately. *Sorry. It's not my habit to befriend strangers. It happened once in North Carolina, and that meeting will last me a lifetime. But I* might *be in Richmond shopping on the days you mentioned and need a place to stay.*

Seconds after hitting Send his response displayed on her screen. *The room is reserved under my name.*

That was it. She put in for leave, rearranged her workload and planned what to pack. Looking at her calendar, she tapped her fingers impatiently. How would she make it another week and a half?

"Do you want to go to the Harbor Festival in Baltimore week after next?" Martha came into the office and flopped in the chair.

"Can't."

"Really. What are you doing?"

"I'm going to Richmond for a few days of shopping. I might hit the museum."

Martha's mouth fell open. "You *live* in the city of shopping and museums." She narrowed her eyes. "What are you really doing?"

The last thing Carie wanted was to share her plans. "I just want a few days away. You know I love history and Richmond has lots of interesting sights."

Martha studied her, then threw her hands out. "Okay. Whatever it is, I hope you have fun."

Carie smiled. "I believe I will."

***

Nine days later, Carie stood in front of the Birkstone Hotel, her rolling suitcase behind her.

"Lost?"

She'd know Todd's voice anywhere. Repeating the question he'd asked her in the North Carolina forest brought the day back. She smiled. "I don't believe so."

From behind, he cupped her shoulders with his big, warm hands and the heat extended all the way to her pussy.

Leaning against his chest she said, "I'm looking for a perfect stranger. Know where I can find one?"

"Well, you might turn around."

She did. He looked wonderful—too wonderful to keep her hands off of. She wrapped her arms around his waist and rose on her toes to brush his lips. "Hmmm. You are indeed perfect."

"I'm so glad you came," he whispered in her ear.

"Did you think I wouldn't?"

He kissed the rim of her ear. "I was afraid the regs would capture you and keep you safely away from temptation."

She turned to face him. "You're leaving for more than six months! Temptation is exactly what I want. Right now, we're just two people, no rate, no rank, no regulations."

He grinned. "Can I still call you *ma'am?*"

"It is kind of sexy, isn't it?"

"Oh, yeah. But then, everything about you is."

"Then, by all means, call me what you will."

He kissed her then. *Finally.* And it was like taking breath after being too long under water. She knew then if she hadn't already recognized it, that Todd Baxter was her life, her love, and if she was damn lucky, her future. Some how, some way.

***

"Do you want something to eat," Todd whispered.

"Yes."

"What would you like?"

"*Something,*" she said with a wicked glint in her eyes.

"Have I told you today that I love you?"

"Not nearly enough."

"No one but you, Carie."

"Todd! I love you, too!"

They didn't waste a moment, kissing in the elevator in the back corner, and not caring who got on or off. In less than five minutes, they replayed the entry into the hotel room in Asheville.

"Todd…? No condom this time?" Carie asked. "I swear to you that I'm healthy. I so want to feel you inside me."

"Oh my God, Carie," he said with a growl. "I'm good, sweetheart. I swear, I'd never hurt you."

"It's just that you'll be gone for so long. I want this memory."

He leaned forward to nip her ear lobe. "Skin to skin. God, I've been waiting for this."

She reached under her skirt and yanked off her panties, he had his slacks unzipped and around his thighs. He lifted her against the room door and over his cock, using the head to tease her opening, pressing in and then pulling out. She braced her elbows on his shoulders and wrapped her hands around his head, pressing her mouth to his, licking and sucking his tongue.

Then he thrust in. Her gasp and then groan of satisfaction encouraged him to go faster and harder. In seconds, she exploded around him. Her pussy gripped his dick hard. The long wait and great anticipation did him in. He drove in and emptied himself.

"Oh, God!" She sucked in air with heavy, labored breathing with her head tucked in the crook of his neck.

"You're mine now," he murmured. "I've never had sex without a condom before."

"Never?"

"I've never been willing to take the chance. I never trusted anyone—or even wanted to."

"I'm yours. You can trust me."

"*Carie.*" He buried his face in her hair, taking in the light scent of flowers. He'd never felt like this, his emotions so close to the surface and his needs insatiable.

"Is the edge off?" he asked.

"No way."

He chuckled. "How about using the bed now?"

"You'll have to carry me because I don't think I can walk."

"My pleasure." Taking careful steps with his jeans hanging on his hips, he moved to the bed where he deposited his wanton lover.

She stood long enough to divest herself of the rest of her clothing.

"Beautiful," he said. "It feels like forever."

"Now you," she said, her voice low and husky. It set his blood on fire. He ripped off his slacks and pulled his shirt over his head, not wanting to bother with buttons.

"My God. You're so hot," she said.

"Hot for you. Come closer. I want to taste you."

Carie scooted to the side of the bed and propped her feet on the edge, much the way she had that first time. The memory burned in his mind as he dropped to his knees and took her with his mouth.

Her clit, extended and firm, slid into his mouth. Carie cried out when he lightly bit down and twirled his tongue around and around. Her fingers squeezed and massaged his scalp as he lapped at her clit. Pressing a couple of fingers into her wet pussy, he firmly stroked her upper lining. In seconds, she bucked under him. He renewed his assault until she moaned. Todd felt the sound along the length of her body.

"I can't get enough of your pussy. You taste so damn good." This time he speared her pussy with his tongue and used his thumb to circle her clit. It took her no time at all to climax again. By then his cock throbbed to get inside her again.

Climbing up her body, he teased her clit with his cock before sinking into her heat. She wrapped her legs around his waist. "The only thing I like better than eating you is making love to you," he muttered and then took her mouth in an intimate kiss, feeding her flavor to her, probing with his tongue as he did with his dick.

Carie met thrust for thrust. Sweat sheened on her body as she strained for yet another climax. He pumped her with long strokes and then short, reveling in the sensation of having her tight sheath surround him. He'd almost believed this would never happen again.

And then she came, in a mind-blowing orgasm that ripped him along with her. He opened his mouth, gulping air, trying to stay with her as she rode out her passion.

When they finally came down, he dropped to her side, depleted. Pulling her into his arms he said, "It's even better than I remember."

"Because we're not messing with condoms?"

"Because we know each other better, and not just each other's bodies." He grinned to the ceiling. "Although that's fucking great in itself."

They lay quietly for a while. Todd thought Carie might even have slipped into sleep. Then she said, "That weekend in Norfolk changed everything for me. Loving you is not fraternization. But I'm not sure the Navy will see it that way."

"I know meeting me here goes against your better principles."

"Principles can go to hell. You're leaving in a few days. How could I let you go without being with you again?"

"You'll write, won't you? And email? I'll call whenever I get a signal."

"I'll email every day. And your mail call won't be empty, either."

He couldn't believe he'd found her standing in the woods. As though she'd been waiting just for him.

"That will be a first. No woman has ever written me before. Well, except family. I've always walked away from anyone when it was time to ship out."

"Not even Jenny?" she teased.

"I just met Jenny a few months ago. And no, I am not encouraging her to write. I had a stern talk with my sister, too."

"Why did you always walk away before?"

"I never cared before." He rolled onto his side. "I was never in love before. Now I'll know what those other guys feel when they get mail. Those guys who have an anchor. Who have someone waiting for them to come home."

"Well, sailor, this time you do have someone waiting for you at home."

"I'm very glad." Their kiss spoke promises he'd never intended to make to a woman. He'd figure out a way for them to be together, and when he came home, if Carie still felt the same, he'd ask her to marry him.

She leaned back so she could see him. "No girls in every port this cruise."

"No, Ma'am. Wouldn't do that." He gave her a shrewd look. "Same for you. No dragon hunting while I'm shipped out."

"Senior Chief," she whispered. "This dragon is tamed and all yours."

He pulled her over him so that she stretched along his length. With tenderness he'd never realized he had in him, he kissed her. "I love you. I never thought I'd say that to a woman, but it feels damn good. It feels right."

"Todd." She murmured his name against his lips. "What are we going to do?"

"Sweetheart, we'll figure it out. Don't give up on us." She sighed and laid her head on his chest, right over his heart. His cock stirred as it always seemed to do whenever he was with Carie or dreamed of Carie or even thought of Carie.

"No rest for the weary," she said with a short laugh, "we have a lot of memories to build up." She slid her hand down his body to his cock. It rose to the occasion, and she caressed it into full attention.

He sighed with contentment. "Just like a lawyer. Taking charge."

"It's what we do. Assertiveness 101 is the first course in law school."

"I like assertiveness."

"You'll like aggression even better." Sliding off him, she turned so that she faced his feet and positioned her mouth at his groin. "Such a handsome cock. Like its owner." She took a long lick, from root to head, laving it with her tongue.

Todd couldn't contain his groan. His hands found her head and he tangled his fingers in her hair. When she took him in fully, he tilted his hips up, meeting her hungry mouth. She grasped his nuts and he almost came off the bed.

Her ass rose with each mouthful. Todd pulled her long legs over his shoulders so that her pussy met his mouth. She squirmed, and he lifted his head to lick her wet furrow. She bore down on him, stroking her tongue along the vein on the bottom of his dick. Todd grasped her hips and ate her hungrily, mindlessly, just going with the sensations. Sucking hard, she wrung a cry from him. God, she was so wet. Pulling her slightly, he took her clit and lightly ran his teeth along it. She jerked her head and gave a long hum that reverberated through his cock and then to every nerve in his body.

He came like a volcano, sending his cum down her throat. She convulsed at the same time, sending a flood of juices over his mouth and chin. And still he couldn't stop lapping, pulsing, letting go in the most extraordinary way ever. He'd never really fucked at all until he met Carie. *No, you never* made love *until you met Carie.* Big difference. Who knew?

At last, she collapsed, falling to her side, her head nestled in his crotch, her nose in the hair at the root of his dick. He gently rubbed her butt cheeks, thinking finally of sleep—and waking up with Carie at his side.

Chapter Eight

She woke him by sucking him off. Not all the way. Just enough so she could enjoy an early morning ride. This was their last day, and she wanted to make the most of every second. The last four days had been a sexual fantasy—though they had spent a large portion of their time just talking and cuddling, catching up on some of the personal information they'd skipped over before. Those times were her favorite.

No, these times are my favorite.

"You think I'm a horse, counselor?" he asked in his sleepy voice.

"I'm going to ride you hard and put you away wet."

He chuckled. "You always do that. And you know I love it." He started to turn to his right.

"No! Don't look at the clock. Time doesn't exist for us." The blinds were drawn tight, so he couldn't tell that it was nearly eight. He'd said he needed to leave at nine, but she couldn't let him go. Not yet.

Slowly she rose over his cock and ever so slowly, sank down again. He sucked in a deep breath and grasped her hips. "Again," he whispered. And she obliged.

"You're so tight, and hot. I burn for you, baby."

"I'm yours, Todd. All yours." Up she went again, straining to keep just the tip of his head inside before sliding down his length again. They were the closest like this. He went the deepest. She wanted to hold him there forever. The Navy couldn't have him back. He was hers.

Then she remembered how he felt about the Navy. It was his life, he'd said. And his mistress. Women always came third. Well, second now, since he had finished his degree. *Two* degrees, her brilliant man. Could she live with taking second place in his life? She'd soon find out.

With the realization that she had to let him go, she hastened her movements, twisting her hips against his groin and reaching behind her to caress his balls.

He used his fingers to rub her clit. As though they'd arranged it, they came together. He clenched her hips, holding her in place. His cock pulsed deep inside, filling her with *Todd.* For days she would have some of him inside her. She'd think of that after his ship pulled out, that a small part of him was still in her body.

She fell forward. He caught her and brought her to his chest.

Stroking her back, he said. "I have to get up and shower if we're going to have breakfast before I go."

"I know." But she didn't move. Neither did he.

"Don't go dragon hunting while I'm gone."

She snorted. "Not a chance. The only dragon hunter I want to be caught by will be on a destroyer halfway around the world."

"About that," he said. "You lawyers can be sneaky. Don't come down to see the ship off."

How did he know she had planned to do just that? "Why not?"

"I have work to do below. But if I know you're there I'll want to be on deck. And I want to say goodbye here while we're both happy. I don't want to watch you fade into a speck as we pull away."

"I won't come," she said past the lump in her throat that threatened to make her cry.

"And don't cry, love," he whispered. "I'll be back before you know it."

She nodded. "I know."

"And remember that I love you, with all my heart."

"I love you, too. Don't forget."

"Not a chance."

Then he placed her to his side and got up. Moments later, she heard the shower running. She thought about going in with him, but then they'd just end up making love again, and he'd be late, and she'd feel guilty. Instead, she dressed, trying to look as good as possible after just getting out of bed. They would have breakfast downstairs and then he'd go. She had plenty of time to come back up to shower. And have a good cry.

***

Time was a funny thing. Some weeks dragged by. Those were the weeks when she received a few quick emails and a letter or two. Then there were times when he was free to call, or she received several emails in a day.

Soon, however, the weeks changed to months.

"I miss you so much," he wrote in an email when he'd been gone around four months. "I was wrong to ask you not to come see the ship off. Right now, I'd give anything to see you, even as a dot in the distance, just to know you were there for me."

His fatigue was obvious in the tone of his words. She knew him that well, she could tell. His next note was more upbeat. When he wrote to arrange a time to teleconference, Carie thought she'd go crazy preparing. Did she look okay? Would she cry and make him feel bad? Would she be able to tell him how much she loved him in their short span online?

When she sat in front of the computer, camera on and waiting, she couldn't stop fidgeting. "How do I look?" she asked Martha.

"Like a woman crazy in love."

Carie frowned. "That's not what I mean. Is this blouse all right? Maybe I should change into something sexier. He hasn't seen me in a while." She started to stand up when the connection came through. And suddenly, Todd was there before her, smiling kind of shyly.

"Carie?"

"Hi, Todd." She was glad she had on her comparatively demure silk blouse when she saw the men gathered around him, all bent over and looking at her.

"By God," one of them said, "there *is* a woman on the other end."

She had to laugh. "You have an audience?"

"Ma'am, did this man pay you to be on the other end of that camera so he could make us think he had a girlfriend?"

"Sorry, Chief. I'm here for him *gratis*."

Todd smiled wryly. "No one can believe that a beautiful woman would be interested in an old sea dog like me."

Smiling, she said, "Gentlemen, I hope you didn't bet money on it."

They laughed. One of the other chiefs slapped him on the back. "She's okay, Todd."

Another said, "We'll give you some privacy now."

A familiar face peered at her through the computer screen. "It's Turner, ma'am. The Senior Chief said I could take a second to say hello and let you know how grateful I am to the two of you for helping me out."

"No problem, Seaman."

He smiled in a way that made his dark blue eyes shine and made him look like an adorable youngster, which, in reality, he was. Then he was gone, and it was just her and Todd. *At last.*

She let out a deep breath. "I miss you so much." Tears threatened but she forced them back.

"Hey," he said in a low voice. "We're over halfway there. Don't give up on me now."

"Never! Have you gotten all my letters?"

"Five or six every mail call. I appreciate it. I wish I had time to write you more, but I hope you don't mind the emails."

"I love your emails."

He stared at the screen for a moment. "You look beautiful, honey. Good enough to eat."

"No sex talk online, Senior Chief," she said with a smile. He laughed. "But I feel the same about you," she said.

"In about two months' time," he said, waggling his brows.

"I'm putting in for leave for when the ship arrives. I'll be there to meet you with open arms."

"No, Carie. Don't come down. There's always a lot of work to do when we dock. I usually take the extra duty so the other guys can go meet their families."

"But…." She couldn't help but feel let down. Wasn't she his family now? Evidently not. "Okay."

He tapped the computer screen, bringing her attention to him. "I want to see you, too, as soon as possible, but I won't be able to get away until a couple of days after we dock. When we're together, I don't want to have to be going back and forth for this little thing and that. I want to have time with you and no worries. A couple days after we get back is a hail and farewell party and I promised I'd be there. The next day"—he checked something behind the computer screen—"that'll be the fourteenth, I'll be able to come to Richmond. Or wherever you want to be. Can you take your leave then?"

"Yes. And I really don't care where we choose as long as we're together."

"The same here, sweetheart." Someone said something in the background, and he frowned. "It's time to go, Carie."

"What? But we've just started. How can our time be up?"

"Don't worry. The cruise is flying by. I'll be with you before you know it."

Not soon enough. "I love you, Todd."

"I love you, Carie." And then he was gone.

"No!" She wanted to punch the monitor or throw something. They'd had barely any time at all. She hadn't told him about her cases or what she and Martha had been doing, or how lonely she was without him. She said all of that in her letters, but it wasn't the same as watching his eyes, seeing his smile, and the little gestures he made when he talked.

"All over?" Martha asked.

"I can't believe how fast it went." She slumped in the chair.

"Well, it *was* only fifteen minutes worth of time."

"Fifteen minutes never went so fast."

"But you said all you needed to say, right?"

"No! I didn't get the chance to tell him about the case I just won, or even about my promotion."

Martha tilted her head. "But you told him that you love him."

Carie smiled. "Yeah, we said that a few times."

Martha stared at her, worry lighting her eyes. "Carie, you're a full commander now. He's an E-9. What are you going to do?"

Anxiety filled her. She picked at her thumbnail absently. "I don't know."

"If you get caught, it'll be bad for both of you."

She took a deep breath. "Martha, I'm thinking of resigning my commission."

Her friend gasped. "You can't. You only have a few years until retirement. You love what you do, and you're damn good at it." She shook her head. "*No.* Huh-uh. I won't let you do it. You'll have to find some other way around this."

She knew that. But what other way was there? Funny as it might sound coming from someone who thought she'd be career Navy, but she wasn't at all sure she could handle being a Navy wife should she decide to get out and Todd stayed in. This cruise had given her a good lesson in being without what you wanted most, and she didn't like it. How did military families stand it, seeing their loved ones off to sea and waiting for their safe return?

"He's worth it, Martha. I can do it. And I *will* do it if it means I can be with Todd."

***

I loved talking with you face-to-face. I loved seeing your smile. Todd e-mailed almost immediately after their teleconference. *Just so you know, this is the first time I've ever counted the days until the ship docks in Norfolk.*

"You got yourself a beauty there, Todd." Fred Maxwell, a fellow chief and one of Todd's best friends came into the mess. He poured a cup of coffee and sat down across from Todd.

"Beautiful and *smart*," Todd said.

"I don't know about smart. She says she loves *you*, right?"

"Prick."

"Yeah, yeah," Fred said. "Like I tell my son, 'Sticks and stones,' and all that. I will grant you though, she *is* sexy," he added. When Todd frowned, Fred held up his hand. "I say that as an impartial observer, not an interested party. I got enough on my hands with *my* wife, without taking on someone else's woman. You gonna marry her?"

"I'm going to ask and hope like hell she says yes."

"Does she know you're retiring?" Fred eyed him.

Todd frowned again. "No."

"That's kind of a big decision to make without talking it through. Will she mind?"

"I hope not. She has years left before she's eligible to retire and she has a profession."

"Hell, you do, too. What are your plans?"

Todd checked to make sure he hadn't received a reply from Carie, and then logged out and closed the laptop kept in the chief's mess. Hell, when had he started waiting like a high school kid for a return note from a girl? *Since Carie.*

He got up to pour himself a cup of strong, hot coffee. Navy coffee. "I've put out feelers to engineering firms. Already have an offer for a contract job in the D.C. area, so that's a start."

"If it's that easy to get a job, maybe I should think about retiring, too."

"*How* many kids do you have?" Todd sat down and grinned.

"Hell," Fred muttered. "Six under ten and another on the way. Damn twins up the number fast." He took a healthy gulp of coffee.

"And how many Med cruises have we been on together?"

Fred grinned back. "Five. One for each pregnancy. Maybe I should stay home for a while. It's the going away part that makes us want to screw like rabbits. Hell, we'd probably never have sex if I was there all the time."

Todd thought about being with Carie. The surge of electric sensations that passed between them when they touched hadn't let up. He had the feeling they'd be having sex when they were old and gray.

"Think this through, idiot. You want to do something that *stops* you from having sex?" he asked Fred.

Fred took another gulp of coffee. "I guess I'd better keep going to sea, just so I can get a little every now and then."

Two other chiefs, Martin and Tolliver, came in for coffee. "Baxter, your girl's real good looking. I don't blame you for wanting out to stay home with her. We've got big plans for your hale and farewell," Tolliver offered.

"Planning already guys? We've got months left."

"You're special," Martin said. "We want to make sure you remember it all—the strippers, the drinking, the karaoke."

Tolliver nudged him and waggled his brows. "The *strippers.*"

Fred tilted his head. "Sounds like a *real* fun time."

"Yeah, for someone else. If Carie finds out I had strippers at my retirement party, she'll skin me alive."

Tolliver laughed. "Not even out and you're pussy whipped already. Put her in her place right at the beginning, Todd, or you'll be asking for trouble later on."

Her place was with him, naked in bed, making his body feel delicious, wicked things. "You know, Tolliver, that's *exactly* what I plan to do."

***

Time crawled. The ship went port to port. Todd looked at each destination from a different perspective now. It might be the last time he ever saw Athens, or Naples, or Nice. He might not come back to visit Egypt or Spain. For years he'd traveled where the Navy took him, carefree and able to see and do what he wanted, and he'd taken full advantage. Could he give it up?

Todd stood on deck, staring at the sun-dappled water of the Mediterranean, thinking about what life would be like without the Navy. Part of him hated the very thought of the change he headed for. The rest of him—the largest part of him—knew that for Carie he could handle anything. Still, it would be a huge change. What if she didn't want him when he got back, or what if she didn't want a change in their relationship, didn't want to marry him? Then he would have given up his life for–

"Senior Chief!" Todd turned toward the sound and saw a seaman first class waving him forward. "Trouble in the boiler room!"

He noticed the tone of the words more than the message. Even with modern technology, the boiler room counted as one of the most dangerous places on a ship. He ran through the hatch and slid down the ladders rather than putting a foot on each step. When he reached the boiler room, deep in the bowels of the ship, the area was chaos, except for Seaman Turner.

"Senior Chief, this boiler is building up steam and we don't know why."

With years of experience, he made a quick evaluation. "The valve must be stuck. Get me that big, mother of a wrench. Anyone who doesn't need to be here, get out."

Turner ran to find the wrench and Todd tossed his hat onto the floor, so he could crawl up under the pipes and lines that ran to and from the boiler. The valve was far under there.

"Here you go, Senior Chief." Turner had crawled under from a different side. He held out the wrench, two feet of heavy steel. "How are you going to twist the wrench with so little room?" he asked.

"Go on and get out, Turner."

"If you don't mind, I'd like to stay here with you. Maybe I can help."

There was no time to argue with the hard-headed idiot. Todd held the wrench in front of him with both hands and slammed the head into the valve, which he could just see. Then he did it again. And again.

"Would it help if I tried from this angle?"

"Give it a shot," Todd said, handing the young man the wrench. The valve had already loosened a bit. Todd could tell from the sound the boiler made that the pressure had been relieved somewhat, so Turner could do no harm and might help.

Slam! The sound of metal on metal rang in his ears. This was why he hadn't jumped at the chance to be an officer. If he had, he'd be in the passageway like Lieutenant Jackson—which is exactly where the lieutenant was *supposed* to be, not under the boiler with one of his men, sweating out the possibility that a line could blow.

God! He loved what he did. He loved the Navy, the feel of the ship when it took on heavy swells, the smell of a spanking-clean floor mixed with the aroma of WD-40, the noise of the boilers when they were underway and the silence that meant they were safely back in port. Soon, everything he loved would be a part of his past. He wouldn't be a member of the "club" anymore. When he met friends who were still in the service, he'd no longer share their kinship, their bond. That was reserved for those who served.

"Good job, Turner. Thanks for the help."

The kid smiled as though Todd had just given him a million dollars. "Thanks, Senior Chief. Glad to do it." He half dragged himself, half crawled out from under the boiler. Todd waited a few seconds and then followed.

"What's the problem, Chief?" Lieutenant Jackson stood before him.

"Stuck valve. We banged it up a bit, so we need to get it taken care of when we pull into Palma."

"Fill out the paperwork and I'll make sure it's done."

"Will do, Lieutenant." They nodded at each other and then Todd picked up his hat and dusted himself off. Hopefully, he'd never have to crawl under that mother fucker again.

Another "last."

Chapter Nine

Carie paced the Richmond hotel room until she couldn't stand it any longer. The ship had docked five days ago. Then Todd had said he had a couple more things to do in Norfolk before meeting her. That meant for seven days she had walked through her job in a haze of desire and frustration. He was home! At last, they were once more in the same country. And yet he was so far away.

She checked her watch one more time. Five minutes had crawled by since the last time she'd looked. Grabbing her purse, she headed out to window shop. She had to do something to make the time go faster.

Shockoe Bottom, the part of Richmond where the hotel was located, had been renovated and modernized but still kept the ambiance of its centuries-old purpose, that of the loading and warehousing area for tobacco. Now boutiques and trendy restaurants lined the streets and cobblestoned alleyways. The area was interesting, but her mind was only half on it.

Carie walked toward Broad Street, looking at the windows but not really seeing. How would Todd take her idea? He'd written, emailed, and called when he could, expressing love in every message, but how would he feel if she proposed they make it permanent? She hadn't given up the idea of resigning her commission, but she had to know, did he love her for what they did in hotel rooms, or as the person she was? After all, they'd really spent little time together. And they were adults, both used to their own lives. Were they compatible in any way other than in the bedroom?

Don't be stupid. He loves you, you love him. What more do you need?

"Carie!"

She spun on her heels at his voice. He jogged up the sidewalk, a bouquet of daisies in his hand. Her heart rate kicked into overdrive and sudden tears filled her eyes. She'd mentioned in one letter how daisies always made her smile, and he'd remembered.

Throwing appearances to the wind, she ran to him and jumped into his open arms. He whirled her around, then set her on her feet and took her mouth in a wrenching kiss.

When they came up for air, she said, "Why Senior Chief, don't you know that the military has a policy of no public displays of affection?"

"That's when you're in uniform, *Commander* Walker." He grinned and held out the flowers, which drooped a little after their exuberant embrace.

"You knew about my promotion?" She took the flowers and sniffed one.

"I read it in the Navy Times. Why didn't you tell me?"

"It was a surprise. I was waiting to tell you in person."

He kissed her again. "Congratulations, sweetheart. I'm so proud of you!" His arm around her waist, they headed back to the hotel. "When did you get here?"

She looked up at him and smiled. "Around nine this morning."

"You've been here all day? I wish I could have gotten here earlier, but everything I had to do took longer than expected."

"I couldn't wait. I guess I thought being in Richmond and at the hotel would make the time go faster." She made a face. "I was so wrong. Did you just arrive?"

"I came around from the parking garage and saw you walking up the street. I left my bag with the concierge and chased after you."

She gave a pouty face. "I hated that you were only a few hours away this past week and I couldn't see you."

He squeezed her waist. "Well, I'm here now. What do you want to do?"

She raised her brows and looked up through her lashes. "You *know* what I want to do." She grinned. "Eat."

"Oh. Okay." His expression showed disappointment.

She knew the moment he understood what she meant. His smile melted her insides. The man was so damn handsome. And all hers. She hoped.

He dropped a quick kiss on her lips. "I'm feeling pretty hungry myself. Shall we dine in the room?"

"We could dine in the lobby if you'd like, but we might be arrested before we finished the first course."

"Can't have that." He opened the front door of the hotel. After stopping at the concierge desk for his suitcase, he dashed across the lobby to catch up with her at the elevators.

"Going up?" he murmured as they crowded against the back wall. Another couple stood in front of them.

She brushed her hand along the front of his slacks. "I think you're already up."

"Decorum, Commander. Remember your prestigious rank." He winked and took her hand, pressing it hard against his erection.

Decorum, hell. She wanted him with a fierce passion. She licked her lips and his eyes darkened.

Ding! The doors opened and the couple sharing the elevator got off. Three more floors. The doors closed slowly, and at last, they were alone. Todd enclosed her in his arms and kissed her as she hadn't been kissed in nearly seven long months. She played tag with his tongue and pressed her hips to his. He groaned. She knew his frustration.

Finally, the door opened on their floor. Their innocent hand-holding did nothing to calm her breath or slow her heartbeat.

Then they were in the room. He barely closed the door before she was in his arms, her legs wrapped around his waist.

He dropped his duffel bag and crushed her to him. His mouth found hers and their tongues tangled as he made his way into the room. When he laid her on the bed, she immediately sat up and undid his belt. The button on his slacks was stubborn, but she finally got it undone, and then she eased the zipper over his cock, straining to escape his boxers. She nuzzled her face against it, blowing through the material, inhaling his fragrance. Her pussy moistened. She needed him inside her, but first, she needed to taste him.

"This is what homecoming should be," he muttered. "Do it, baby, please."

His *please* did it for her. She released his cock from his clothing only to capture it immediately in her mouth. His male scent drove her mad with desire. He tangled his fingers in her hair. She wrapped one hand around his hip, tense with the need to move. Then she slowly took him in, all the way in, tickling him with her tongue and following with a firm caress, twisting the tender skin at the root.

"Oh God!" he groaned. "Stop, honey, stop. I want to come inside you."

That suited her fine. With a final squeeze and lick, taking that bead of pre-cum off the head, she lay back and undid her slacks. Todd stripped while she removed everything but her bra and panties. She'd carefully chosen them for his homecoming—black lace bikini underwear and matching lace underwire bra. She raised her arms over her head, completely spread out before him.

His eyes narrowed when he examined her, and he licked his lips.

"You're the most beautiful woman I've ever seen."

"And how many women have you seen, Senior Chief?"

He smiled. "Oh, thousands and thousands."

"Well, then. I'm honored."

"As you should be, Commander Walker. I'm a connoisseur of women. And you are definitely the most beautiful, the sexiest, the smartest, the— God, that underwear is hot."

"I bought it just for you."

"I hope you don't mind if I take it off now and admire you in it later?"

She undid the front hook of her bra and let it fall open. "Please feel free to remove whatever you want."

Todd wasted no time pulling her panties down her legs and off, tossing them behind him. Then he crawled onto the bed, gazing into her eyes, making silent promises, she hoped he'd keep. When he pressed into her, gliding in easily on her cream, she forgot about the world outside the room. Her life, her heaven on earth was right here, between her legs taking her to dizzying heights of passion.

***

Todd pounded into Carie. He tried for finesse, but couldn't seem to come up with it. And she seemed to want him as much as he did her. The light sheen of sweat, her gasping breath, and wet pussy all showed her need. A light, rosy color covered her tits and collarbone. She'd gone over the edge once and was about to a second time. Then he'd come with a vengeance. He'd dreamed of this moment for months, and he didn't want it to end on a single orgasm for her. He wanted to make sure she was happy to see him home.

"Todd! Oh, God, yes!"

She squeezed his cock like a vice, pulling him deeper. He thrust forward and froze while he filled her with his cum. He might have been in port for a week, but now he was home.

When she relaxed her grip and her arms fell from his shoulders, he slid off and to her side. Pulling her close, he took comfort just in knowing she lay beside him. He'd never felt like this with a woman. There was a need to fuck now and then, and he had friends who were women he could talk and laugh with. But he'd never felt such a sense of contentment. A desire just to *be* with someone—a desire to have her, yes, but also a desire to share time and space with her. That's how he knew he'd done the right thing.

"Welcome home, sailor," she said.

He felt her lips turn up in a smile on the skin of his shoulder.

"Thank you, ma'am. Happy to be here. And by that, I mean happy to be *here* I mean naked with you. I can't believe how much I've missed you."

"Me, too. These have been the longest, most horrible months of my life. I hate to even ask, but when do you ship out again? How long will I have you here?"

He turned onto his side so he could face her. He hadn't planned the timing like this, but now was the moment to tell her.

"Forever, if you want."

Her eyes flew open and met his gaze. "What do you mean?"

"Two things. First, I want to marry you. I love you, Carie. The time we spend apart is not what I think life should be. I want to spend my life *with* you. And there's only one way that can happen. If you'll *have* me, that is."

Confusion filled her eyes. "You know I love you. Of course, I *want* to marry you. But we still have a problem."

"Well, that's my second thing. The hale and farewell party was for me. That's why I had to be there. I put in my retirement papers."

She blinked. "You what? What do you mean?"

"I'm retired." This was not the reaction he'd expected. Why wasn't she laughing, covering his face with kisses and swearing she'd always be his?

"From the *Navy?*"

She was beginning to worry him, and fear brought out irritation. "Of course, from the Navy. What else would I retire from? I have more than twenty years in. I was eligible."

Amazingly, she pulled away from him, turning onto her back. "That was a big decision to make without discussing it, wasn't it? I mean, if we marry, isn't it my future, too? I've been thinking of resigning my commission so we could be together, but I was going to talk to you about it, not just run off and do it."

He sat up and turned so he could see her face. "Are you crazy?" At her astonished expression, he changed tack. Look, we couldn't be together as things were. I fixed it so we *can* be together. What about that don't you like?" His voice was low and calm. A sure-fire signal of how upset he was. And confused. Didn't she *want* them to be together? Did she want him to continue going on cruises, being away for months at a time when they didn't have to go through that again?

She sat up, too. Her naked body called to his, but even that couldn't get past the cold fear crawling up inside him. Was she going to turn him down because he didn't ask her if he could retire?

"There are important questions in life, Todd. Things that two people who are in love discuss before answering. What one will do with the rest of one's life is pretty damn serious. You made a choice of what to do with your life without asking me if it was what I wanted. I think that's clear."

"I think it's bullshit. Yes, retirement affects the rest of my life. The Navy has *been* my life since I was a kid barely out of high school. You think it was an easy decision to make? It wasn't. But I made the sacrifice for you. For you and your regulations."

The color drained from her face. "You think I want you to *sacrifice* to marry me? You think I want your resentment in years to come because you gave up a life you loved in order to be with me? Well, I don't. Stick your sacrifice up your ass, Senior Chief."

Before he could stop her, she flew off the bed, gathered up her clothes and went into the bathroom, slamming the door behind her.

"Carie, don't be foolish. Come back out and talk."

"*Foolish?* Who's foolish, when one of us *changes our lives* and doesn't bother to mention it to the other one until it's too fucking late?" Her voice rose until she shouted the last few words. The door flew open and she rushed out, dressed and flushed with anger. She opened her purse for lipstick and applied it, never once glancing at his reflection in the mirror above the dresser.

"Well, you know what? It's not *too* late. The ink has barely dried on my separation papers. I can have them rescinded if that's what you want."

"I was wrong," she said, ice in her tone. "I am hungry, but for *food.* I'll be back later." And she was gone.

"Goddamn, mother fucking regs!" Todd raved at the empty room. But he wasn't mad, he was fucking scared. What should he do now?

Raking his hand through his hair he had to admit. He was screwed. And not in a good way.

***

I will not cry. I will not cry. Carie repeated the mantra as she rushed through the lobby and out onto the street. She had noticed a sandwich shop a few doors down. She would be able to eat and have some coffee and think through this whole thing with Todd.

How could he do something so rash as retiring and not tell her about it? Granted, she had thought about giving up her commission, but she hadn't filed the paperwork. Of *course*, she would want to talk to Todd first. Why couldn't he have given her the same consideration?

She had so looked forward to their reunion, and now it was all ruined. She didn't even remember if she had agreed to marry him or not. Would he rescind the proposal like he had threatened to rescind his separation papers? What would she do then? She couldn't stand the thought of life without him.

She entered the shop and approached the counter where the day's menu was displayed. "Turkey and Swiss on rye, please. And strong, black coffee." She searched out a table. The restaurant held a surprising number of people, considering that it was mid-afternoon. But she spotted a tiny round table with a couple of high stools a few rows away from the counter. She paid, took her coffee, and indicated where she would be sitting.

What to do now? Well, she had to go back. She only hoped Todd would still be there when she returned. She should get the sandwich to go. Already, her anger abated, she missed having his arms around her.

"Lost?" a voice asked from behind her.

Carie closed her eyes and dropped her head back against his chest. "Only when I'm not with you." As she had wished moments before, his arms came around her. He kissed the top of her head.

"I'm sorry," he whispered.

"No. I'm sorry. I overreacted. I-I don't know what was wrong."

He walked around and took the stool across from her. "I've read that a lot of couples argue on their honeymoons. There's all the anticipation of being married, combined with the stress of planning the wedding, and then the vision of perfection they have of what comes next. And what comes next is just life. Or I should say life-changing. The nerves take over."

"I wanted everything to be perfect," she said, reaching across the table and taking his hand. "I wanted you to want to be with me."

He shook his head and stared into her eyes. "Honey, every minute of every day since we met I've wanted nothing more than to be with you. Since I found you in the woods we've been headed for this moment."

"I was going to give up my commission so we could be together." The look of wonder on his face made her smile. "Did you think I didn't want to sacrifice for you, too?"

He grimaced. "Let's not use that word. Bad choice on my part." The waiter brought her sandwich. When he left, Todd began again. "You were just promoted, Carie. You have a good profession and you're respected. I don't want you to give that up. You're only a few years from retirement yourself. Don't waste it, honey."

"It wouldn't be a waste if we were together." The tears welled up again. She took a harsh breath to try to control them. But of course, Todd saw, as he seemed to notice everything about her.

"Why don't you eat?" he asked softly.

"Want to share?"

"Maybe in a minute. I'll get some coffee, though." He left, returning a few minutes later with a steaming cup.

"Maybe I'll get them to wrap this up and we can have it later. I'm not as hungry as I thought."

"Okay."

"Todd, what will you do?"

"Well, I *did* want to talk to you about that. I have an interview in D.C. next week to be a consultant for an engineering firm. There are other promising prospects for a man of my talents and skill." He smiled, and she nearly died with longing.

"Your *engineering* talents and skills. Your other skills and talents are all mine."

"No question there. But now that you've been promoted, do you think they might transfer you somewhere else? This company is international. If I get on, I can follow you anywhere Uncle Sam chooses to send you. I've already mentioned that to them and they still want to talk to me."

"That sounds about perfect. But I think I'll be in Washington for another two years or more."

"I can show you the company when we get to a computer, and then we can talk about it." He looked down into his cup and then back at her.

"You are going to marry me, aren't you? I mean, if you want me to, I'll get down on one knee and ask traditionally, right here."

She laughed. "I appreciate the offer, but it won't be necessary. I want to marry you, Todd. But there's one thing that still bothers me." He raised his brows, waiting for her to continue. "The Navy is your first love, your mistress. You told me that, remember? You *love* the Navy."

"Not as much as I love you. The moment we met, my separation was in the works, though I didn't know it until you came to Norfolk for Turner's case. When I was so miserable I couldn't sleep, knowing you were only a few miles away, I knew what had to be done eventually. No stupid regulation was going to keep me from you. I'm really sorry I didn't ask your opinion about it beforehand." He half-shrugged. "I thought it would be a happy surprise."

"Now that I've gotten used to the idea, it is. We'll be together."

"Married. Forever, Commander. It's what I expect."

"It's what will happen, *Mister* Baxter."

He laughed. "Now *that* will take getting used to."

She smiled back at him. "No worries, love. We have a lifetime to accomplish it."

Anchor Home

Chapter One

Pat Welles stopped dead as she entered the elevator. An instrumental rendition of "The Way You Look Tonight" played on the Musak. She hadn't heard the song in years, and immediately she went back in time, back to her senior prom and the boy who'd held her close.

"Excuse me," a voice said from behind her, and she gave herself a mental shake to bring her back to the present. But as she moved to the corner and plastered herself to the elevator's mirrored wall, her heart took on a staccato beat and she drifted again. Sam Turner. Lord, she hadn't thought of him in years. But the magic of music—of that song in particular—led her to feel his arms around her once more, if only virtually.

That night he'd held her tightly. They'd done little more than sway to the melody, her body molded to his. He'd whispered in her ear that he loved her, how much he wanted her. Shortly after that, up a rural, secluded road, they'd shared their love in a Roanoke hotel room. Two stupid virgins, fumbling and tangling arms and legs. It had been exhilarating at the time—*beyond* exhilarating to know that Sam Turner loved her. Now, with the song, those same feelings charged through her like a speeding train.

Then the music changed, and the nostalgia train screeched to a halt. "That was then, and this is now," she muttered. The elevator door opened on her floor and she nudged people aside to get to the exit before they closed again. The door for the Office of Community Partnerships stood before her and she walked up to the receptionist's desk.

"Good morning, Brenda. Any messages?"

"Morning. Nope. But I put the paperwork for the military outreach program on your desk. Looks like we'll have three service people here for the school assemblies."

"Good. I'll take a look at the profiles right now." Pat took a left down the hallway, away from reception and past six offices, three to a side, all the way to the end. She stuck her head in the open door directly across from her office. "Ben, good morning. How's Melanie?" Ben Goodman, her friend for the last six years, had recently demonstrated male sympathy pains for his wife, who was six months pregnant.

"Melanie is fine. I'm the one you should be worried about. My back is beginning to kill me, and I'm still nauseated every morning." Looking up with puppy dog eyes, dark brown and sad, he did seem a bit green around the gills.

"Are you sure you don't have flu or something?" Pat leaned against the door frame.

Ben signed. "No." Then he quirked a half smile. "Melanie thinks I hung the moon since I started sharing some of her symptoms. Thinks I'm sharing in her physical misery to make her life easier. You're not buying it though, are you?"

"Let's just say that I think sharing in *symptoms* is possible, but no matter what, you can't know what it really feels like. Still, if it makes her happy, you're doing a good job." Ben held up his right hand for a high five and she stepped in to slap it. "I hope you're doing some stuff to really make her feel better though, like helping around the house and rubbing her swollen feet."

"Oh, hell yeah. The woman wants for nothing."

"You're a good guy, Ben. And you're going to be a great father." The wistful look in his eyes made her envious of his wife. Just a smidge. Then she got past it.

"Do you really think so? Because I can't wait. As long as we've been married, this feels like a miracle, Pat, and I'm so damn happy."

"I'm glad. You and Melanie deserve this."

"Look at this." He pulled a tiny football from a bag stashed beside the desk. "If it's a boy, I'm ready."

Pat laughed. "And if it's a girl?"

"Girls can catch footballs. It's good for hand/eye coordination."

"You're such a guy," Pat said shaking her head.

"Well, yeah. I mean, one look at Melanie and you'd know that. Only a guy can put a bun in the oven." He wiggled his brows and smiled.

"For a small fee, I will swear not to tell Melanie you just said that, thus preserving your life."

He nodded. "Oh yeah, she'd kill me. Did you stop in to say hi or did you need me for something?"

"Work with me on these military visits? They'll be with us for only a couple of weeks, but I've scheduled lots of city school events and I also said I'd help with a few schools in Henrico and Chesterfield counties. I think I bit off more than I can chew."

"Will do. Let me know what you need, and I'll be there."

"Thanks." Pat pivoted toward her office.

First things first, she poured water from a filtered pitcher into her individual coffee maker, plopped a K-cup into the holder and pushed down the magic lever that produced a perfect, hot cup of French roast every time. In less than a minute, she lifted her Best Mom Ever mug to her nose, taking in the aroma before sipping. Ah! Now her day could start for real.

Picking up the papers Brenda had left on her desk, she skimmed the boilerplate text that the Commonwealth Department of Education added to all documentation. Then she read the conditions for the particular project where the community reached out to its military members. Career days and job fairs provided students the opportunity to interact with participants in a variety of occupations. The city set aside two weeks each spring for servicemen and women to explain what military service was all about, something especially important for the high school students who might need a job after graduations but who weren't ready or interested in heading to college. In the six years Pat had worked with community outreach, she had heard of several students who'd found maturity and a place to grow and learn after they'd joined up, the benefit of this program.

The program consisted of three to four service members to be available to visit all of the nearly forty schools in the city system. This year, Pat had offered to share time and resources with the high schools in the surrounding counties of Henrico and Chesterfield, meaning she would be stretched to the limit since she would be with the team each day through all of their school visits. "Thank heaven Ben agreed to help," she murmured, turning to the second page.

Jennifer Holden, a female marine, would certainly be able to share with the students the difficulties and the benefits of being a woman in a service that had such a tough reputation. Pat studied the woman's stern picture. The Marine Corps photos she'd received in years past never featured smiling people, and Jennifer's was no different. Dark brown hair, up off the nape and tucked under her hat, barely showed, and her posture was ramrod straight. Still, in Jennifer's milk chocolate brown eyes, she saw a glimmer of fun. She looked forward to meeting her.

Flipping to the next page, she examined the photo of Thomas Preston, a representative from the Air Force. He looked young to hold the rank of staff sergeant, but that would play to his benefit when visiting the high schools where the girls would pay attention because he was so cute, and the guys would pay attention because the girls thought he was cute.

"Uniforms do seem to add something to a guy's appearance," she said. "And Staff Sergeant, you are damn cute in that uniform." His sparkling blue eyes showed mirth even though he wasn't smiling. Or not really smiling—the ends of his mouth tipped up just a bit, as though he knew a joke and couldn't wait to share it. Black hair skimmed the top of his ear and he sported a small mustache.

Turning to the last page, her heart stopped. In response, the blood drained from her head and dizziness assaulted her. Nausea rolled through her stomach and her hands turned clammy.

"Pat, will you sign this—Good Lord, what's wrong?" Brenda rushed to the desk. "Put your head between your legs," she said as she turned Pat's chair and forced her shoulders forward and down. "Ben," she called across the hall, "can you come here?"

"No," Pat protested weakly. "I'm okay." *Liar!* She'd just had the shock of her life and nothing was okay.

"What's wrong?" Ben sounded more worried than curious. Was her feeling faint such a big deal?

"Nothing's wrong," Pat insisted, sitting up. "Everything's fine. I just had a moment, that's all." Brenda stared at her, frowning, and Ben stood behind her visitor chair, his brows pulled up in question.

"Are you sure?" he asked. "Because I can do a mean bear hug. Or I can run out and pick up some pickles and ice cream."

She managed a short laugh. "I wasn't choking, Ben, and I'm sure as hell not pregnant. But thanks for the offer. If I have strange cravings or can't breathe, you'll be the first person I call."

The question in his expression eased somewhat. "Okay. If you think you're really all right, I'll just go back." He and Brenda exchanged a look that *said find out what's up* as surely as if one of them had said it aloud.

"Nothing's up," Pat said, and she hoped she said it plainly enough for them to leave it all alone. Ben gave a half shrug and as he left sent Brenda another pointed look that said, *yeah, right.*

Brenda sat in one of her visitor chairs. "He's gone now. You can tell me what upset you."

Pat smiled. "I appreciate the concern but really, I have no idea what brought it on. What is it you want me to sign?"

Brenda stared a moment and then gave a sigh that indicated she relented. "This allowance for those service members to stay at the Birkstone while they're here. It only covers the weekdays since their bases are close enough for them to go home for the weekends. And the Navy fellow lives in town, so we were able to cut some expense."

Pat signed the form and handed it back. On unsteady legs, she rose. "Thanks for your help on this Brenda, and for coming to my aid. Don't give it another thought, though. I'm fine."

As graciously as possible, she ushered Brenda out the door and closed it. Then she took her seat again and pulled out the final profile of her military team. Lieutenant Samuel Turner, USN stared back at her from his color photo. Same dark blue eyes, same blonde hair—short now, and unlike the somewhat wild mess that used to flop in his eyes in that adorable way—and same broad shoulders that proved so effective at diverse tasks as blocking opponents on the football field or serving as a pillow at the movies.

It seemed impossible, but she would be hosting Lieutenant Turner for ten whole days while trying desperately to hide the fact that she had never stopped loving him.

***

"So, Monday you're on vacation, huh?" Master Sergeant Josh Henry propped his feet on his desk and grinned at Sam.

"Vacation, hell. I'll be spending the next two work weeks with a bunch of kids, being led around by the nose by some school teacher sort who probably doesn't know the difference between sailors and jarheads."

"Hey! Knock that profanity off," said First Lieutenant Mike Barber. "You squids should know by now that we're leathernecks, not jarheads."

"More like leather*heads*," muttered Josh. "Maybe this 'teacher sort' is hot, Turner. You ever think of that?"

"Not my luck," said Sam. "She'll probably be like my tenth grade English teacher. Pointed chin, wart on her nose, hard, cold eyes, missing teeth, and a cackle."

"You sure that wasn't the character in *Wicked?*" Mike toyed with the pen on his desk.

"Pretty sure. She wasn't green, at least."

"Probably hadn't been laid in years, either," added Josh.

Looking toward the front entrance of the recruiting office on Broad Street, Sam said, "Now, that's exactly the kind of talk that will get your Army ass kicked back to Fort Polk." Fort Polk, Louisiana, was widely regarded as one of the worst duty stations in the army.

Josh shivered. "Crap. Forget I said anything."

"How do you know it's a she? Maybe it's some dipshit guy that's taking charge of you for two weeks." Mike yawned, indicating he was about ready for the weekend to begin.

"Letter says to report to a Mrs. Welles at the city school offices at oh-eight-hundred Monday morning." Sam frowned. "How did I get stuck with this duty? Why not one of you guys?"

Mike laughed. "Just like Walmart inventory. Last in, first out. In this case, the 'out' means you get the crappy jobs, Newbie."

"Don't worry," Josh spoke up and pointed to Mike. "Mr. Leatherneck over there—"

"That's Lieutenant Leatherneck to you, asshole."

"—will be going back into regular duty in a couple of months and then we can pass crap jobs to the next new person."

"Well, buds, see you in a couple of weeks." Sam closed his briefcase and headed out.

"Hope things aren't as bad as you seem to think," called Josh.

Yeah, me, too.

Chapter Two

Pat couldn't calm the butterflies in her stomach. She'd seriously considered calling in sick—and she'd actually felt the need to vomit a couple of times before breakfast. But she'd dragged herself into work on Monday morning because she couldn't face being a coward. And because she didn't want to stick Ben with the task of managing the first day of their community outreach with the military team. And because she needed to set a good example for Timmy.

But most of all because the program lasted two weeks and she had to bite the bullet sometime. Might as well get it over with. *Yeah, that's the spirit!*

"Good morning, Brenda," she said with a forced smile. "Any messages?" *Please let there be one that says Sam has been replaced by someone else.*

"No messages. The service people are here and Ben is with them in the conference room." Pat frowned. She wasn't late. Ben always arrived first, but it appeared that her military group was early, too. Great, just great. No time to settle her nerves with an early morning coffee fortified with a splash of bourbon.

"Good! Wonderful! That's really…really good." Pat gripped the edge of Brenda's desk. If she never let go, she'd never have to walk into that conference room. Spending the rest of her life holding onto Brenda's desk was beginning to seem like a great idea.

"Pat, are you alright?"

"Of course. Why wouldn't I be alright?"

"For one thing, you suddenly turned pale, kind of like last week, and for another, you're going to break the desk if you don't let loose."

Pat stared into Brenda's eyes and knew that it was do or die. Sink or swim. Face her past or hide.

Hiding sounds good.

She took a breath and released her death grip on the desk. "Right.

I'll uh… I'll just drop off my things in the office and go down to meet them, shall I?"

Brenda's questioning gaze hadn't left her face. "You should, yes."

"Okay. Here I go." Fortunately, she'd decided on low heels that morning or she might not have made it down the hallway. As it was, just the thought of seeing Sam again had her off balance. Stilettos would have had her flat on her ass.

Dropping her briefcase on the floor beside her desk, she drew in a deep breath. Then she hung her coat on the coatrack inside her door, gathered the program paperwork from her desk, and reversed course.

"On my way to the conference room now," she trilled, passing Brenda's desk.

"Glad to hear it," Brenda replied.

At the last moment, just before entering, she stopped to listen to the low hum of voices. They spoke too low for her to make out words, but she caught the sound of Sam's voice, and then his laughter as one of the others said something funny. *You can do this. It's been thirteen years. You've moved on and he's moved on.*

Before she could do anything else, she stepped into the room and closed the door. Conversation stopped, and all eyes turned to her. Ben, who had been perched on the conference table near the group, stood.

"Here she is," Ben said. "Right on time. Pat, welcome to a room of early birds." The military group stood at the opposite side of the room holding coffee cups. Almost as one, they placed their cups on the table.

"I might be right on time, but I'm sorry to have kept you waiting. I feel I know you all a bit from the profiles I've received." She walked to the only other woman in the room and held out her hand. "Sergeant Holden, I'm so happy you could come. I know there will be a great deal of interest in what you do and what life is like in the Marine Corps for a woman."

"Pleased to meet you, ma'am."

Pat smiled. "Please don't call me ma'am. *Please.* Pat will be fine." She extended her hand to the man who was not-Sam. "Staff Sergeant Preston, nice to meet you."

"And you, *Pat.* And please, for the next two weeks call me Tom." When he smiled, dimples appeared in his cheeks. Good Lord. She'd been right in her earlier assessment.

"You're going to make a big splash, Tom. I predict enlistment in the

Air Force will increase from the Richmond area after this program." He laughed and released her hand.

"Well, that is what we're here for," he said. "I think it will prove to be an interesting two weeks."

If not for the next man to greet, Pat might have thought so, too. Thomas Preston was handsome as sin and charming enough to make a woman want to find out how much sinning was on his mind. But there was someone else in the room, and that someone eclipsed every other man. He always had for her.

Pat stepped to the right. "And Lieutenant Turner. Thank you for taking the time to inform our students about the Navy."

He took her hand. A question clouded his eyes but no recognition. Had she changed that much?

"My pleasure," he said. After a moment he added, "Have we met? You look very familiar."

"Leave it to Navy to use a standard line," Preston whispered to Ben and Jennifer Holden.

"It's not a line, it's..." Sam studied her, his intense gaze stripping away the years and changes.

Pat smiled. "You don't remember me, do you?"

"No, I do, I—Oh my God, it's Tricia. Tricia Smith. Right?" In a matter of seconds, his eyes went from surprise, to shock, to happiness, to reservation. And reservation is where they stayed.

"How have you been, Sam?"

"Fine. And you?" He'd released her hand already but now he took a step back, adding a little physical distance to the years already between them.

"Real good, thanks. I'm happy you're part of the program."

"As I said, it's a pleasure. I'll try to represent the Navy well and redirect some of the kids from flocking to the Air Force." He raised a brow in challenge to Tom Preston.

"Don't count out the Marine Corps." Sergeant Holden cracked her knuckles and gave the other two a savage stare.

"Well, okay," murmured Pat. "All countries heard from. Let's take our seats and I'll review what the next two weeks will look like."

She and Ben sat side by side while the other three sat across from them. "Each day we'll attend assemblies at two schools. The ages of the students will range from elementary middle school through high school. So, you can see that questions will vary. In years past, we've had children ask what the team does, do men and woman kiss when they are fighting"—the group laughed at that—"how much money you each make, whether you've ever killed anyone, and who knows what else. No one is more imaginative than children. Do any of you have problems answering off the wall questions like that?"

"Nope, it's all good to me," said Preston.

Holden shrugged. "I can deal with it."

Pat looked to Sam. "Lieutenant Turner?"

He stared at the table for a moment and then focused those midnight blue eyes on her. "To tell the truth, I don't have trouble with the questions, but I kinda have trouble with this assignment. I don't get along with kids well, and I'm not sure why I was given this task. I'd really rather not participate. Can't we get someone else from the recruiting staff to take my place?"

Pat's heart stuttered. Had Sam felt this way before she arrived, and he discovered she would be heading up the program? She stared back, hoping her emotions didn't show on her face.

"I'm afraid for today at least there's no way to switch. If you feel strongly, we can see what might be done within the next few days," Ben said when she'd remained silent for several seconds. Thank God for Ben!

Sam nodded his understanding and dropped his gaze.

"Either Ben or I will drive us from school to school. Each of you will give a brief introduction to your branch of service and what you do. We have a video sent along by the Department of Defense, and then we'll open it to questions. Each stop shouldn't last longer than an hour and a half or so." Pat looked at each team member. "Any other questions before we start?"

"Nope, Pat," intoned Staff Sergeant Preston, "let's get this show on the road."

***

"Dude, what's wrong with you?" Tom Preston asked Sam on the way to the minivan idling at the curb outside the school offices.

The last thing Sam wanted to do was talk to the Air Force asshole who'd openly flirted with Tricia. *Excuse me, Pat.* She'd always be Tricia to him, though. Sweet little Tricia with the soulful brown eyes, shiny, silky brown hair, and perfect body that fit his, the way a woman's body was supposed to fit a man's. Of course, she hadn't actually been a woman and years of living and maturity had proven in his own mind that he hadn't been a man. That night of their senior prom though, age and maturity hadn't mattered. They'd been old enough, and their body parts had easily known just what to go. Tab A had fit into slot B just as God intended. As they'd demonstrated over and over that summer.

But to see her now? After what she'd done to him? It wasn't going down well.

He shrugged to Preston's question. "I have other work I'd rather be doing," he said.

"Not me," Preston said smiling. "Hey, Sergeant Holden. Are you sorry to have a few days away from Quantico, or sorry to spend a few days down here?"

Posture erect, the sergeant turned before entering the vehicle. "It's a good thing to explain what military service is about. You know, here we have a chance to correct misunderstandings and encourage positive opinions. And besides, I go where the Corps sends me." Without a smile or another word, she climbed in and sat near the window on the opposite side of the van.

Tom rolled his eyes at Sam. "Marines are such suck-ups. Anyway, I see this as a good break for a couple of weeks. And"—he waggled his brows—"the hostess is hot as shit. You know her, right?"

"*Knew* her. In high school. I have no idea who or what she is now." Seeing Tricia had been a shock, and for a brief moment, all he'd wanted to do was pull her into his arms. Fortunately, the memory of all she'd put him through overrode that initial impulse.

Preston rubbed his hands together, delight showing in his eyes. "Well, I plan to get to know her better. She's got my name written all over her."

Prick. Sam took the center of the long bench seat. Preston stepped in and slid the door shut. He'd thought to serve as a buffer between the flyboy and the marine, but as soon as he looked up, he noticed that he was smack dab in Tricia's view when she checked the rear-view mirror. Shit. Thoughts of her were much easier to avoid when he wasn't meeting her gaze every few minutes.

"We're going to the west side first, to one of our high schools. Y'all will be on the stage, and the staff there will provide microphones to the students for the Q and A part of the assembly." Pat smoothly merged onto the downtown expressway and headed west.

"So, what is the age range?" asked Sergeant Holden.

Ben, the co-host answered. "Ninth grade through twelfth. In our system, we have four-year high schools. Later today we'll visit a middle school."

High school had been their time, his and Tricia's. They'd met in sixth grade when her parents moved to the small town where he'd lived in western Virginia. She'd been a scrawny little girl with a stutter that made her shy and introverted. Sam had befriended her right away because she lived a few houses down from him and his mother kind of forced him to welcome her to their town and to show her around. But once he'd discovered that she liked watching football—which she did every Sunday with her dad—and not only that she enjoyed reading science fiction but also had tried writing her own stories, he'd willingly stuck by her side.

Sam had been a popular kid and his cachet opened doors for Tricia. He'd taken pride when she started making friends, blossomed in class as her interests and talents became known, and she came out of her shell. When she became so comfortable and sure that she was able to meet strangers and control her stutter, Sam swelled with pride, but for her accomplishments, not for his part in them.

Then came the betrayal and everything changed. He'd never thought of her the same way again but even he couldn't avoid noticing how the beautiful girl had flourished into a stunning woman. Her flawless complexion displayed little makeup, her more than shoulder-length hair, a rich, dark brown, accented her heart-shaped face, and her figure came straight out of a wet dream. Sam would be as interested in her as Tom Preston if she'd been anyone other than Tricia Smith. *Pat Welles.* It would take some doing to get used to her new name. But tomato, tomahto. A cheat by any other name was still a cheat.

"Pat, are there many good places to eat around the hotel where you've booked us?" Preston asked.

"Several," she answered. "There are bistros, little holes in the wall, or full-fledged, high-end restaurants. Anything you want, you'll be able to find it in the Bottom."

Sam knew from the couple of months he'd lived in Richmond that "the Bottom" meant Shockoe Bottom, an old section of Richmond near the James River where tobacco warehouses had been built to hold hogsheads of tobacco before they were shipped out to the rest of the world. In more recent years, those warehouses and cobbled streets had become home to restaurants, boutiques and tourists. As fun as it could be at night in the Bottom, Sam would enjoy being in his own apartment and sleeping in his own bed rather than holed up in a hotel. And as for eating out, when he got home tonight he had a rib eye steak ready to kiss his charcoal grill and a cold beer waiting.

"Pat, why don't you join me this evening and show me the sights?" Preston asked.

Sam observed the raised eyebrows of Tricia's friend Ben as he swiveled in his seat waiting for her answer. Tricia made the turn into a school parking lot.

"I'm sure you can find your way around, Tom." Was that satisfaction on Ben's face? Her slap down of the slimy bastard sure filled Sam with satisfaction. Though why it might bother him that she would go out with the Air Force guy escaped him.

Preston slid the door open and exited the van. Sam followed, and then held out his hand to help out Sergeant Holden.

"She's a marine, dude. Newsflash. If she can fight her way out of a village in Iraq, she can get out of a car by herself."

"Being polite, *dude*. She didn't fight in a *skirt* in Iraq." God, this guy was stepping on his last nerve.

"Thanks, Lieutenant," she said. "And dude," she said, addressing Preston, "stop hitting on our host. For God's sake, anyone can see she's not into you."

"Yeah?" Preston asked, sounding more curious than irritated. "How do you know that?"

"Because a blind pig could see that she's interested in the Lieutenant here. I'm sure an Air Force staff sergeant could see it, too, if he got over himself." With that, she walked to the back of the vehicle to join Ben and Tricia. Sam hid a smile.

Preston slapped Sam on the shoulder. "Well, Lieutenant, lucky you. She's hot and ripe, ready for picking." He tapped his nose. "I can always tell about women."

As much as Sam wanted to knock Preston's block off, he couldn't help a smidgen of male pride. He didn't want her, but evidently—if the only other female in their group understood the situation—Tricia still wanted him.

Preston leaned in closer. "But don't think I'm not going to wear her down." Then the asshole ambled off to join the group at the back of the minivan.

Chapter Three

"Why do you have to wear your hair like that?" asked one of the eleventh graders of the female marine.

Offstage, Pat sighed. She shouldn't have expected it, but she had hoped for a few more insightful questions other than those about makeup and hairstyles and why Sergeant Holden's skirt couldn't be shorter. That last question had come from a boy. Well, she'd warned the group that the questions could be off the wall.

"Regulations require that female service members wear their hair off the neck. It isn't a hardship to keep my hair up when there are so many more important problems in the world," Jennifer Holden replied. "Why don't we ask the male team members why they wear their hair as they do." With a raised brow, Jennifer turned toward Sam and Tom.

Sam smiled, and Pat's heart nearly stopped. Regardless of what other changes had taken place, his smile remained as she remembered from high school—warm and sexy enough to take her breath away. God help her.

He stood up from one of the stools placed on stage for the three guests. "Just as Sergeant Holden said, the military has strict regulations about all kinds of things, hair length being one of them."

"But the Air Force guy's longer than yours," called out a boy from the back of the auditorium.

Chuckling, Sam glanced back at Tom and then faced the sea of faces. "Well, let's just say that within those regs there is a certain latitude. The Air Force is known for being a law unto itself when it comes to things like hair, duty stations, and the like. I'd say that Staff Sergeant Preston's hair is maybe on the edge of being too long."

Tom aimed a dimpled smile toward the audience and said, "Yeah, Lieutenant, I'll get right on that." The students laughed, as did Sam.

Another boy raised his hand and one of the teachers with a mic walked to him. "What do you all make?"

Ah, the question asked at nearly every assembly in the years she'd been hosting the program. Pat checked her watch. They were over the hour she'd allotted, but as long as questions continued, and the group didn't appear tired—or annoyed—she liked letting things go as long as the school allowed.

Tom handled the question first. "Pay grade is made up of a variety of things. I'm a staff sergeant, which is an E-5 in how the government assesses its pay grades. I've been in the Air Force for sixteen years. Right now, I make about forty-five thousand dollars a year. But I also receive free health care, I get to travel the world, and I have thirty days of leave—that's vacation—a year."

Sam stepped up next. "I went into the Navy as an enlisted man thirteen years ago. I don't mind telling you—as long as you keep it a secret"—he stage-whispered the last part—"that I got into a bit of trouble at the beginning. But I had a great mentor and eventually, thanks to his influence, I took advantage of the military's offer of college. Then four years ago I was accepted into OCS—that's Officer Candidate School—and that's how I became an officer. I hold the rank of O-3 now, and make an annual salary of around seventy-five thousand. We all carry the same benefits, so it mostly boils down to length of time, schooling, and your fitness reports as to how high you rise. It pays to do your best, whether in school or in any job."

Jennifer rose and stepped forward. "I have the lowest rank of the three of us."

"Though in Sergeant Holden's defense," Sam offered, "the Marine Corps is probably the hardest branch to advance in."

Jennifer flashed him a smile. "I'm an E-5, I've been in the Corps eight and a half years, and make about thirty-six grand a year."

"That's not very much," the same boy who'd asked the question commented. "My dad makes more than that and he's a mechanic."

Jennifer quirked a brow. "Yeah, but I get to go out and shoot things as part of my job. I'll bet your dad doesn't do that."

The boy laughed. "True."

Pat saw the principal near the back of the auditorium now, pointing to his watch. She walked onto the stage and up to the microphone in the center. "As we close, I'd like to ask our guests to take one last moment to say why they joined the branch of service they did and what they would recommend about it. If any of you are interested in more information, there are brochures about the services available in the guidance office. Or ask your guidance counselor, Ms. Rodgers, to contact me if you have a specific question for one of our team." She turned to her side. "Sergeant Holden, will you start us off?"

Jennifer stepped up to the mic. "I joined the Marine Corps because I wanted a challenge. I knew being a female member of the Corps would be hard, but that was what I wanted, to prove to myself that I could handle the strain of being one of the few and proud. I would recommend the Corps to anyone who wants to be part of the best and isn't afraid of a challenge."

Tom stepped up next. "The Air Force is probably the best branch of service for families. For the *most* part, we're stationed on actual bases and families travel with service members. Of course, not all of those places are in great parts of the country. Minot, North Dakota comes to mind, where winters are severe and summer mosquitos carry off small animals"—he waited for the laugh, which he got—"but we're also located in some great parts of the world, like Germany, and Hampton, right down the road." He grinned and Pat could almost hear the girls in the audience sigh.

Then his grin faded, and his gaze roamed the audience. "I joined because I wanted to make a difference in the world. And I signed up right out of high school because of nine-eleven. The world is in a bad place, people, and we need good men and women willing to step up and do their parts to keep us all safe. It sounds corny, but I believe it."

Sam went last. "I couldn't agree more with what my colleagues have said. We need good people to join the military. If not for us, who will preserve our country and those who need help in the world? It's a daunting task but a necessary one." He took a breath. "As for me, I joined up for one of the oldest reasons in the world, a broken heart. I thought going on board ship would get me the farthest away from the situation."

Pat felt the blood leave her face and she sucked in a breath in an effort not to keel over. It took all of her willpower to keep from turning her gaze on him. She didn't, knowing her expression would reflect all of the sorrow she'd kept well-hidden through the years.

"It seems silly looking back on it now. But what I found is, just like they say, that girl wasn't the only fish in the sea—and I've been back and forth across the seas, so I know what I'm talking about." He smiled, and the crowd responded with a laugh. "I found a home and family in the Navy. Also, an education and what I think is an important place in the world. I wouldn't trade these years for anything."

"Not even for that girl?" called out a guy from the middle of the auditorium.

"Nope. Thomas Wolfe said that you can't go home again. Meeting her after all these years wouldn't mean anything now. She's different and so am I. It's best to remember that." Not once during that rebuke had he snuck a glance at Pat.

On shaky legs, she stepped back to the microphone. "Please let's thank our guests." She led the applause, all the while wondering how she could possibly make it through two weeks of this.

***

"Here's to our first day out and living through it!" Tom held up his glass of beer. Sam and Jennifer tapped it with their glasses.

"It's what I expected," Jennifer said. "How about y'all?"

"'Y'all'? Where are you from, Marine?" Tom sat back in his chair and fixed his gaze on the lady at their table.

"Alabama," she said. "How about you?"

"Massachusetts, born and bred," Tom responded. "The birthplace of our liberty." He nodded affirmatively and took another sip.

"Fighting words for a native Virginian," Sam said with a smile. "'Give me liberty or give me death,' remember that? Spoken just up the hill right here in Richmond. We're the mother of presidents, don't forget."

"We had Sam and John Adams, and Revere, and—"

"Okay, guys, give it up," Jennifer said, laughing. "I absolutely understand northerners and southerners refighting the Civil War—"

"War Between the States," Sam corrected.

"Whatever," Tom added.

"But refighting the revolution? Give me a break. We won, and that's the most important thing about that war."

"You're right, Sergeant. To America!" Sam held up his glass this time.

"America!" Tom clinked his glass.

"Semper fi!" Jennifer smiled and added her glass to the mix.

"Oh, good," came a female voice from behind him, a voice he had not anticipated hearing tonight. "I'm glad to see you all here and relaxing," Pat said.

When Tom invited him and Jennifer to join him for a drink in the hotel bar, he'd also invited Tricia. She had declined, which was the only reason he had accepted. Getting through these two weeks would be hard enough without having to be around her in the evenings, too. Against his reasoned judgment, all day he'd been torn between totally ignoring her or finding a time and place to kiss her senseless. He knew that giving into old feelings would be bad—very bad—but he still felt the tug of the past and the girl he'd once known. Mind won out over heart in that battle and he'd ignored her.

He'd meant what he'd said that morning. He had found that there were other fish in the sea. He'd dated and bedded fewer women than some sailors he knew, but he'd definitely done his part to forward the reputation that sailors had a girl in every port. However, he'd never forgotten his first. Tricia had been everything to him. Until she wasn't.

Tom stood. "Hey, boss! Glad to see you're joining us." A grin had brought out Tom's dimples, but Sam watched as that grin faded. "And who's this?"

With that, Sam turned in his seat. Tricia stood there with a man. Could his day get any fucking worse? Sam stood, also. Just being polite, not joyful over the company.

"This is Mark Welles. Mark, this is my team for the military outreach. This is Staff Sergeant Tom Preston, here is Sergeant Jennifer Holden, and this"—she lost a bit of her composure as her eyes met his—"is Lieutenant Sam Turner."

Mark shook hands around the table. It wasn't Sam's fault if his grip turned crushing when Mark shook his hand. It just happened.

"Hey, guys, I have to go," Sam said. "This has been great, though. See you in the morning."

"I was just getting ready to order another round," Tom protested.

"Please don't leave on our account," Pat added.

The Mark Welles character shot him a shrewd look. "If the lieutenant needs to go, he needs to go."

"That's right," Sam said, assessing the man with a look of his own. "Someone needs to."

"I'm sure you have other things to do." Mark shrugged and then addressed Jennifer and Tom. "Well then, the next round is on me." He looked at Tricia. "We have time before our dinner reservations and you did say you'd like to spend some time with your team informally."

Tricia slid her gaze to Sam. "Do you really need to go? Can't we even have a drink?"

The past came crashing down on him. Her hairstyle was different and her figure was near perfect, though honestly, she no longer had the cheerleader body he'd adored when they'd first dated. Now she had the curves and softness of a woman. Instead of the clear innocence of before, her face now displayed the glow of a woman who had blossomed, who'd handled responsibility, and who had seen life's ups and downs. To his mind, she looked even better than when they'd rocked each other's worlds.

Sadly, she still showed enough of the old Tricia to draw him in. A part of him wanted to be back in the vortex of the feelings they'd had for one another. She knew him as no other woman ever had. He'd known her, too. Just not well enough.

Hurt flashed through her eyes, and for a moment, Sam thought he saw a bit of longing, too. He'd have to fight against giving in to old feelings for the time they had to deal with each other, and it was already harder than that morning, when he'd first realized who she was.

"No, sorry," he answered in a low voice. "Same time tomorrow?"

"So, you're going to see it through?" she asked him in a low voice.

"Yes. I'll stay for the two weeks. But let's stay out of each other's way, all right?"

She nodded. "Seven tomorrow morning, please. At the office." Then she turned from him and took the seat he'd vacated. "Instead of you two meeting at the office," she told Jennifer and Tom, "I'll come and pick you up here. It will be a few minutes before seven." Mark gave him a final dismissive glance and then waved his hand to signal the waiter.

Before moving away, Sam nodded good night to Jennifer and Tom. Tom held his hands up as if to say *what the fuck, man?* but Sam just shook his head. He'd be far better off going home and building his emotional strength than he would be hanging here and drinking with Tricia and her damn husband. It would be a cold day in hell before he'd willingly spend time with her and the man she'd betrayed him with.

Chapter Four

"Are you sure you're all right this morning?" Ben lowered his voice so as not to alert Tom and Jennifer who were in the back seat. Pat drove the van from the Birkstone Hotel to the office where they would pick up Sam.

"I'm fine. Why?"

"I don't know. You seem nervous. I thought yesterday went well, so don't be nervous today."

She seemed nervous to Ben? Ben, who has his mind so full of his pregnant wife and sympathy pains that he barely noticed if the sun was out or if it was raining? She must *really* seem a wreck. And not just physically. She'd barely slept last night. This morning she'd changed clothes twice before settling on a dark brown suit with a light blue camisole and black pumps. She'd taken extra care with her makeup and hair, too. And all because of Sam, damn him. Why, of all the sailors in the Navy, had she ended up with *him* on her team?

Pat flashed Ben a smile. "No worries. How's Melanie feeling this morning?" Ben started off on a litany of Melanie's status—every pain, swollen ankle, craving for foods. Pat felt mildly guilty for the easy nudge off topic, but the last thing in the world she wanted or needed was prodding into why she was nervous this morning.

She pulled up to the curb and Sam stepped out from the doorway of Richmond's City Hall. Tom slid open the back door and Sam slipped in.

"Good morning," she said, just as she had to her first passengers when she'd picked them up.

"Good morning," he replied, his rich baritone sending shivers through her body. He used to say that to her every morning in the hallway outside her homeroom, his mouth close to her ear, his voice deep, low, and sexy enough to make her heart race. How could she let herself fall into that same trap now, all these years later?

She turned on her signal, checked her side mirror and pulled out into traffic. "We have a high school to visit this morning and a middle school this afternoon. Sadly, I don't think you'll find the questions all that different."

"Pretty much like yesterday?" Jennifer asked.

"I think you'll find most all of the school visits will be pretty close to what you've already experienced."

Tom spoke up. "That's cool. Yesterday was fun."

Ben laughed. "I hope you still feel the same after ten days."

"Maybe we can shake things up a bit. Come up with some questions for the kids instead of only being on the receiving end," Sam offered. "We can gauge their knowledge and their preconceived ideas before we start taking their questions and then build on how they answer."

"That's a great idea, Sam." Pat berated herself for not thinking of that herself. These school sessions, after so many years, had become a little stale for her, too. "Could each of you come up with three or four questions to toss to the audience?"

"No problem," Tom said right away.

A glance in the rear-view mirror showed a big smile on Jennifer's face. "This could be fun."

The three in the back started throwing out ideas right away, and by the time they arrived at Tucker High they'd organized the questions and who would ask them.

Pat stopped at the front of the school. "Ben, will you go in and make sure things are set up? I'll park the car and meet all of you inside."

"Sure," he said, opening the door. The others exited from the back and just like that, Pat was alone, able to take a breath and clear her mind.

As she pulled into a parking space, the realization hit her. She wasn't going to make it. Two weeks of being around Sam would kill her. He looked like a poster boy for the Navy in his uniform, but when she saw him, heard his voice, felt his laugh in every nerve, all she pictured was the young man he had been, in his letter jacket, golden hair falling into his eyes and a killer smile, leaning his shoulder against her locker, his eyes shining with love.

Pat flipped the ignition and removed the key. Instead of getting out, she rested her forehead against the steering wheel and let her mind drift back. Funny, she hadn't consciously spent time thinking about the past in years. Something would strike now and then, like the song in the elevator, but for the most part, she'd shut off the past and the pain that remembering brought. Now, though, she wanted to remember the sound of his sigh when he'd kissed her senseless and whispered how he wanted her. He'd meant sex, of course, but Sam had wanted much more for them. He'd spoken of marriage, and a nice house, and children, and a future with her, Tricia, the girl he'd called his soul mate.

His arms had wrapped around her the night of his senior prom. The theme had been the 1950s, and they'd danced to "The Way You Look Tonight." Sam told her that he wanted to make her his. His hands had roamed up and down her back while she twined her fingers at the back of his neck and swayed with him to the music. She'd felt the evidence of his desire, long and hard against her stomach, and unknown feelings had swelled within her. Instead of moving away, she'd stepped even closer, purposely rubbing against him, exalting in the way his arms tightened and a low moan escaped him.

Shortly after the song ended, he'd taken her hand and led her from the ballroom of the hotel in downtown Roanoke where the school had scheduled the prom. Since they lived about twenty miles outside town, and because parents wanted their kids to experience "prom night" in all its glory—and coincidentally didn't want them driving curving mountain roads back home after the dance—a good many kids had rooms in the hotel. Sam held her hand as they made their way to the elevator, only kissing her once as they rode up to the floor where he had a room.

Once inside, instead of tearing at her clothes, he'd sat her on the bed and kissed her again and again, whispering how much he loved her and never wanted to leave her, though they both knew he would be off to the university in Charlottesville in September while she stayed in their hometown. Her breath came in pants and heat filled her. The area between her legs tingled with some kind of need, and she wanted to touch herself to make it stop. Fortunately, she fell back onto the bed and Sam went with her. Lost in the thrill of his kisses, she still somehow knew that his hand was under her dress and that she no longer had to touch herself because Sam did it for her.

"Sam?" she'd whispered, afraid and yet not afraid because she knew he would never hurt her.

He'd raised his head and stared down at her, his eyes midnight blue and heavy-lidded. His fingers had found the core of her own need, and he slid them under the elastic of her panties and through the moisture she felt there. A strange, arousing scent filled the air. Sam bent to leave hot, open-mouth kisses along her neck.

"Tricia, I love you so much. Do you love me?" After assurances that she loved him more than life, he said, "I want to make you mine. I want to be your first one, your only one, as you'll be my first, my one and only. I'll love you forever, Tricia."

"Yes, Sam, please!"

And that had been all the encouragement he'd needed. They'd given themselves to each other. She'd cried with joy and with the promise of their lives together. Somehow, in their fumbling, they'd each come. Glorious fireworks burst in Pat that she hadn't imagined before that night. Without even trying, she'd found her Prince Charming that fulfilled every wish, every need, for the rest of her life.

"Or for at least one summer," she muttered now. Then things had gone all to hell.

She sat up, wiping tears from her cheeks that she hadn't known were there. A knock on the window caused her to jump. When she turned her head, Sam Turner stared at her through the class.

***

"We're waiting for you," Sam said when she opened the door. He narrowed his gaze. Tricia had been crying. What was that all about? Despite his not being happy to be working with her, he didn't want the woman to *cry*, for God's sake.

She stepped out and hit the key fob to lock the van. The color of her business suit highlighted the rich brown of her eyes and the blue was a nice contrast. Her cheeks blushed a sweet dark pink and even her flustered attitude as she took a final swipe at her wet cheeks added to her beauty. And no mistaking it, Tricia Welles was beautiful. She looked up at him and blinked, her wet lashes sweeping her cheeks drew his gaze as a candle flame drew a moth. For a moment, he was back in the hotel room where he'd taken her the night of their senior prom. After they'd had sex for the first time, she'd cried, and he'd kissed her until she smiled and kissed him back, swearing she'd marry him when he graduated from college and they'd love each other forever.

Yeah, that had lasted. They'd both been stupid kids. Only, he'd been a *loyal* stupid kid, unlike Tricia.

"Sorry to hold everyone up," she said.

"It's okay. Ben was talking to the principal, so I volunteered to come and find you. Are you alright?"

"Yes! Of course. I just have a few things going on, is all." She dabbed the puffy area below her right eye with her pointer finger, blinked and started off at a brisk pace.

Okay, then. Nothing to worry about. He'd done his duty by asking after her, and he shouldn't have to do anything else. But being alone with her for the first time in years, he just couldn't keep his big mouth shut.

"I haven't heard about your family in a while. Are they doing well?" He hadn't heard anything about her family because he never asked, and his mother knew better than to bring up anything to do with Tricia. It was as though their world had split, with her going east and his going west and never the twain meeting, just like the poet said.

"Daddy died a couple of years ago. Mother moved to Atlanta to live with my aunt Elizabeth."

"I'm sorry to hear about your dad. He was a fine man." They'd reached the building and Sam held open the door.

"Thank you. I miss him a lot." She strode through and down the hall toward the auditorium.

Up the steps and behind the stage, they caught up with the rest of their group as well as Tim Gote, the principal of the high school. Sam could only imagine what the kids made of that name, and didn't envy the guy a bit.

"Are we ready?" Gote asked them.

"Ready, fire, aim," Tom noted with a smile. "Lead the way."

"No wonder the Air Force leaves the fighting to the Marine Corps," joked Jennifer. "You guys don't even know the right end of the gun to hold."

"Hey, we've got the air support when you need it."

Sam peeked around the corner of the stage curtain while the other two bantered. Kids were pouring in. Some found places and waved for others to join them. Some took seats and propped their heads on their fists, and even from a distance, Sam could see that they wanted to be anywhere but here, having to listen to a bunch of old idiots talk up the joys of military service. He could sympathize. Back in the old days, if he wasn't on the football field or snatching a few minutes alone with Tricia, he wasn't a happy camper, either.

The noise in the auditorium was earsplitting, but it all came to a halt when Gote walked out to mid-stage and tapped the microphone. "May

I have your attention?" He waited a few seconds and then continued, introducing Tricia, who in turn introduced each of them. While Sam had gone out to find Tricia, Gote had provided a few students' names that they could call on for answers to their questions. Nothing like putting people on notice that they would have to stand in front of their classmates and provide answers to ad hoc questions. Sam smiled. This should keep the twerps awake.

Watching Tricia on stage, the image of her tears came back to him, flooding him with curiosity and a swift, unwanted need to protect her. Something was upsetting her, and he wanted to find out what. And then he wanted to put a stop to it.

Then he wanted to forget her. Again.

Hearing her call his name as through a fog, he stepped to the mic and smiled at the kids in the audience. Glancing at his card where Principal Gote had noted that a kid named Mike Foster liked ships and military stuff, he called on Mike to ask if he could name a major characteristic of the Nimitz class aircraft carrier. Mike stood, looked a little nervous and then said that they were nuclear powered. "Good job," Sam said and then proceeded to explain that a Nimitz class carrier based in Norfolk was the duty station he had just left. He talked for a good ten minutes about ships he'd been on and what various people did on them.

All the while, he wished that he were still on board. That he'd turned down coming to Richmond as a recruiter, and thus coming up smack dab against his first love. His *only* real love, if he were being honest.

Damn it. He should have begged to stay aboard ship.

Chapter Five

"I like that reverse question and answer thing," Ben told Pat as they finished lunch that Friday afternoon. "When the kids get their turn to ask questions, they're better ones."

"I agree." Pat thought that Sam's switch in the program at Tucker High had continued going well the rest of the week. It wasn't anyone's fault but her own that during the bulk of their time at the school her mind had been elsewhere. After her memory about their prom night, seeing his face so close to hers through the window had been too much for her to handle. Now she suddenly couldn't shake old feelings she'd locked away thirteen years ago, and she didn't know what to do.

"Pat," Ben said with a frown. "Something's wrong. What is it? Something's been off all week. Do you want me to handle the rest of the day so you can go home?"

How about all next week so I can hide for the rest of the program? Then it struck her. Sam lived in Richmond now, and would for the next year or two, probably. She could bump into him anywhere, at any time. Her gasp sent the sip of coffee she'd just taken down the wrong way and she coughed, trying to catch her breath.

Ben stood up and beat her on the back, making things worse while thinking he made them better. The last thing she wanted was attention drawn to her, especially the attention of the man sitting with his colleagues at the next table. All three of her team members looked over in concern, but it was Sam's gaze that bore into hers as she tried to gain her breath. For a brief moment, she could have sworn that he saw right through her, right into her broken heart and the sadness of what she'd done to him.

Then it was over. Jennifer jumped up to come to the table and check on her. Tom switched tables, pulling out an empty chair at her and Ben's table. Sam turned back around and picked up his coffee cup.

Why had they sat at different tables, anyway? Right. It had been Sam's idea, of course. He hated her, hated any moment he had to spend with her. Sure, he'd politely asked after her family the other morning, but he hadn't asked about *her*, how she'd been the last many years. He had been civil, but there was no love lost on his side of the equation. She'd be well off to make it the same on her side. Shove the memory of Sam Turner back into the box of childhood where it belonged and forget it. Thank God it was Friday and she'd made it through half of their forced association. The program was her baby. She couldn't foist it off on Ben just because she couldn't handle her emotions.

"Sorry! I'm fine. Thanks." Ben gave her another swat between the shoulder blades. She choked out a laugh. "Enough, Ben!"

"You're sure?"

"I'm sure." Pat looked up into the faces of her crew. "Truly. Just a case of my coffee going down the wrong pipe." She dabbed at her mouth with the napkin and took a deep breath. "But on that note, maybe we're ready to go? I think I've had enough coffee if everyone else is ready."

Tom stood and pushed his chair back under the table. "Let's get this show on the road."

"I'll meet you out front," Jennifer said, and then leaned in closer to Pat. "Little girl's room pit stop first."

"I'll be out front, too," she told the men. She followed Jennifer to the ladies' room.

Meeting up at the sinks after taking care of business, Jennifer stared at Pat's reflection. "Is there some trouble between you and Sam?"

Pat couldn't stop her startled stare. "Why do you ask?"

Jennifer grabbed a couple of paper towels and leaned against the counter as she dried her hands. "Nothing too much. He has an interesting expression when he looks at you—and he does that a lot, when you're looking away from him. Then there's the way he seems to avoid talking to you. You do the same to him. Y'all are too intense for there to be nothing."

Pat shook the excess water from her hands and then tried to use up time drying them. "He and I went to high school together. We dated for a while." She shrugged. "Then he went to college and we split up. This is the first time we've seen each other since then." If only things could be as simple as two old friends meeting up for the first time in years.

Jennifer stared at her, as though trying to measure what she said with what her own observations had indicated. Then she faced the mirror and tucked a few loose strands of hair back into her chignon before fitting on her cap. "I don't mean to pry. I'm a good listener if things get to the point where you want to talk." She faced Pat with a smile. "And if you need to do more than talk, I'm a crack shot. Men can be so infuriating at times."

Pat laughed. "I don't think I'll need him to be shot, but thanks for the offer." She moved to the door and opened it. "Shall we go and see what trouble they've gotten into?"

The men were chatting outside the minivan but stopped talking as soon as the women joined them. Jennifer nudged Pat and then said, "I enjoyed meeting your brother-in-law the other night, Pat. Do you think we can meet for dinner again before the program is over? Maybe Sam can join us this time."

Sam's brows shot up. "Brother-in-law? That wasn't your…?"

"Husband? No," Pat said, curious of the expression on his face. He looked as though someone had just slapped him. "I'm divorced."

Sam's jaw clamped shut and he turned away, staring at the traffic flowing on Three Chopt Road, past the restaurant's parking area. Did her status have any effect on him? And if so, why should it?

Instead of speaking again, Sam opened the door. Jennifer sent her a telling glance before stepping in, followed by Tom. "Is everything okay?" Ben asked in passing, as she moved to the driver side of the van.

"Fine, thanks." She climbed behind the wheel and they started off for the middle school she had scheduled for the afternoon. This time, she had a few questions for her team members—or for one member in particular—and not ones she could ask in front of a school assembly.

***

Tricia was divorced. Why should that matter to him? *It didn't.* He couldn't care less whether she was married or not and who the asshole was taking her to dinner the other night. Still… There was something about that guy, something possessive in the way he acted toward her. She might not be married, but was she totally free?

Not that Sam gave a shit either way. Nope. She'd made her bed years before. He'd been happy to let her lie in it and she could stay there for all he cared. Still, he wondered what the story was.

Lost in thought, he hadn't noticed that they'd arrived at their destination until Tricia pulled into the parking space. Tom and Jennifer were discussing the kinds of questions they might ask of and expect from kids this age, but he'd zoned out the whole ride. He slid open the door and stepped out. They walked into the building as a group, although Sam hung in the back. From there, as though with a will of their own, his eyes had focused on Tricia's hips and their gentle way as she walked. Her hair made the same swing across her shoulders with each step.

He forced his gaze from her backside to the building. Standard brick, typical for Virginia, the single-story building had been constructed with lots of windows and even skylights. Sam imagined the intent to be that a light and airy building made students more open to learning. In contrast, the high school he and Tricia had attended had been a two-story brick structure with wooden floors and stairs. It hadn't provided a particularly pleasant place to study, cast in the shadows of the mountains, but he didn't remember his years there as being bad. With the help of football and adequate grades, he'd escaped the shadows for the university. However, when he left home for Charlottesville, he'd never dreamed he'd leave Tricia forever, too.

But then he hadn't left Tricia, had he? She'd left him. Was their being thrown together now fate throwing him a bone or putting him in the middle of a cruel joke? If he should take this as a second chance with his first love, did he even want it? Maybe.

"There're a few things to straighten out first," he muttered. The rapid beat of his heart told him to investigate it.

Tucking his hat under his arm when he entered the lobby, he followed the team to the office and then joined in the introductions. He tried to catch Tricia's eye, but couldn't. And then they were ushered to the auditorium and all chance to talk with her was lost.

He started off asking the two hundred or so middle school kids what they thought the Navy did. He took a few answers and then expounded on them, letting them know about the different types of positions a sailor could hold. He half-listened as Jennifer and Tom went through the information on their services, all the time building courage to swallow his pride and ask Tricia to dinner. Now that he knew she was no longer married, he wanted to know—he *needed* to know—what had happened between them. It might lead nowhere. But it might at least give him closure on an episode that had changed his life forever. He felt free to ask the questions now that he knew he wouldn't be causing trouble in her marriage.

Finally, the session ended. The kids began exiting the auditorium in a burst of noise. The team gathered backstage where the principal thanked everyone and especially Tricia for coming today. He'd enjoyed this session better than the others. The kids had seemed more interested, more alert, and they'd asked really good questions. Tom and Jennifer walked down the steps and opened the doorway into the brightly lit hallway, letting in light and the sound of the student body. Sam touched Tricia's arm. "May I speak with you a moment?"

"Sure." She took his arm and nudged him. "But let's talk out in the van."

He stopped and brought her to a stop, too. "Let's talk here. It's a little more private."

With a look of resignation, she turned to Ben and handed him the van keys. "We'll be right out." He nodded and let the door close. It wasn't silent but the change in volume made it seem almost as though it were.

"Is there a problem?" she asked. She seemed more nervous than she had been before. Was she acting that way because she was alone with him?

"Problem? No. Not really." Suddenly he felt like a fifteen-year-old asking his first girl out on a date. "I wondered if maybe you'd like to get together. Maybe for dinner? Just to catch up."

Her startled expression told him all he needed to know. "That's okay. It's been too long. Don't know what I was thinking." He took a step toward the stairs and the safety of other people.

Tricia grabbed his wrist and halted him. "I'd like that. I was just surprised. You—you haven't seemed very interested in touching base since the team got together."

He looked down at her and found himself lost in her rich brown gaze. Her face was small but expressive. She'd never been able to hide her emotions. What he saw now was wariness. But interest, too.

"I've been acting like an ass, and I apologize. Would you have dinner with me tonight?"

She looked away and bit her bottom lip. "I don't think I can tonight."

Instantly, Sam remembered the look of possession on Mark Welles' face and he was filled with irrational jealousy. Was she seeing him tonight? Had she given up one brother to take up with the other?

Tricia faced him again. "I wish I could. Maybe another night?"

Sam studied her face. She was hiding something but damned if he knew what. If she was dating someone else, he'd be finished with her for good. Being dumped once was quite enough. "Do you mind if I ask why you're busy tonight?"

Just then a boy ran up to her. "Mom, hi. Mister Goodman said you were back here."

An instant smile lit her face and she reached out to ruffle the boy's hair. He frowned and ducked out of reach. "Mom." He drew the word out in the time-honored way every boy has when he's embarrassed at being treated like a child.

Smiling, but with that wary look back in her eyes, Tricia looked up. "This is why."

Sam stepped back, stunned. He'd known she was married, but he'd never heard that she had a child. From his size and weight, he was around twelve or thirteen, which meant she'd dumped Sam and gotten pregnant right away. Remembering the things they'd talked about all those years ago, the life they'd planned, the family they'd hoped for, he felt a sudden flash of pain rip through him. He wanted nothing more than to escape and never set eyes on her again. And just now he'd asked her out again. What a fool!

"Sam, this is my son Timmy. Timmy, this is Lieutenant Turner, an old friend." Did she sound even more nervous than before?

The boy stuck out his hand and Sam shook it, looking down into blue eyes and a friendly face with a few freckles dancing over his nose. *My God!* Sam knew that face. He'd seen it in his mirror as a child.

"It's Tim, Sir. I keep telling my mom that, but she insists on calling me by my baby name."

"That's because you'll always be my baby," Tricia said fondly.

Tim rolled his eyes and Sam forced a laugh. "Nice to meet you, Tim. My mom still calls me Sammy sometimes."

"For real? Even as old as you are?"

"Tim!"

The boy ducked his head. "Sorry. I didn't mean that you're *old.*"

Sam laughed again. "Well, I am, kind of."

Tim turned his attention to his mother again. "Mom, Mike wants to know if I can stay at his house tonight. John is going, too."

A wrinkle marred her brow. "Does Mike's mom know he's planning to have you and John at her house tonight?"

"Yeah, of course! Please?" He adopted a puppy dog look that Sam imagined the boy used often to get what he wanted.

"I want a call from Mrs. Cooper. And I'll come tomorrow. Early, if they have plans."

"Well…" Tim scraped his foot on the stage. "We hope his parents will take us to the mall."

"I know why you want to go to the mall, Timothy. That movie is opening, and you know I don't approve." She glanced up at Sam. "Slasher film." *Nightmares*, she mouthed.

"Oh, Mom." Tricia had a stubborn set to her jaw, a look Tim must have been familiar with. "Okay," Tim grumbled. But then he went up on tiptoes to give her a kiss on the cheek. "See you later!" He'd taken two steps before calling over his shoulder, "Nice to meet you, Lieutenant! I enjoyed your talk." And he was gone.

Tricia stared after him and then took a deep breath. Slowly, she faced him again. "He's like a tornado."

Heart in his throat, Sam fixed her with a glare. "He's just like *me.*"

Chapter Six

Oh God. Pat had never wanted to tell him about Timmy like this. She'd never wanted to tell him about Timmy at *all*. Now he knew the truth and she had no way out.

"This is neither the time nor place to talk about any of this."

The left side of his clenched jaw ticked and nothing showed in his eyes but fury. "Tonight then. Where?"

Nowhere. She didn't want to have this talk but if she did she'd rather have it on home turf and privately. "Come to my house, about six. I'll give you the address before you leave."

They walked back to the van, she an emotional mess just trying to hold herself together long enough to figure out how to explain, and he a walking mountain of tension. When they got to the car the rest of the group cast them one look and then Jennifer and Tom climbed into the van silently. Ben studied her worriedly and opened the passenger door while Sam slammed the sliding side door.

After they got back on the road Tom said, "That was fun. I think I liked the younger kids better than the older ones."

Jennifer chuckled. "That's because they weren't so jaded about what we do. They still have some sense of wonder. Don't you agree, Sam?"

"Sure."

Jennifer waited for more, but he didn't elaborate. "You headed back to Langley for the weekend, Tom?"

"Yeah. Not that I don't appreciate your hospitality, Pat, but it will be good to get back to my own bed for the weekend."

Pat tried on a smile and hoped it didn't look as strained as she thought it might. "I understand totally."

"And I assume you have a hot date?" Jennifer teased.

"I won't disabuse you of that idea," Tom answered, teasing back. "How about you?"

"Target practice tomorrow, and then I might be heading into D.C. to check out the nightlife with a friend."

"Sounds like fun. What do you have planned, Sam?"

Pat had to hand it to Tom and Jennifer, they were trying to draw Sam out, but he would have none of it.

"Nothing much," he replied. "A little history lesson."

"Oh-kay," Tom said.

Ben pulled into the drive for the hotel where Tom and Jennifer had their cars and bags.

"Thanks so much for helping to make this a great week," Pat said. "So far, I think this is the best program we've ever hosted. Have a great weekend and I'll meet you back here on Monday morning."

"Have a great weekend," Ben added.

Sam let them out and then climbed back in. Tom headed inside but Jennifer reached in through the window and gave Pat a quick hug. "Remember my offer," she whispered. Then with a final wave to Ben and even to Sam, she disappeared behind the automatic sliding doors of the hotel.

A few minutes later, Ben pulled the van into the school district lot. "Do you have everything, Pat?" he asked.

"Yes, I think we're good. Take good care of Melanie this weekend."

Ben smiled as she knew he would. "You know it. If I get through a weekend of not having to go out for ice-cream, I'll feel we're making progress."

Pat laughed. At least with Ben she could. Not so with the man standing by her side.

"Well," Ben said, flicking his gaze between Pat and Sam, "I'll drop off the keys, so unless you need to go to your office for something I think you're free." He glanced at Sam's stony expression and then back to her. "Get some rest this weekend, okay?"

"I will. Thanks so much for helping out this week, Ben."

When he had gone, Pat found a slip of paper in her purse. Quickly, she scribbled her address and cell number. "Here. I'll see you later." She turned to go. If she spent one more second in Sam's company she'd scream. Or cry, which would be even worse. Or...

"One more thing." She swung around to tell him to come with an open mind and a willingness to understand. But he was gone.

Tonight was the beginning of the weekend. Usually, if Timmy spent the night with a friend, Pat would have the whole night free. She didn't indulge in much. An extra glass of wine, a pedi, or pizza and sappy movie. Sometimes she called Mark to see if he was free for dinner. But in every other instance, she felt a lightness that accompanied an evening all to herself. Tonight, not so much. Whatever else happened this weekend, and despite Ben's suggestion, she wouldn't be getting much rest.

***

"Come in." Pat held open her front door to Sam. Fortunately, he hadn't come in his uniform, dressed for battle. Sam wore fitted, worn jeans and a navy-blue tee shirt with a San Diego Chargers logo. Impossibly, the shirt made his eyes even more blue. The tee shirt didn't hide his fine physique or toned muscles the way his uniform did. He was in the same great shape he'd been in high school only better. He had filled out not only with age, he carried himself with confidence in a way kids can't. Pat knew without a doubt that women everywhere drooled over this man. Hell, she would herself if things weren't so serious between them.

Sam stepped through the door and walked into the living room. Pat's house was in a good neighborhood but not the best the city offered. Neither was her house expensive or high class. But it was comfortable and big enough for her and Timmy, and she loved it. She wasn't a fussy decorator, preferring to stay within the clean lines of the arts and crafts style. She tried to envision the place through his eyes and hoped he saw the comfort that showed people lived there and not her lack of *Architectural Digest* styling.

Then again, if he doesn't like it who cares? He doesn't have to.

Right. "Can I get you something to drink? A beer or glass of wine?"

"A beer, please." He swung around, taking in everything from her living room and open kitchen, to the dining room off to the right. His shoulders were rigid, and his stance showed every bit of the strain he'd exhibited earlier in the day.

Pat slipped into the kitchen and withdrew a bottle of Sam Adams from the refrigerator. She'd planned to have a glass of pinot, but now that he was here she saw that this was no time to go for a frou-frou drink like wine. She pulled out a second bottle of Sam Adams.

Handing him one, she said, "I didn't have time to make dinner, what with helping Timmy get packed and driving him over to his friends'. I thought we could order a pizza after we've talked a bit."

Sam twisted off the top of his beer. "Let's see if we feel like eating after we talk."

"Okay." He wouldn't make this easy for her. But then, she hadn't really expected him to, had she? "Let's go out to the patio." She opened the sliding door and led the way to the glass table covered with a garishly striped umbrella. Here he was. Here she was. Suddenly, she couldn't think of how to begin.

He flipped his hand out. "This is your show, Tricia."

Tricia. "No one's called me that since I left home." Thirteen years ago, she'd started a new life with a new name and had tried to leave all the hurt and bad feelings she'd caused behind her. Now it seemed like a lifetime ago. She'd fought the memories all this time, until this past week when she'd been confronted with Sam Turner again. Now she had to go back and not only remember, but tell the story she'd never told anyone else.

* * *

Sam tried not to look at her too carefully, knowing if he did, if he saw a glimmer of the old Tricia, that he'd start to lose the head of anger he'd built up and he didn't want that. "Just come out with it," he said gruffly.

"Okay. I must have become pregnant that August, just before you left for Charlottesville. I didn't know before you left for Charlottesville. I knew a few weeks after."

"And you didn't think to write and tell me."

"What would you have done?"

"Married you, of course. I'd have come home and found a job and we would have raised our family, together." Damn! He wanted to pound something, wanted to *break* something. How could she have done this to him?

"Sam, you were the first person on either side of your family to go to college. You were your parents' pride and joy, the big football hero who'd become a great Cavalier and get a degree and take the world by storm. You're all your mother could talk about, how well you were doing, how you were on the starting line-up even though you were just a freshman, how everyone just knew you were going to be someone great. How could I have destroyed everyone's hopes and dreams?"

Wait. *What?* He could only stare at her, dumbstruck. "Do you mean to tell me you had my child, my *son*, and never told me about him because you were trying not to break my mother's heart? Tell me that is *not* the fuck you are explaining to me."

"I'm sorry."

Sam stood fast enough that his chair fell back and crashed into a flower pot. Stomping out into the center of her backyard, he planted his hands on his hips and bent his head, trying to catch his breath. The Tricia he'd known couldn't have done that. She couldn't have ruined his life and thrown away his love and his heart because his family was proud that he'd gone to college. And all without even giving him a say in his own future, without giving him a chance to hold his son in his arms, without giving him the chance to have her as his wife and maybe give her more children. She'd decided on her own what he deserved and what he wanted or needed. Fuck, fuck, *fuck!*

Suddenly he heard the sound of Super Chief Baxter in his head. *Calm down, son. Not everything is the way it seems at first glance. Take a breath and hear the lady out.* The chief had never given him bad advice and he should probably take a chance on it now.

Sam raised his head and forced a deep breath. Then another, and another. Each one came easier than the one before. He turned and walked back to the table. A trace of tears was evident on Tricia's face, but fortunately, she wasn't crying now.

"Go on," he said, righting his chair and taking a seat again. He took a long pull on the beer for the courage he'd need to hear the rest.

"I couldn't destroy your dream of college, but I didn't know what to do. My daddy would have come after you with his shotgun if he'd known you were the father, and that would have destroyed your whole future. As it was, Mama and Daddy were so disappointed it almost killed me. Your parents were probably happy you were rid of me when they found out about the wedding.

"One day, Susie Jordan said she had met a guy who went to Tech and he had invited her to a frat party. She was sneaking out of her house that Saturday night to meet him and a friend up at the crossroads. She wanted me to come. Her date's friend was Brian Welles. He seemed to like me, and I thought he was okay." Nervously, she kept her gaze on her bottle while she tore off the label. "We, uh, did it, and a few weeks after, I told him I was pregnant."

Sam begged for the chief to give him some more virtual advice, but his head was silent. "So, you lied by omission to me, and you lied straight up to his face."

"Someone was going to be hurt whatever I did. I couldn't give up our baby. I certainly couldn't stand the thought of an abortion. So, instead of taking away your dream of college, I took away Brian's. We married right away. He was a junior and his family was furious about his dropping out. But they had contacts, so he was able to get a banking job here in Richmond. Timmy was born a little under eight months after the wedding."

"And he didn't know?"

She choked out a mirthless laugh. "Oh, he knew. Right away. The early birth, Timmy's blue eyes—both his and mine are brown—and even later as a toddler, he resembled no one else in our families. He always looked like you."

"God damn it all, Tricia. You had no right to keep this from me. Do you have any idea what you put me through?"

She looked up at him. Tears glistened in her eyes and tipped her lashes. "We were young, Sam. Would you have been happy coming home and working in Gus Wilson's garage? Could you have given up football, and your plans to become an engineer? Could you have been happy, or would you have become bitter and ended up hating me?"

Another piece of sage advice the super chief had given him back when he was wet behind the ears and in a hell of a lot of trouble was to tell the truth. He did so now. "We'll never know, Tricia. You took that choice away from me. And it tore me up so much to hear that you were married and had moved away that I dropped out of school and joined the Navy. So, I still lost football and that engineering degree, and the woman I loved. I'm only now learning what it feels like to lose a son I never knew I had."

"I don't know what to say except I'm sorry. I wish you'd never found out, truthfully."

How could she say that? Wasn't it bad enough that the kid was twelve without knowing his real father?

He sat back in his chair and stared at her. "I want you to tell him."

Tricia sat up, too, and stubbornness marked her face. "We can't. I *won't*. You have no rights to him. Your name is not on his birth certificate. He knows nothing about you. Hell, *I* don't know anything about you anymore." Standing, she said, "Maybe dinner is a bad idea. You'd better go."

He got up slowly, without breaking eye contact. "I want to know about him. How has he grown up? Does he like athletics? Is he good in school? Was he sick as a baby? Was your husband good to him, knowing that he wasn't Tim's father?" That was the first time since that afternoon he'd dared mention his son's name, even to himself. It felt weird and strangely good, too. He tried it again. Tim. *Tim Turner.*

Tricia looked nervous again, as wary as she had at the school that afternoon. "Brian made me pay for my deception, but he also tried to be a good father to Timmy. As good a father as he knew how to be."

"What do you mean you paid?" Sam didn't want to feel that need to protect her again, but he did, nonetheless. Something bad had happened to her.

"Turns out, even with a good job, Brian wasn't a happy man. Who knows what he would have been like if I hadn't come into his life and messed everything up? As it was, when he couldn't stand life, he drank. And when he drank, he liked to use his fists. He had always taken his temper out on me, but when Timmy was five and a half, he did something—I don't even remember what, right off, but something any little kid would do—and Brian raised his hand. I stepped between the two and took the blow. The next day I saw his brother and filed for divorce. Mark got Brian out of the house and watched over us until the marriage was legally over. The week the papers were signed, Brian moved to California."

Sam's mind filled with rage. If he ever met the son of a bitch he'd kill him. His hands already formed fists. He saw Tricia's gaze drop to them and then snap back, filled with fear. He forced himself to release the fists, flexing his fingers to show her that he was okay. If only he could calm his internal anger as easily.

"What is this Mark to you now?" He really meant to ask what Mark was to Timmy, whether he'd stepped in as father to Sam's son.

"He's a very good friend. Mark is always here to help when I need it, he takes me to dinner now and then, and fills in for Timmy on things I can't, like scouting and ballgames."

"I see." All the things a dad would do. All the things *he* would have done. He took yet another deep breath. That's how things had been. The question was what could he do now?

"I want to know about him, Tricia. Every little thing. Can we order that pizza now, and maybe, I don't know, look at some pictures or something?"

She studied him. He knew when she'd made up her mind to trust him. Her shoulders relaxed, and she breathed steadily. "I have lots of pictures." And then she led him back into the house.

Chapter Seven

Pat pushed the empty pizza box into the trash and took two more beers from the fridge. This would make their fourth, but after the emotions of the night, who was counting? She could put Sam into a taxi soon and then settle in bed to reflect on where she stood in life.

She'd started the evening in terror of what she had to explain to Sam what had happened when they were foolish, careless kids. Then she moved into despair that even though she hadn't seen or heard from him in over a decade, Sam hated her—*hated* her. The thought of his bitterness, that somehow Timmy would be affected with it through her, filled her with trepidation. Irrational, sure, but after the day they'd had, who was to say osmosis of negativity couldn't happen?

Then she pulled out her photo albums and shared them with Sam as they ate. Pat hadn't looked at the pictures for years either, and seeing Timmy's dear little face just after birth and through all the years since choked her up. She loved her little man! She only hoped that the early years spent living with Brian hadn't affected him too adversely. Even though Brian had never hit their son, children always knew more than adults gave them credit for. He had to have heard their arguments, the sound of Brian's fists striking her, her tears, sometimes late into the night. She should have divorced him sooner—like after the first time he'd hit her.

Pat took the beers into the living room where Sam sat on the couch poring over Timmy's current school pictures. She held out a bottle and he took it. "He didn't want to have his picture that day," she said, explaining the frown in lieu of the smile that more frequently covered Timmy's face.

"Why not?"

"Who knows? Maybe I hadn't washed his favorite shirt, or he wanted to wear glasses. Sometimes the mind of a child is a wild and crazy place."

Sam looked up. "Does he need glasses?"

She shook her head. "No, but his best friend Mike has glasses and hates them. Timmy wants to wear a pair in solidarity."

Sam laughed and lifted the fresh bottle of Sam Adams to his lips. "Good kid," he said after taking a swig.

Pat leaned back into the sofa, fully relaxed for the first time since that afternoon when Timmy and Sam came face to face. "He *is* a good kid," she affirmed, reaching out to touch her finger to the photo. "I'm lucky." Immediately she felt Sam's posture tense. "I'm sorry. I didn't mean—"

"Stop saying you're sorry. It's done. I just wish I'd known. I wish I'd had a chance to be a part of all this." He sighed and closed the album, placing it on the coffee table. Adjusting his position, he sat sideways so he could see her face. "Are you happy, Tricia?"

She took a moment. "It sounds so strange to hear that name again."

He gave a half smile. "You'll always be Tricia to me."

"It's nice," she murmured. Then added, "I guess I'm happy. Happy enough, anyway. I have the love of my life. Timmy gives me not only joy but purpose. He centers me. And I have a good job, great friends. I love my house. There isn't anything I truly need."

"Nothing, Tricia?"

Was it her imagination or had he moved closer? And had his eyes darkened and his lids dropped to half-mast?

"There are things I miss," she said.

"Like what?"

The scent of his aftershave burst on her like fresh wintergreen. He licked his lips and she felt it on her lips. All evening she had blocked him from her senses. Bad enough to have to see his beautiful eyes and the ripple of muscles as he moved. Hearing his rich, deep voice had been torture because she wanted to close her eyes and remember the sound of his saying how much he loved her. But at least she hadn't touched him or taken in his scent, or tasted him. Not until now.

"I miss…"

"What, Tricia? Tell me." Now he did scoot closer. He placed his beer on the table and then reached out for hers and put it on the table, too. Suddenly, his hand slid under her hair and to the back of her neck. His gaze slipped to her mouth. "What do you miss?"

"This," she whispered. "What we used to have. What I've never had with anyone else. What I've never *wanted* with anyone else."

Her heart beat like a kettle drum when he tugged at her gently until his breath claimed hers. The kiss was nothing more than a brush, lips barely touching, but she felt it to her toes and every place in between. Especially one place in between. Her panties flooded with moisture. Her nipples hardened and even the cashmere softness of her old tee shirt proved suddenly too rough.

Sam pulled back but when Pat opened her eyes she saw he was close enough to kiss her again. "What are you doing, Sam? Just an hour or two ago you were furious with me. Where are we going?"

"I'll be damned if I know." He sighed and released her neck. She wanted to cry out not to let her go but despite all the evidence her body was sending her, things were a little too late for them. As he'd pointed out at one of the school assemblies, you can't go home again. They'd both changed too much.

He moved back but not to where he had been sitting. "I think seeing those pictures of Tim's babyhood got to me. You look exactly the way I always remember you. It's like I was looking at the girl I'd just loved the week before I left home, with my baby in her arms." He laughed and pointed to the coffee table." Or maybe I shouldn't have had that last beer."

Disappointment stabbed at her. *What did you think, idiot? That he'd say he still loved you?* "Maybe you shouldn't drive. Let me call you a cab."

"Nah, I'm okay." Pulling out the bottom photo album, he flipped it open to the pictures of when she'd first brought Timmy home. "You look so beautiful."

Pat glanced to the picture. She had been happy—delirious, really—to be holding Sam's baby. But despite loving Sam, she had committed to making her marriage work. Even Brian looked happy, smiling behind her. That hadn't lasted long, but those days had been good ones.

"You always said that."

"Beautiful is how you always looked to me." He faced her. "You still do."

She forgot to breathe. What did she want? She knew what she should do. She should tell him to go home and then contact her lawyer first thing Monday morning to see how she could protect herself and Timmy from any actions Sam might be contemplating. The last thing she could allow is that he would disrupt Timmy's life with news of who he was. Later, when Timmy was old enough to understand, yes, but not now.

But that was what she should do, not what she wanted to do.

"Let me stay, Tricia."

"What?"

He turned to her fully now, his eyes intense, his shoulders squared. "Let me have tonight. Let me pretend if only for a few hours that that's me in this picture, holding you as my wife, and smiling down on our baby boy."

* * *

Sam never imagined he would feel this again. The desire to hold Tricia, to touch her and kiss her senseless, to lose himself in her body rode his senses like an addiction. It took every ounce of willpower he could muster to keep from wrapping his arms around her and pushing her into the sofa like a wild man. Impatiently, he waited for her response.

"Sam," she whispered, "I'm not sixteen anymore. A lot has changed since then."

"Hell, Tricia. I'm not seventeen anymore, either. And a lot has changed, you're right. I've fought my baser instincts all week, but I'm defenseless now. Seeing these pictures and being with you tonight has stripped away the past thirteen years."

"We can't bring the past back. It won't be the same."

How could he make her understand? "For years I've hated you, did you know that? I thought you betrayed me in the worst possible way, and tonight, when you told me that Tim is my son, I discovered a pain I'd never imagined before. I had a son and didn't know it." She threw her hand over her mouth and her eyes filled with tears. *Yeah, that's the way to win her over.* "But now that I've truly heard you out, now that I know the reason for everything, I can see that you did the best you knew how. And you protected and raised our boy to be someone fine."

He used his thumb to swipe away her tears and then held her hand on his thigh. "No more hatred, Tricia. It's too exhausting and we have too much between us. What's left is the love that's never really died over all these years."

"Sam..."

"And it won't be the same, I know that. It will be better, I hope. Give us this night?"

Tricia closed her eyes and slumped against him. Sam took his opportunity and pulled her closer, letting her scent and warmth surround him. Rocking until he felt her relax, he kissed the top of her head and rubbed his cheek against her hair.

"Are you sure?" she murmured.

"Positive. I don't want to be alone. Hold me for the night. And let me hold you."

She pulled away and stood up. Taking his hand, she led him down the hall to her bedroom. Once she closed the door and then turned on the bedside lamp, all he saw was her.

Without looking at him, she began undressing, pulling her tee shirt over her head. When she reached back to unhook her bra, he put out his hand. "Let me."

That's when she cast him the briefest of glances and he saw the disquiet in the way she bit her bottom lip and wrinkled her brow. "It's been a very long time," she said. "Not since Brian."

Tricia had been seven years or so without sex? That answered his question about what kind of relationship she had with Mark Welles. But at the moment, all he cared about was the relationship she would have with him.

Sam unhooked her bra, brought the straps over her shoulders and let it fall. Tricia raised her arms to try to cover herself, but he took hold of her wrists. "No, let me look at you." And look he did.

She was fucking beautiful. Her breasts were still firm and high, her arms toned, and silky-smooth skin tapered to a narrow waist. Using both hands, he palmed her breasts, gently kneading, pulling, rubbing her nipples. She let out a moan as she closed her eyes.

"I can't say it's been that long since I've been with a woman, Tricia, but I can say that it's been thirteen years since I've been with so beautiful a woman. I've missed you."

He bent to take control of her lips and when she gasped, he moved to conquer her mouth too, his tongue stroking and exploring until he felt her acquiesce and use her tongue, too. She wrapped her arms around his neck. Sam smoothed his hands down her back and under the waistband of her jeans and panties until he cupped her ass. She pressed herself against him. He ran his kisses to her jaw and down her neck. Tricia threw back her head to allow him greater access. At the pulse point where her neck and shoulder met, he bit her lightly and then licked the spot.

Bending lower, he took advantage of her bare breasts, sucking and licking a nipple, twirling his tongue over it and using his teeth to lightly scrape it. She cried out but threaded her fingers through his hair and held him tighter.

His cock was so hard, he thought it might break off by the time she handled it, and he so wanted her to handle it. His balls ached with the need to be inside her.

Now it was a race. Placing her on the edge of the bed, he pushed her back to remove her jeans. Quickly, he stripped them off along with her panties. She toed off her sneakers. He stood over her, panting. Slowly, she spread her legs, opening herself to his gaze. He dropped to his knees and nestled his nose in the light brown hair at the apex of her thighs. Using his tongue, he finally found the center of his need.

Spreading her legs further apart with his hands, Sam hungrily lapped at her pussy. Her arousal assailed him, and he inhaled deeply. He stroked her clit with his thumb and was pleased and surprised that she came almost immediately, crying his name, and jerking her hips off the bed and to his greedy mouth. No other woman had ever come apart so quickly. No other woman had filled him with such pleasure and pride when he hadn't even been inside her.

"Sam!"

"Shh. That's just the beginning," he said. And then set out to prove that statement.

Chapter Eight

While Pat came down from her splintering climax, Sam stripped, retrieving a condom from his wallet before tossing it on the night table and throwing his pants toward the foot of the bed. He stood over her, stroking his erection and looking at her like she was a Big Mac and he was a Biggest Loser dieter.

"Tricia, are you sure—"

"Sam, please come here." She held out her arms and braced her feet on the edge of the bed to push back toward the center. He crawled between her legs and then propped on one elbow. Taking her left nipple in his mouth, he used his free hand to swish his sheathed cock through the cream coating the folds of her pussy. She raised her hips, trying to capture him at her entrance but he had other thoughts and ground against her clit instead. A few more seconds of that and she would come again before he even entered her.

Finally, with a groan of surrender, he slid inside her, far enough for her to feel her channel stretch and stopped. Propped on both elbows now, he raised his mouth to hers and took her in a deep kiss, angling his head to allow his tongue the greatest penetration while burrowing his cock in her pussy a few inches at a time.

"More," she begged when Sam swept his mouth over her cheek to the tender skin beneath her ear.

"You're so damn tight! I don't want to hurt you," he whispered.

She stretched her arms down his back, grabbing his ass and pulling him. "You won't hurt me."

Sucking in a breath, Sam thrust hard. The slice of pain that did penetrate was overridden by the pure bliss of having Sam inside her again. He held still, breathing hard along her shoulder. "Fuck, Tricia, *fuck!* I have to move."

"Yes." For her part, she could have stayed just like that forever, filled with Sam Turner and knowing that he wanted to be right where he was, deep inside her and about to take both of them to heaven. How had she ever given this up? If only she hadn't lied all those years ago. If only she had asked him what he wanted, they might have been married all these years, raising their son and maybe other children. They might have been happy instead of sharing one night after more than a decade of hard feelings and guilt.

Sam pulled out and slid back in, erasing everything from her mind except what they were doing right here and now. Pat pulled her knees up and over his hips. The muscles across his shoulders rippled under her fingers as he kept his weight off her but still moved within her. Each stroke of his cock, moving in, moving out, brought her closer to release as tension built inside. Sam lavished attention on her right nipple now, swirling his tongue around it and then lightly biting down. Pat threw back her head, her mouth open and reaching for air.

His pace increased. Heavy breathing and the slap of their bodies coming together filled the otherwise silent room. Their bodies slid over each other on a light sheen of sweat but nothing reduced the friction going on inside her pussy. Glorious, wonderful friction! She didn't even have to reach for the orgasm—it enveloped her without thought or effort, like an out of control bullet train racing through the night. At the same time, Sam slammed into her and went rigid, pulsing strongly. As he settled his weight on her, Pat wrapped him in her arms, holding him tightly while tears ran from the corners of her eyes and down into her hair.

How could the very feel of Sam loving her be so different and yet the same as all of her memories? The different part—the part where he kissed her "down there"—comprised the stuff of erotic dreams she'd experienced over the years. He'd probably not known how to do that back in the days when they were high school lovers, and for sure she'd never imagined anything like that, or how delicious it could feel. Brian had refused to try it, though he'd loved for her to go down on him.

Their foreplay techniques had greatly improved—the kissing, the touching, the mind-blowing caresses—since they'd been together long ago. But the filled-to-the-brim-with-love sensation felt as though they'd never been apart. Through no fault of her own—in fact, despite her efforts—she'd been given a second chance to know what being loved meant.

Sam rose to his elbows and rolled off her. "I'd better take care of this," he said, holding the condom on as he made it to the edge of the bed.

"The bathroom is right through that door on your left," she said. He closed the door behind him and switched on the light. The toilet flushed and the water came on in the sink. All the while, Pat wondered what would happen when Sam emerged. Would he do as he'd said he wanted and spend the night, or did "giving him a night" mean a round of sex? If that was all he wanted, all he'd allow her, she'd take it and be grateful.

For her, having sex with Sam was more like making love. She'd never felt that way with Brian, probably because she'd built their relationship on a lie from the beginning. For Pat, the word love had always meant Sam. She only hoped that they'd dispelled the bad feelings of the past and could be at least friends.

The door opened, and she stared at him silhouetted by the bathroom light. Even without detailed definition, his body displayed muscle and a trim shape. He turned out the light and walked back to the bed. Pat held her breath, letting him take the lead in where they went from here. She didn't think she had the right to make assumptions or demands. She had wronged him. Now he had to decide what he wanted their association to be.

Sam seemed totally comfortable in his nakedness. He stood by the bed looking proud and in control. Lazily, he reached out and ran his pointer finger across her lips, then down her chin and across her collarbone. Following his finger with his gaze, he circled one breast and then the other. Lightly scraping his nail over one nipple, he smiled when she sucked in a breath.

"You're so responsive, Tricia. I don't remember your being quite this fast to light up before. But I like it. I like it a lot."

"I told you that it's been a long time."

"You did, indeed."

Could she be brave enough to tell him the rest? How did she know if this was serious on his part or just a night of fun? Maybe a night of revenge, taking something from her because of what she'd taken from him and given to another man.

"But it's only with you that I've been this responsive, Sam. I want you to know that. Only you."

He didn't say a word, just rolled her nipple between his thumb and index finger until she moaned. Then he continued his finger stroll down her torso, through her pubic hair and between her legs where he stroked her clit until fire once again raced through her body and she came hard and long.

My God! Three orgasms in less than half an hour. When had that ever happened before? Never—not even when they were young and captured by the new sexual experiences they explored.

Sam skewered her to the bed with his stare. He ran his finger through her furrow and then raised his finger coated with her juices to his mouth. "You taste so fucking good, Tricia."

"I do?" Was it wrong of her to hope this night never ended? She wanted to debauch herself with Sam. To feel his arms around her, to feel his cock deep inside, filling her, and to eat him and taste his cum going down her throat. She wanted every XXX film experience she'd ever seen, and she wanted it all with Sam. She wanted to feel dirty, she wanted to feel fulfilled. She wanted to let go and live every fantasy she'd ever had with the only man she'd ever loved or wanted. And tonight might be all she had.

"I'm going to eat you out again later, Tricia. I want your juices on my tongue and in my mouth before I fuck you like you've never been fucked. I want to leave you tomorrow too sore to walk, and know that I did that to you."

Pat pulled down the sheet and comforter and scooted beneath them. She held them open. "Join me?" Sam hesitated long enough that she feared he might leave after all. Then he climbed in beside her.

***

I've come home. That thought brought him awake after a second fitful session of sleep.

After Tricia invited him into her bed, they'd spent some time kissing and took time to explore each other's bodies. Hers was different than he remembered. But different in a better way. She had curves that hadn't developed when she was a teen. Though she was soft, she must exercise because he felt toned muscle in her arms and legs. Her hips swelled from her waist, but not with extra padding. He couldn't get enough of touching her. Sam mapped her body and recorded all the markings in his mind, including the small sexy noises she made as his hands traveled her hills and valleys.

He detected the remnants of a subtle perfume between her breasts. When she touched him, it was with the certainty of a woman touching a man, not the tentative way a girl touches a boy when she doesn't know what to expect or how to bring about a reaction she wants. Tricia was all woman now, and he wanted her. Every bit of her.

He also wanted their son to know who he was. For that, he had to earn her trust. And he had to determine whether he could trust *her*. He needed her to understand his side in this issue and to make right what she'd done.

In the meantime, he'd never been so turned on. Being inside her felt so damn *right*. And he meant to feel "right" as often as he could in the night they had. Before he'd last dropped off to sleep, he'd eaten her out and then fed her flavor to her with deep kisses. Now he wanted to come deep inside her. But he'd brought her to completion quite a few times and now deep breathing indicated she slept soundly.

Sam glanced at the clock beside her bed. It was only a little past midnight. They'd started their night together early, but he registered that they only had a few hours left. One night is all he'd asked for, and maybe all Tricia would give him. He had to take what he could get now. This night might be all he has in memories for years to come.

He dipped below the covers and took her breast into his mouth, taking care to abrade her nipple with his tongue. Still asleep, she arched her back, inviting him to continue. Switching breasts, he gave the other the same attention.

"Sam," she murmured, and her hand came down on his head to hold him in place. "Yes, love, yes."

Sam barely heard the words, but they set his heart galloping. Was she dreaming or was she awake enough to mean it? And if she did mean it, did he feel anywhere like the same? Sure, the sex had been beyond belief, but could they have anything meaningful after tonight?

He let his hand slide down to her pussy, inserting first one finger and then two, curling them to search for that sweet spot that women loved. The way she jerked her back off the bed and her breathing quickened told him he'd found it. Using his thumb, he rubbed her clit. He sucked her nipple into his mouth and tantalized it with his teeth and tongue. Crying out, she shot off like a rocket, bathing his fingers with her fragrant juices.

"Get on your hands and knees." Sam's voice was hoarse with need. When she'd positioned herself, he pushed her head down to the pillow and spread her knees. He swiped his second condom from the nightstand.

Seconds later, he'd plunged into her pussy, gaining a depth he couldn't get when she was on her back. Foregoing finesse, he drove into her. His nuts slapped her with each thrust. He wouldn't last long. Reaching around to her front, he found her clit and pinched it and then pressed it hard to her body.

"Sam!" Tricia screamed, gripping his cock like a vise. He gritted his teeth and came like a wild man.

Coming felt good. Hell, coming felt great. But nothing filled him with so much satisfaction as hearing Tricia scream his name in the course of her orgasm.

Chapter Nine

"Sam," Pat murmured, not wanting to wake him.

Light filtered in below the shade in her bedroom window, letting Pat know that morning had finally arrived to end their night. For the first time in years, a man slept beside her, his steady breathing like a balm to her soul. Very slowly, she turned over, so she could watch him. A peaceful expression hid the humor he'd shown with the kids this past week and the nearly hostile intensity with which he'd treated her. Here, he looked like the boy she'd once known. And yet, not him. Not exactly. This was like Sam 2.0.

His hair, short as it was, still looked tousled. Long, charcoal lashes rested on his cheeks and his mouth hung slightly open to let out a very soft snore. He'd slung one arm over his head at some point, and his other arm rested on his chest. She hadn't had enough time last night to adequately admire his chest. Sculpted hardly described it. Soft brown hair sprinkled his pecs and led like an arrow over hard, washboard abs to the treasure between his legs. Speaking of which... The bed covers draped his hips, but a morning erection was clearly evident.

She wanted to touch him. No, she wanted to taste him. He'd dipped his head between her legs three times since they'd come to bed last night and hadn't asked the same of her. It hadn't been a task she enjoyed with Brian, but maybe because he had demanded it of her and then set out to punish her with the way he handled her. Somehow, she knew that Sam would be different.

All night he'd alternated between worshipping her body and treating her with a desperation that didn't allow for the soft and tender. Her body had responded to both approaches, but the times he'd taken charge, when he'd driven into her as though he couldn't get enough, those were the times her orgasms registered off the charts. Maybe because that was how she wanted him to feel about her? Being worshipped had its place, but being needed as though he would die unless he had all of her, that was heart altering.

As slowly as she could, Pat slipped under the sheet until her head was level with his cock. Semi-erect, it lay on his thigh and twitched lightly. Pat ran her finger very softly along his length and immediately noticed a difference in length and thickness. Smiling, she scooted closer. She lifted his cock to her mouth and licked the head. Sam's hips bolted off the bed and he straightened his legs. Holding the root of his cock, she took him in, using her tongue to lick the pulsing vein that ran the full length. By the time she reached the root, the head touched the back of her throat.

Heat consumed her. She closed her eyes and raised her head, sucking slightly all the way to the head. Sam groaned and flexed his hips against the mattress. She swirled her tongue across the head, licking the pre-cum from the slit and then started down again as Sam pushed up into her mouth.

He lifted the bed covers from her head and swept her hair away from her face. When she used her tongue to stroke him on the way up, she opened her eyes to see his gaze settled on her. His eyes showed desire and wonder, and she wanted nothing more than to make him feel as satisfied as he'd made her. To that end, she sank onto him again, her tongue flicking and stroking. When she reached her hand, she inhaled and took his scent deep into her lungs. She stayed there a few seconds, bobbing her head and wondering at how different this was than the times Brian had insisted she do this. Sam's scent drove her crazy. His taste filled her with a need that surprised and almost scared her. Never had she wanted a man more. A moan came from deep within and she raised her head, faster, sucking hard.

"My God, Tricia. More."

More was what she wanted too. She used her other hand to grasp his balls, rubbing them in her palms. Her head dropped over him again, her lips clamped against his hard length, her tongue mapping his cock like a GPS. On the uptake, she twisted the root and pulled as though she wanted to keep him in her mouth even as she pulled away. His balls tightened in her hand.

"I'm going to come, Tricia. Stop now."

His words drove her on and she took him again, licking, sucking, pulling. As she sunk over him the next time, Sam grabbed a handful of her hair and held her down. Pat's throat filled with his cum as he exploded in her mouth. Her heart pounded as she swallowed, lightly stroking his balls and using her other hand to reach up his body to one of his nipples.

When he finished she rested her head there, her nose buried in his pubic hair, Sam stroking her hair. He tugged her arm and she climbed up to snuggled under his arm.

"That was the most amazing way to wake up ever." He kissed the top of her head. "You didn't have to do that."

"I wanted to." Shyly, she ducked her head. "I never realized how it would turn me on, too."

Sam was silent for a few seconds and then he chuckled. "So, you're turned on right now?" He took control of her right breast, caressing her in a way that made her pussy tingle. He moved down in the bed a bit and rolled onto his side. "I wish we could fuck again, but I only brought two condoms." His hand roamed from her breast to the junction of her thighs. "But I can still make you feel good." He replaced the hand on her breast with his hot, wet mouth. Pat spread her legs and Sam took full advantage. Unerringly, he found her clit. His thumb controlled it while he inserted two fingers into her pussy.

"Sam, are you good? I mean, are you, you know, healthy?"

He lifted his gaze from where he'd been focused, on torturing Pat with his tongue on her nipple. "Are you asking what I think? Because yes, Tricia, I'm good. I promise. But what about you? Are you on birth control?"

"It helps keep my cycles regular, so yeah, I am." Pat moved against his fingers, feeling the familiar spiral of need spread from her center through her nervous system. He took her nipple into his mouth, sucking hard and pressed her clit. In seconds, she rode his hand to a wild orgasm. Before she came down from her high, Sam settled between her legs and thrust into her.

Propped on his elbows just inches above her, his eyes were glazed with lust, lids half-mast. "Tricia, my God, Tricia. This is fucking heaven."

For Pat, his words couldn't have been more right. Sam hooked his arm under one of her knees and opened her farther than she could have imagined, but the man knew what he was doing. His cock hit her just right, going deeper than ever before and stroking her clit with each stroke.

"Oh my God!" She came so hard it felt like an internal explosion. Sam groaned at the same time and Pat felt him pulse, felt the warmth of his cum spurting inside. "I love you!"

Sam had just collapsed on her, breathing hard. But with her words, he raised up and then rolled off her. Saying nothing, he reached out and took her hand.

"Tricia, I never stopped loving you. Even when I hated you, I knew that no one would ever take your place in my heart."

Pat sat up to see him better. "Sam, is this our second chance? Do you think we could make a relationship work?"

His eyes were solemn. He took her hand before speaking. "I don't know where this is going, but I know that I want to get to know my son. And I want him to know me."

***

Sam waited for Tricia to reply. He hadn't explicitly said he wanted Tim to know who he was, but he hoped she'd get the hint because that was what he meant.

She took back her hand and moved off the bed. "He's only a little boy, Sam. He won't understand."

He sat up and tucked a foot under him. "We can be careful in how we tell him." Her lips flattened into a line and she looked away, pulling on her bathrobe.

"At least let me spend some time with him."

"Okay." She'd spoken so low that he had to ask her to repeat it. "But I don't want you to tell him. Promise me."

Sam fought to keep the smile from his face. He had a son and now he would get to know him better. "I swear I won't tell him without your agreement."

Before Tricia could say anything else, the phone rang. She glanced at the clock. "Oh, gosh. It's later than I thought."

"I'll take a shower," he said, and slipped into the bathroom.

"Hello?" That was all he heard of her call before closing the door and giving her privacy. Sam heaved a sigh of relief. He hadn't made love to Tricia as a way to coerce her into letting him spend time with Tim, but he was damn glad things had turned out that way. He had no doubts that eventually he could talk her into sharing with their son who Sam was. After all, he was stationed in Richmond for almost two more years, and they lived here, too. Looking into the mirror over the sink he congratulated his reflection for being a lucky bastard. Then he turned on the water, adjusted the temperature, and stepped into the shower.

He'd hoped to shower with Tricia to finish out their night together, but that was another thing he hoped would work out—that this wouldn't end up being their only night. Surely if he spent more time with her and with Tim things would lead to a natural conclusion. And who knew, they might really fall in love again, not just play with feelings from the past.

When he finished, he went into an empty bedroom to find his clothes from last night. The smell of coffee and bacon drew him into the kitchen as soon as he was mostly decent. He didn't hear voices, so he ventured out without his tee shirt.

He walked up to Tricia at the stove and slipped his arms around her from behind. "That smells delicious."

"Hmmm, you smell delicious, too."

Sam kissed Tricia's neck and then let her go in order to pour a cup of coffee.

"That was Mike's mother calling. First, she asked if I minded Timmy's going to the movies with Mike. Not the slasher film, some shoot-'em-up adventure thing. And if it would work out for me to pick them up."

"So… That means we have the morning free?" Did his voice sound as lecherous as his body felt?

Tricia removed the bacon and dropped the slices onto a paper towel-covered plate. She drained off most of the bacon fat. Sam watched her, amazed that she handled even something as mundane as fixing breakfast with a certain gracefulness. Her mama had taught her to cook and she'd always enjoyed it.

"That's exactly what it means, except I do have chores to do today." Picking up an egg she turned to ask, "How do you like your eggs?"

"Any way you feel comfortable fixing them. Can I help? Maybe make toast or something?"

"That would be great, thanks. The bread is over there," she said using the egg to point to the other side of the counter. Then she turned and broke the egg into the pan followed by three more. Sam started the toast.

Opening drawers until he found silverware, he set two places at the breakfast table and left a couple of plates beside the stove for when Tricia finished the eggs and then buttered the first slices of toast.

"What's second?" Sam asked.

"Second?"

"You said 'first' Mike's mother asked about picking up the boys. What's second?"

She turned off the burner and stood still, staring into the pan. "Oh, yeah. She said that her husband sprung a dinner obligation on her, so she wondered if the boys could stay here tonight. Not John, just Mike."

"I see." Uncertain of where he stood in the family dynamic, Sam stared at the floor and then raised his gaze to her. "I don't suppose you'd consider letting me hang with you and the kids? Obviously, I'd behave myself." He waggled his brows.

"I'd love it," she said quietly. "Thank you." Then as though gathering herself up, she slid the spatula under the eggs and deposited them on the plates. Sam brought the last two pieces of buttered toast to the table and then filled their cups with coffee. "I thought you said you didn't care to be around kids that much?"

Sam half smiled. "This is different." He sat down. "This looks good. So, what do you need to do today?"

"Saturday is my grocery day. Usually, I do most of my cleaning on Saturday, too." She looked up with a twinkle in her eye. "But this Saturday I'd like to stay in bed late. Too bad you've already showered."

Sam smiled. He'd get his wish after all. "A man can't have too many showers. And a shower with company is the best kind."

Chapter Ten

"Mom! Did you hear what I said?"

Pat came out of her reverie with a jolt, looking first at Timmy, with his wrinkled brow and stern little face, and then at Sam, who raised one brow and smiled, indicating that he knew exactly where her mind had been—back at her house in the shower with him, up against the tiled wall with him deep inside her. She fought the heat flooding her cheeks.

"Mom, are you okay? You look funny."

"I'm fine, Timmy. It's just hot in here." They sat in the food court of the local mall, and it was anything but warm in the building. No way would she look at Sam after making *that* remark. "I'm sorry, ask me again? I'm listening."

"Can Mike and me go over to the fountain? We're finished eating." They'd picked up the boys from the theater and acquiesced to their request to stop for ice cream in the complex's food court.

"*May* Mike and *I* go over to the fountain." Timmy sighed and nodded. "Just for a few minutes. Sam and I are almost finished with our coffees and then we're heading home."

"Okay," Timmy said with a smile. "Come on, Mike."

"Your mom is as bad as mine," Mike muttered to Timmy. The two boys took off, stopping at the fountain in the center of the mall and well within sight. Pat watched Timmy point at something in the water and he and Mike broke into laughter that had them bending over with hilarity.

"Thank God they're still too young to be interested in girls," she confided to Sam.

"They're not far off," Sam replied, gesturing toward the boys with his Styrofoam cup. Pat turned to see a group of three girls standing with Timmy and Mike. The girls were probably about the same age as the boys but somehow looked older. The two boys looked star struck.

"Oh, no," she groaned. "Can't he stay a little boy forever?"

"Nope." Sam took a sip. "I'd say you have about a year, year and a half before you'll have to give him the birds and bees talk." They watched as one of the girls smiled and reached over to take Timmy's hand. "Maybe sooner," Sam added.

Pat let out a huff. "What is it about girls these days?"

"They grow up fast, that's for sure. I used to listen to shipmates talk about their kids and the trouble they got into and thought how lucky I was not to have that worry." Pay swiveled to face him and he concentrated on her face. "Now I know that the rewards are greater than the trouble you have to put up with."

"You really think so? Sometimes I've hated raising him all alone. He was only six when Brian left, and except for Mark, he's had no male role model. I feel like I've cheated him."

"And maybe you've cheated yourself too, Tricia." He took her hand and linked their fingers. Warmth flowed through her. Sam leaned closer and she thought he might even kiss her, right there in the mall food court. "I wish I'd known."

"I didn't think I'd see you here. What a surprise." Mark's voice came from behind Sam.

Startled, Pat looked up into his face. His smile was tight. When he looked at Sam he wore no smile at all. But polite at all times, he stuck out his hand. "Have we met?"

Sam stood and shook Mark's hand. "Yes, last week at the restaurant."

"That's right. You were the guy who wouldn't stay for a drink." Mark glanced back at Pat. "How have you ended here, with my sister-in-law?"

"I believe she's your former sister-in-law, right? And I'm here with Tricia because we're old friends. Very *good* old friends."

Pat's heart pounded. Surely Sam wouldn't tell Mark their secret.

"We share…a history."

Thank God he hadn't said what she feared. Pat couldn't stand the idea of his spilling the truth about Timmy in the middle of a bunch of shops filled with strangers. And especially not since Timmy had spotted his uncle and come running up.

"Hey, Uncle Mark."

"Hey, Tim. How's it going? Hello, Mike."

"Hi, Mr. Welles."

"We went to the movie and then we're just going home. What are you doing today?"

Mark held out a bag. "I needed a couple of shirts, and then I saw your mom and stopped to say hello."

"Want to come and have dinner with us?" Timmy wouldn't see the harm in the invitation. Mark had often eaten with them, and she hadn't told him that Sam was going to grill dinner for them.

Mark focused on her. She all but saw the question in his eyes, but her relationship with Sam was really none of his business. Not yet, anyway.

"Well, maybe I could—"

"Normally I'd love to have you join us, Mark, but Sam is hosting dinner tonight. We picked up some hamburger at the grocery store and he's grilling." She turned to Timmy. "I hadn't told you yet, but Lieutenant Turner is having dinner with us tonight."

"Lieutenant Turner is such a mouthful," Sam said to Timmy. "Why don't you call me Sam?"

Pat saw it all. The hopefulness in Sam's eyes, slight confusion in Timmy's, and disappointment in Mark's. She hated being in the middle but what could she do? She was grateful to Mark for all the help he'd given her, both through her divorce and in the years since. She knew he had wanted more from her, but she'd never felt right giving in. The fact was, she'd always loved Sam. But even that love didn't compare to her love and devotion to Timmy. She didn't want to hurt any of them.

"May I see you a moment in private?" Mark asked.

"Of course." She stood and walked a short distance away with him.

"Do you know what you're doing?" he asked.

"I don't know what you mean. Sam told you, we're old friends."

Mark shook his head and fixed her with a glare. "Don't dance around the truth with me, Pat. And don't do it with yourself. I've always known that Tim wasn't Brian's son." Pat gasped. Her hand flew up to cover her mouth. "And I think seeing the two of them together that I know whose son he is. Do you think it's wise getting involved with him again?"

"What do you mean 'wise?' Sam and I…we loved each other."

"He *abandoned* you, Pat. He left a pregnant teenage girl alone while she carried his baby. Think about what you're doing."

Pat's heart sank. How could the day start so perfectly and go to crap so suddenly? She took a breath. "Mark, Sam never knew I was pregnant. He didn't know he had a son until last week when he addressed the students at Timmy's school. I never told him. I'm so sorry. I know you must think the very worst of me."

Mark didn't say anything, just used his lawyer-courtroom face on her. She saw why he was so successful—all he had to do was focus that laser gaze on a witness and they'd confess.

"I will always appreciate all you did for me, Mark. I'll always consider you a good friend—if you still *want* me as a friend after what I just told you. But I love Sam, and I always have."

His shoulders slumped, and the fire went out of his eyes. "Are you going to tell Tim?"

"Someday. I think he's too young now. And besides, I don't know where this is going. Until last week I thought Sam had graduated from UVA and had forgotten me. We hadn't seen or talked to each other since my senior year of high school." She touched his arm. "I'm sorry if this hurts you, Mark. You're the last person I'd want to hurt. Do you think you can ever forgive me?"

"It's okay. After all these years, I should have known we were never going to get together. Still, I guess I hoped." He gave a small smile. "If you ever need me...?"

"Thank you. You're Timmy's uncle, and you know how much he loves you." She stood on tiptoe to kiss his cheek. Then, heart heavy, she went back to the boy and the man she loved more than anything in all the world.

***

"Are you my father?"

Sam almost dropped the grill spatula he was using to flip the burgers. Tim's friend Mike had gone into the bathroom. Tricia was inside getting the rest of the meal ready. Sam quickly took care of the meat and then sat across from the boy. Not "the boy," he reminded himself, his *son*. How in hell could he answer that question?

"Why would you ask that?" Okay, that was a good start. Maybe this question was like the joke where the kid asks his father where he came from. After the father goes through the whole egg and sperm explanation, he finds out the boy just wanted to know which *city* he was from.

"My dad—I mean my first dad—got mad one time and said that I was too stupid to be *his* kid. That I *wasn't* his and he was damn glad." Tim shot a quick look toward the kitchen. Then he leaned closer and whispered, "Don't tell Mom I said damn. She'd be mad."

Sam almost laughed. The boy had just revealed that the man he'd thought was his father had told him that he wasn't, and the thing that worried him was that Tricia might find out he'd sworn. "Your secret is safe with me." He sucked in a breath. "Are you sure you didn't misunderstand?"

Tim looked down. "He kinda made sure I understood. I was pretty little but it's something that stuck with me, you know?"

"The bastard!" He said it in a low voice, but Tim still jerked up his head and stared with wide eyes. Sam smiled with chagrin. "Don't tell your mom, okay? She'd be mad at me, too."

Tim grinned. Then he said, "It's okay that he's not my real father. I don't want him to be. He made Mom cry all the time, and he hurt her. Uncle Mark isn't like that, but I don't look anything like Uncle Mark, so I can't be his." Tim stared at him like he would examine a specimen in science class. "But I think I look a little like you. Our eyes are the same color. Mike thinks we look alike, too."

God, please tell me the right thing to say. "Well, Tim, kids don't always look like their parents but I kinda think we look something alike, too. I hope you know, I'd never make your mom cry. Not on purpose. I love her, and I have for a long time." *Shit!* He'd never been so scared of doing the wrong thing. He'd faced being thrown in the brig for driving a forklift off the Norfolk pier with less trepidation than he did this conversation. He folded his hands in his lap, so Tim wouldn't see them shake. "Would you object to my being your dad someday?"

Tim thought for a minute. Such a serious kid. The question *was* too much for him. Tricia had been right when she said that Tim was too young to understand their relationship. But then Tim smiled. Kind of. It was hard to tell if his expression was a smile or a grimace, but Sam was going to take the positive outlook.

"If you're good to my mom. If you love her and take care of her, then I think you should be my dad."

Sam wanted to cry. He blinked back the tears though and held out his hand. "Tell you what. Let's agree man to man. I'm going to do my best to love your mom forever. And I know you're too old for all the things a *little* kid does with his father"—he watched as Tim straightened his shoulders and sat up a little straighter—"but I'll try my best to be the best dad possible, too. Is that all right?"

Tim grinned then and shook Sam's hand. "Deal," he said.

"Of course, you know how women are. We might need to let your mom think this is her idea, and she might need some time to come around to it. We'll need patience."

"Okay." Tim grinned at him. How had Sam lived his whole life without knowing this kind of love?

Mike walked out then. "What's going on?" he asked.

"Nothing," Tim replied. "I'm getting a dad."

"Cool," Mike said as though Tim announced he was acquiring a father every day. "Wanna toss the football around until dinner?"

Shit! The burgers! Sam jumped up to check the meat on the grill. He flipped them and moved them to the edge of the charcoal fire. Tricia walked out carrying a bowl of potato salad and a bag of chips.

"I have tomatoes, pickles, onion, and the buns ready to come out. And we have water, iced tea, and Coke to drink. What do you want?"

Riding on the high of his talk with Tim, Sam dragged Tricia back into the house and around the wall into the living room, out of the boys' line of sight. He took her in his arms and kissed her, skipping the soft and tender and going straight to the hard and urgent. Tricia cupped his cheek with one hand and his nape with the other, stretching her fingers up into his hair. Open-mouthed, tongues dueling, she molded herself to him and rubbed against his erection.

"God, I love you," he murmured into her ear when he gave up her mouth in favor of her jaw, her ear, and finally her neck. He felt the thunder of her heart and it matched his.

"I love you, too," she said. "I wish—"

"Sam, is it almost time to eat?" Tim called from the backyard.

They broke off kissing. "Almost, buddy!" Sam called out. "We're bringing out the rest of the stuff now." He took another breath and rested his forehead on hers for a moment. "This might take a little getting used to," he said to Tricia with a smile.

"It comes to you after a while," she answered back. Then she stepped out of his arms. In the kitchen, she grabbed a couple of bowls and headed to the patio. "Boys, go and wash up."

It might take a bit of adjustment on his part, holding back his own desires in order to be around his son, but Sam was ready to take on the challenge. Starting with their first dinner together.

Chapter Eleven

"Did you have a good day today?" Pat asked Timmy. Mike had gone into the adjoining bathroom to get ready for bed and Timmy was about to climb into bed. She had no illusions that the boys would settle down and sleep, but at least if they were in the big double bed Timmy had in his room, falling asleep would come more naturally.

"Yeah, a really good day. Thanks, Mom."

"You're welcome, sweetheart. I hope you remembered to thank Mike's parents, too."

"I did. And Sam," he added.

"Yes, and Sam, too. He grills a great hamburger, doesn't he?"

"Thanks for liking Sam, Mom," Timmy said in a low voice, as though he didn't want Mike to hear. "He's my dad."

What? Pat went cold. Sam wouldn't have told him, he'd promised not to. "Where did you get that idea, Timmy?"

"Sam said—"

"Can we play some Xbox before going to sleep?" Mike came dashing out of the bathroom with his pajama top wet where he'd splashed water, probably while brushing his teeth.

"Just for a little while," she said. Timmy and Mike fist-bumped each other. "I'll check on you in a little bit."

Closing the bedroom door, she walked downstairs in a cold fury wondering what to say to Sam. She heard the sounds of dishes from the kitchen and found him there filling the dishwasher, having cleared up both the patio and the counters.

He looked up. "There you are. Are the boys settled in?" He closed the dishwasher door, wiped his hands on a kitchen towel and came to her. When he tried to slide his hands around her waist, she pushed him away.

"How dare you!"

He looked as though she'd slapped him. Maybe she should have started with that. She was angry enough to do it. More than heartbroken, more than sad that what they'd started wouldn't continue, she was just plain furious.

Sam stepped back. "What are you talking about? What's wrong?"

Even in a rage, she tried hard to keep her voice down. Not only didn't she want Timmy to hear their argument, she didn't want to embarrass him in front of his best friend. "You promised you wouldn't tell Timmy about you. Then you went and did it. I can't deal with a man who lies, Sam."

Planting his hands on his hips, he glared at her. "You can't deal with lies? That's rich, Tricia. But just so we're clear, I did not tell Tim about me."

"He says you did."

"He must have misunderstood because I didn't." He changed his position to cross his arms over his chest. "But even if I had, what would be so terrible? I *am* his father."

"Not that he knew before tonight. And not legally. Your name isn't on his birth certificate."

"So you've already told me. But please, keep reminding me." Sam twisted around and braced his hands on the counter. "You'd rather he think his father is a wife beater, Tricia? I might not be a banker or a lawyer like the sainted Mark, but I'm a decent guy. I don't kick dogs or rob little old ladies of their social security checks. Why can't my own son know who I am?"

Breathing hard and unable to stop herself, Pat attacked. "It doesn't matter *who* you are or *what* you are or aren't. You have no control over how I raise my son." Sam slowly turned. The pain in his eyes nearly ripped out her heart but fear kept her going. The truth of it was, if Timmy found out that Sam was his father, he also discovered who she was—a woman who'd cheated and lied. That was one truth too many for her to face.

"I'll call your office Monday morning and ask for a replacement in the program, so please don't come to the office. I won't make it a bad reflection on you, I promise, but I just don't want to see you anymore."

He reached out. "Tricia, please—"

Pat stepped out of reach. "You asked for a night, Sam, and I gave it to you. I'd like you to go now."

After staring at her for long, painful seconds, he stalked past her. At the door, he looked straight ahead but addressed her. "I will try not to cause you or Tim any trouble or harm, Tricia, but this isn't over." Then he opened the door and left.

Pat dropped onto the couch, her elbows on her knees, her hand over her mouth. "I'm called Pat now," she whispered. Her tears fell off her chin and into her lap. "Oh, God, what have I done?"

Through the closed door upstairs she heard the boys laughing and the sounds of virtual laser guns. Because she wanted Sam so much, she'd put Timmy in danger. Now that Sam knew who Timmy was, he would fight for him. That much about Sam she hadn't forgotten—he'd fight for what he wanted. Had he known she carried his child before she married Brian, he might have fought for her back then and her life would have been very different. Now, because of her desire to have what she didn't deserve, Timmy's life would certainly be changed.

Did Sam have a point? Was it better for Timmy to think his father was a man like Brian rather than someone like Sam? "He was too little to remember Brian's cruelty," she said out loud. But was that true? At least he'd grown up mostly with Mark to view as a role model, but was that enough?

Too emotionally tired to think anymore, she flipped out the light and curled up in a corner of the couch. She'd let the boys have another half hour before encouraging them to go to sleep. She wanted just a few minutes to herself to clear her mind. And her heart.

***

"Mike, your parents are here," Pat called upstairs. Suddenly, two pairs of feet came pounding down the steps. Mike had his backpack over his shoulders. Pat opened the door just as her friend Elise, Mike's mother, reached the porch steps.

"Thanks so much, Pat. Hope he wasn't any trouble." She hugged Mike who scrambled out of his mother's arms just as Timmy always did with her. She and Pat smiled at each other.

"None whatsoever. This was a great idea, our trading nights like this. Maybe we can do it again sometime."

"Bye, Mike!" Timmy stood by her side. "See you tomorrow!"

Mike ran backwards and waved. "Tomorrow, dude!" He climbed in the backseat of the Volvo. Pat could see his dad talking to him, then he laughed and they high-fived.

"That's a good idea. Let's see if we can work it out." Elise glanced back at the car. "Well, we're on our way to brunch, so I'd better get a move on. Talk to you later."

"See you, Elise." She and Timmy went back into the house. "What would you like to do today?" She had skipped housecleaning yesterday. Now that her anger had burned itself out, Pat allowed herself one moment to remember why she'd skipped dusting and vacuuming. Sam had fucked her one way to Sunday. He'd brought her to life. He'd made her feel. He'd made her remember what it was like to love and be loved.

Damn him.

"I don't know," Timmy said. "Can we call Sam and see what he wants to do?"

"No, honey. Sam has his own life just as we have ours. He's an old friend but he was just visiting yesterday." This was why she'd been nearly seven years without a man. It was too confusing to Timmy to see a bunch of men with her. She surely hadn't wanted any boyfriends building up his hopes and then disappointing him when things didn't work, and she'd somehow known things wouldn't work out because she loved Sam. Oh God, would she never get over him?

"But Mom, that can't be right. I told him that I wanted him to be my dad as long as he promised to take care of you and not make you cry, and he said he would. We shook on it."

Pat felt the blood drain from her face. "What? Timmy, what are you talking about? Sit right here and tell me exactly what you and Sam said."

As Timmy talked, Pat's stomach started churning. She'd gotten it all wrong. Timmy *did* remember Brian. Sam had both the conversation and her misunderstanding of it right. She'd made a fool of herself. And she'd pushed away the only man she'd ever loved with hateful words and accusations.

"You *want* Sam as your dad?"

Her son nodded. "I like him. And I think he would be good to you." His face looked younger suddenly and unsure. "You're the best mom ever," he said. "But I really want a dad. Sam understands that I don't need a father like I did when I was little." He looked proud of that fact, though in her eyes he'd always be her little baby.

"But still," he went on, "Mike's dad does things with him, guy stuff. They take me with them sometimes but it's not the same. And Uncle Mark is cool, and I love him, but well, he's my *uncle*. We don't look alike, and to tell the truth, we don't really like the same things. Sam has a cool job. Plus, we look a little alike, so I know people would believe I'm his real son. You know what I mean, Mom?"

Pat sobbed in a breath. "Ah, Mom," Timmy said, stricken. "I didn't mean to make you cry."

She swiped at her eyes. "It's okay, honey. Let me tell you a story about Sam. And then we'll call him because I didn't treat him very nicely last night and I have to apologize."

He awkwardly put his arm over her shoulder. "Sam is nice, Mom. I'm sure he'll forgive you."

Pat could only hope Timmy was right.

***

As shocked as he'd been to receive Tricia's phone call earlier that morning, he was even more shocked at her appearance at his front door. Her eyes had circles under them and strain showed in the set of her mouth and the tightness of her jaw. Her tan slacks and light brown, short-sleeved sweater looked neat, but she wore only one earring.

"Come on in," he said. "Can I get you something to drink?" He could offer her tea or coffee but maybe she'd prefer something stronger.

"No, thanks. And thank you for agreeing to see me after the way I treated you last night."

"No problem. Sit down." She took the sofa. He sat in the opposite leather chair. "If you're going to warn me away from seeing Tim again, I feel I should tell you—"

She held up her hand. "That's not why I'm here. I need to apologize. After Mike left this morning Timmy told me your whole conversation. I was wrong, Sam. Wrong about what you and he had said, and wrong not to let you explain. I'm so, so sorry."

Sam folded his hands between his knees. That was the easiest way he knew to keep from reaching for her. "I said some words I'm not proud of, too, Tricia, and I'm sorry."

"I was just so mad, Sam. I didn't think he would understand, but you were right. He does. Or at least, I think he does."

"You told him?" His heart picked up speed. He not only had a son, but his son knew him as his father.

"Yes. Maybe you can kind of feel him out and make sure I didn't do more harm than good?"

"Absolutely." Damn. His eyes stung with tears. "What changed your mind?"

"He did." She fumbled with the strap on her purse. "He said he really wanted a dad. I think I've been so used to being the only parent that I didn't see that his needs were changing. Or maybe I didn't want to see it." She looked away. "And of course, I was ashamed. I didn't want him to know the kind of girl I was. I wanted him to think well of me."

At that, Sam rose and moved beside her. He wrapped his arm around her and pulled her head to his shoulder. "He loves you very much, Tricia. As do I."

It broke his heart to hear her sniffling, knowing she had passed from one phase of Tim's life to another. "You weren't any *kind* of girl, honey. You were just a girl. One who found herself in a bad situation and handled it as best you could. And Tricia, if I become part of Tim's life, I hope that means I will be part of yours. You don't have to be alone anymore. We'll share life, all of it. For better or worse, okay?"

She nodded. "Are you sure, Sam? I don't want you to marry me just because of Timmy."

He laughed for the first time since she'd arrived. "If you don't know how much I love you by now, I don't know how else to show you." He raised her chin so he could kiss her. "Except to remind you every day for the rest of our lives. We've wasted so much time, Tricia. Say you'll marry me and say it can be soon."

"Yes, Sam."

They kissed. Gently at first, but then hotter, more greedily. "Where's Tim now?" he asked, breathing hard.

"I asked if he could stay with his friend John for a few hours." She sounded no more in control of her emotions than he did.

"Good. Then we have time for this." Standing her up, he quickly unzipped her slacks and pulled them off her. He unfastened his jeans and ripped them to his thighs. Then with her knees on each side of his thighs, he tested her with his fingers. "So fucking wet," he whispered before taking her lips again. She slid onto his cock and they groaned in unison.

Though he'd wanted her beyond reason, he didn't force their tempo to match his desire. Instead, he wanted her to know that he was in this relationship for the long haul, so slow and steady was the pace he set, a gentle rocking into her, an easing out, skin against skin.

The Navy had a term for when the ship was underway, and the anchor was safely in place. It implied that all was well, that all was as it should be. For the first time in a long time, Sam felt that way. He'd explain it to her later, this feeling of peace, of rightness, knowing that at last they would be each other's family, as they'd intended so long ago.

"This is anchor home," he whispered. And he knew it to be true.

The End

About the author

A few years ago, Dee S. Knight began writing, making getting up in the morning fun. During the day, her characters killed people, fell in love, became drunk with power, or sober with responsibility. And they had sex, lots of sex. Writing was so much fun Dee decided to keep at it. That's how she spends her days. Her nights? Well, she's lucky that her dream man, childhood sweetheart, and long-time hubby are all the same guy, and nights are their secret. Dee loves writing erotic romance and sharing her stories with you. She hopes you enjoy!

More of our titles

Their Lady Gloriana by Starla Kaye
Cowboys in Charge by Starla Kaye
Her Cowboy's Way by Starla Kaye
Punished by Richard Savage, Nadia Nautalia & Starla Kaye
Accidental Affair by Leslie McKelvey
Right Place, Right Time by Leslie McKelvey
Her Sister's Keeper by Leslie McKelvey
Playing for Keeps by Glenda Horsfall
Playing By His Rules by Glenda Horsfall
The Stir of Echo by Susan Gabriel
Rally Fever by Crea Jones
Behind The Clouds by Jan Selbourne
Trusting Love Again by Starla Kaye
Runaway Heart by Leslie McKelvey
The Otherling by Heather M. Walker
First Submission - Anthology
These Eyes So Green by Deborah Kelsey
Dark Awakening by Karlene Cameron
The Reclaiming of Charlotte Moss by Heather M. Walker
Ryann's Revenge by Rai Karr & Breanna Hayse
The Postman's Daughter by Sally Anne Palmer
Final Kill by Leslie McKelvey
Killer Secrets by Zia Westfield
Crossover, Texas by Freia Hooper-Bradford
The King's Blade by L.J. Dare
Uniform Desire - Anthology
Safe by Keren Hughes
Finishing the Game by M.K. Smith
Out of the Shadows by Gabriella Hewitt
A Woman's Secret by C.L. Koch
Love Times Infinity by K.L Ramsey
Her Lover's Face by Patricia Elliott

__Black Velvet Seductions__

See a full list of our titles at
www.blackvelvetseductions.com

Come and like us at
Black Velvet Seductions on Facebook
and follow BVS books on Twitter